ONCE UPON A THYME

JANE LOVERING

Boldwood

First published in Great Britain in 2025 by Boldwood Books Ltd.

Copyright © Jane Lovering, 2025

Cover Design by Alexandra Allden

Cover Images: Shutterstock and iStock

The moral right of Jane Lovering to be identified as the author of this work has been asserted in accordance with the Copyright, Designs and Patents Act 1988.

All rights reserved. No part of this book may be reproduced in any form or by any electronic or mechanical means, including information storage and retrieval systems, without written permission from the author, except for the use of brief quotations in a book review. This book is a work of fiction and, except in the case of historical fact, any resemblance to actual persons, living or dead, is purely coincidental.

Every effort has been made to obtain the necessary permissions with reference to copyright material, both illustrative and quoted. We apologise for any omissions in this respect and will be pleased to make the appropriate acknowledgements in any future edition.

A CIP catalogue record for this book is available from the British Library.

Paperback ISBN 978-1-83533-250-4

Large Print ISBN 978-1-83533-251-1

Hardback ISBN 978-1-83533-249-8

Ebook ISBN 978-1-83533-252-8

Kindle ISBN 978-1-83533-253-5

Audio CD ISBN 978-1-83533-244-3

MP3 CD ISBN 978-1-83533-245-0

Digital audio download ISBN 978-1-83533-247-4

This book is printed on certified sustainable paper. Boldwood Books is dedicated to putting sustainability at the heart of our business. For more information please visit https://www.boldwoodbooks.com/about-us/sustainability/

Boldwood Books Ltd, 23 Bowerdean Street, London, SW6 3TN

www.boldwoodbooks.com

This book is dedicated to Wendy, of Twigs and Twine, Helmsley, whom I consulted on the general subject of a commercial herb garden, and who came up with the wedding idea, and also to Tessa, who let me shamelessly steal her name.

1

There was a pig in the kitchen, with its trotters on the table and its snout in the fruit bowl. But this was fine – well, maybe not *fine*, I wasn't happy about it, but at least the pig was a known quantity. The man, on the other hand, standing watching the pig eat a satsuma, was not.

'There's a pig in here,' he said, as though observing a strange scientific phenomenon. 'Eating an orange.'

'It's a satsuma,' I said, helpfully pedantic.

'Oh.' He eyed the pig again. 'Is that a rare breed?'

'I meant the orange, not the pig. She's a Tamworth.' Then I regained my sensibilities, like suddenly putting on a pair of glasses and being able to focus. 'But who are you and why are you in my kitchen?'

He blinked a couple of times, while the pig honked happily around the remains of the fruit bowl, making the kind of slurpy chomping noises that sounded like a toddler eating porridge. 'Er,' he said finally. 'Do you not think that having a pig in your kitchen is a slightly more pressing problem right now?'

'Probably.' I stared at the pig again. She was happily snaffling down the last of the fruit with one eye rolled towards me to check whether I was about to eject her with a broom handle. 'But I can handle the pig. It's you I'm questioning. Who are you?'

The man, who now looked a little uncertain himself about who he was and why he was here, blinked again. 'I came about the job, but I seem to be caught up in a cartoon. *Why* is there a pig in the kitchen?'

'Someone left the gate open, I expect. What job?'

I put my hands on my hips in an inquisitorial stance and ignored the issue of the pig. It wasn't unheard of for various animals to infiltrate the house; the kitchen door was always open because the kitchen was also my office and I needed to be alert to customers driving into the gardens. It had never been the pig before though; I was more used to a rabbit or guinea pig intrusion, but the oddness of this situation being pointed out by a strange man was not welcome.

The man in question, who had tousled dark hair and a half-beard, as though he'd leaped out of bed to come here, just kept staring at the porcine incursion. 'But... it's a *pig*!' he eventually expostulated, as though somehow he was insulted by the presence of said creature. Okay, it's not every day you find one in a kitchen, least of all with its head amid the fruit, but, even so, hardly a velociraptor in the bath.

'Yes, but who are you, and what job?' I repeated with as much patience as I could summon.

Two pairs of eyes rested on me. One pair was brown and looked worried. The other pair was blue, fringed with ginger lashes and wore an expression of hopeful bliss. 'And you can bugger off,' I addressed the sow. 'You're not getting anything else.'

I got a wet nose-blow of a noise in reply and she rotated on her haunches, dropped from her snuffle-examination of the table and trotted out, delicate as a duchess in stilettos, over the flagstones back to the yard, where noises of incipient pig-recapture were going on.

'Er,' said the man again. 'I'm not entirely certain I'm in the right place. I've come for the herb farm job? Drycott Herbs? I was sure the sign said...'

'This is Drycott Herbs.' I began putting the table back together again. Four hundred pounds of pig had disarranged the surface somewhat. 'I'm Tallie Fisher, I run the herb farm. But I don't know which job you mean, I've not advertised for any... Oh.'

Mother had been at it again, clearly. I was going to take to her internet connection with a pair of secateurs. I had bought her out of the business four years ago and she was supposed to be taking life easy. Instead, she'd found a new hobby: gross interference. 'You're always so busy, Natalie,' she'd said. 'You should be able to relax more. Get yourself an assistant. Apart from that Ollie, he's as much use as Bournemouth. He's not an assistant, he's an impediment.'

She'd presented it as concern, but the subtext had been 'and then you'd have more time to come by and keep me company'. Which, experience had told me, meant 'do all my housework while I lounge around on the sofa telling you how fragile I feel and watching daytime TV, then hint heavily that I'd like a roast dinner that I then won't eat.' My mother was *complicated* and our relationship was a cat's cradle of obligations, guilt, affection and duty. And Ollie wasn't useless, he was excellent with the plants, even if he did have a tendency to hide from customers. Plus, she didn't even seem to enjoy my company, she just liked having someone there in the house. She could have got a Labradoodle, and not needed me at all.

'So, who are you?' I continued my questioning. My mother's controlling nature and desire to have me permanently within calling distance wasn't his problem.

He glanced very quickly away from the window, where he was watching the pig's progress. He seemed afraid that taking his eye off her might result in her coming back inside and attacking him. 'My name is Zeb. Short for Zebedee, and I've heard all the *Magic Roundabout* jokes already, thank you. Zebedee McAuley-Wilson. I've just moved to Yorkshire and I'm looking for a creative kind of job that I can do part time alongside my online work.'

Zebedee McAuley-Wilson. Flippin' heck, as Mother would say, because she'd had any kind of swearing knocked out of her by Granny. His parents must have gone right through the baby naming book before they'd found one they liked. I could never employ someone whose name used up all the boxes on those stupid forms that we had to fill in.

He was watching me hopefully now, presumably hoping I'd ask what his online job was so he could mutter about being a content creator or an influencer or something. Although, from his appearance, I had no idea who he could influence, apart from maybe some gullible teenagers. He looked a little bit like David Tennant's *Dr Who*, if the Doctor had had a sudden bout of low self-esteem and a quick trot through ASOS.

'Well, you're thinking about it, that's a good start.'

I wanted to say that I *wasn't* 'thinking about it', that there was nothing to think about; I was busy but there wasn't a job for Mr 'Part time alongside my real work' and that my mother should butt out of my life, but I realised that the moment had passed. I'd spent too long thinking.

And there actually was a lot to do. I hated to admit it, but on this point my mother was spot on. I'd been stretched to the limits lately and, in the depths of the night, had even wondered about recruiting someone to mind the shop. But I knew I wouldn't, because that would mean someone else having input, someone else's ideas sliding under the door. Drycott Herbs was *mine*, and I'd rather be overworked and in control than having to think of tactful ways not to implement someone else's 'brainwaves'. Least of all an agent of my mother's.

'Do you know anything about herbs?' I asked, my eyes following the pig's retreat and ending up gazing out across the carefully laid gravel paths and two acres of hand-planting. Ollie was running around with a brush, as though sweeping the sow back into her enclosure was a possibility.

'A bit. But mostly on the culinary side, and you seem to deal more with the aesthetics.' Zebedee nodded towards the bunches of herbs which hung from the ceiling rafters, heads down, drying in the gentle breeze.

'Customers cut their own herbs, and we sell arrangements and pre-packaged...' I tailed off. Why was I going into the sales spiel for a man I didn't want here anyway?

'Great idea,' he said robustly. 'When can I start?'

I gave in. I *always* gave in. 'I'll give you a trial shift. Just now I think Ollie – that's Ollie, the blond bloke out there with the broom handle – could do with a hand getting the pig back in.'

'Ah.' He didn't move. 'Herbs I can do. Pigs, less so.'

Here was my get-out. 'To work here you have to multi-task. We've got a little animal corner for children; it's mostly the pig, a few rabbits and guinea pigs, that sort of thing. They need looking after just as much as the herbs, so...' I trailed off because he was nodding. I'd hoped he'd go more for the polite refusal and head home, but apparently he was prepared to overcome his swinophobia in the interests of having a job. Bugger. That probably meant that his 'influencing' wasn't going well and he'd want all the hours I could give him to work, rather than the odd half hour here and there doing some pruning that I'd been grudgingly preparing to offer – just to satisfy Mother that I did take her advice, sometimes.

'Catch the pig. Yes. I rather thought that was going to be my induction.' He straightened his back. 'Right. I suppose we can deal with all the paperwork and everything later?'

Again I looked out on my sunlit acres. The pig was calmly snuffling her way across a path, having heavily trampled the variegated sage, on her way towards the far more fragile fennel bed. The air was filled with the scent of crushed stuffing and the cries of foiled recapture. Thankfully, the main gate to the road was closed, and the stone walls which surrounded the gardens were ten feet high and enough to withstand even a pig that had watched *The Great Escape*.

'Yes,' I said weakly. 'I suppose so.'

2

The catmint was in full flower, trailing gracefully over the gravelled path in buoyant swathes as though in a passionate but thwarted relationship with the pineapple mint in the opposite bed. I cut an armful, ignoring the pungent smell. The little purple and white flowers and the dusty-green leaves made a good backdrop for bouquets, and there was always a market for the bunches I made up, a woven mass of flower and decorative foliage that we sold from the polished galvanised buckets neatly lined up by the fence. I straightened up, resting the dots of nodding heads against my forearm and looked out across the garden. To my left was the tiny cottage where I lived and worked, and on the right the old stables which I'd converted into the shop area. Their rooflines were dipped and buckled with the contours of aged beams echoing the line of the moors which embraced our little enterprise in its valley like a burly chef's arm encircling a mixing bowl. Apart from the wonky roofline and the encircling moorland hills everything else was geometric. Herb beds were divided by well-ordered pathways and trimmed box edging, as though the Tudors had gone down-market and now lived in a two-up-two-down but had kept the gardeners on. The pet barn was straight and true in all its corrugated-roofed glory, the fencing and walling so horizontal that you could have danced the samba along the coping stones. Everything was neat, everything was tidy. Apart from the herbs, and I cut those a lot of slack because flouncing and flopping over the gravel like drunken bridesmaids was what they did at this time of year.

Over at the far side of the acres, our reluctant recruit, Zeb, had been put to work by Ollie, and the pair of them were clearing weeds from the saxifrage, Ollie's blond head bent next to Zeb's dark, untidy one. Ollie was explaining something. I could see his mouth moving in his almost constant stream of monologue, to which Zeb appeared to have adjusted, judging by his head-down occasional nod. I watched them work for a few moments – it really didn't take two people to weed and I wondered again at my mother's presumption in advertising a job that didn't exist. But then, that was my mother all over.

I tucked the nepeta further into my arms, letting its smell of musty mint float by me. No, it didn't take two to weed, but I knew I really *could* do with someone to help with the sales side; a dichotomy I was trying to get my head around. Zeb seemed to have been accepted by Ollie, he seemed keen to work – maybe I could find a slot for him. He might not be the kind of person to have ideas. He seemed, like Ollie, content to work without expressing opinions on how things were done, so perhaps I could use him as just another pair of hands around the place for now. I'd have to tell Mother he was only here for a couple of weeks; maybe I could tell her I was giving him some work experience? I couldn't let her think she was right about me needing help or she'd think she'd won. Well, no, she'd *know* she'd won. Not knowing best simply didn't cross her mind; after all, she had had her whole life to understand the business, she'd been born into it. I'd had herbs thrust upon me and it was purely the luck of the draw that I enjoyed the work, was good at it, and had the kind of temperament that meant pleasing my mother was more important that heading overseas to pick grapes, or going off to university to study marine biology.

I'd not so much taken over the family firm as had the family firm squeezed into me until the impression was so deep that I couldn't get it out.

Resentment heated the back of my neck in the same way as the sun warmed my shoulder blades. I bent to add a few stems of lavender to my makeshift bouquet and wondered again why I'd gone along with it. *Why* hadn't I just turned on my heel, like those heroines in the books I read, all snappy and professional? Why hadn't I told Zeb that there wasn't a job and held the door ajar for him to push past me, offended and annoyed in a macho way? Why hadn't I rung Mother and snapped out a stream of unanswerable questions – I'd bought her out of the business, why did she think that there was any need for her to interfere any more? Why did she not consider me a grown woman who could run my own affairs? Why couldn't I *tell her anything*?

The mental picture broke down about there. Whilst I could imagine dismissing Zeb – after all, I didn't know the man – the mental image of offending my mother went all wobbly and pixelated, like the TV in the cottage when the weather was bad, accompanied by a sense of dread.

I looked back over at the slightly untidy and lanky dark figure, now hunched over some stubborn couch grass. I didn't want him here, but I needed him and my mother knew it and that made me itchy somewhere inside. She had no *right* to make decisions for me. She was still, despite four years of my sole ownership, trying to hang on to control over Drycott. Then, to stop myself from thinking about my mother, I tried to imagine telling Zebedee he could only stay for a few days, a fortnight at most. He'd be fine about it, I was sure. I'd have grounds, too, he'd been alarmed by the pig, rendered semi-speechless by her presence in the kitchen, and odd though it might seem, the pig was as much a part of Drycott Herbs as – well, as the herbs. Or me. I bet my mother hadn't mentioned *that* in whatever she'd put in the job advert.

Ollie saw me looking and stood up to wave. 'Hey, Tallie! Nearly finished this bed, would you like us to start doing some cutting? We've nearly sold out of herb posies; we could top up the buckets?'

Before I could reply, there was a commotion in the small car park outside the stables. Customers drove directly in off the road, and as the farm was situated on a vast sweeping bend in the narrow moorland lane, sometimes people not steering with enough concentration could be gathered by accident. We were used to vehicles arriving in a confused state then trying to reverse amid the herb buckets to make their way straight back out again, but this kerfuffle seemed worse than usual and I turned around to see a minibus nudging its way into a spot opposite the doors.

Ollie and I stared. High summer meant that we generally expected a glut of customers coming and going but a minibus was a new one on us. Herb lovers aren't usually the coach trip type.

The bus door opened and there was a gradual procession of people getting out, all of which was too much for Ollie. He bolted, heading off to the compost corner to busy himself with tidying and turning the compost heaps, while Zeb watched his sudden retreat from the saxifrage with a startled expression.

The bus continued to disgorge passengers, until they were

crowded in the car park, a collection of long hair, embroidered jackets, tight jeans and flapping skirts, as though the 1960s had come on an outing. Overhead, swifts screamed in dark streaks across the sky above our heads, darting their way into their nests under the eaves of the old stables, intent on feeding their newly hatched young. Several of the new arrivals ducked, which told me they were unused to the countryside, although their clothing had already given me the heads' up that they weren't exactly expecting the pig snuffling over her gate in their direction, or the bunches of herbs grouped in buckets outside the shop.

They all looked baffled and a bit shell-shocked. Maybe it had been a white-knuckle minibus ride. The road down into our steep-sided valley was precipitous in places and you hung on to your seat and hoped that smell of burning was from local bonfires, not from your brakes.

Zeb glanced over at me, then back in the direction that Ollie had taken. Ollie himself was now invisible; most likely he was crouching down behind the bins. Zeb's expression was still registering the same shock as it had when he'd encountered the pig, probably wondering what the hell he'd let himself in for, working for someone who hadn't even wanted a worker, and with a workmate who either monologued for Britain or ran away. You didn't get this sort of thing from influencing.

'Hi there!' An older man, long greying hair gathered into an unwise ponytail, who seemed to be in charge of the rag-tag group of visitors, saw me and approached. 'Who's in charge around here?' I saw him look towards Zeb, then back at me again, clearly not wanting to assume, but assuming pretty bloody hard that it must be a man.

I stepped forward. 'Me. I am. Tallie Fisher, I run Drycott Herbs, Mr...?'

The man looked me up and down slowly. It was an assessing look with widening eyes and a slight smile. Not sexual, not leering, which was just as well as he had to be in his fifties and, well preserved he may be, but I was not about to be letched at. 'I'm Simon Welbury.'

He said it as though I should know who he was. I didn't, so I just stared. My catmint drooped.

'I manage the band,' he went on, with a nod towards the collection of people in the car park, who were now beginning to filter through the gate in ones and twos, peering in at the stable building and staring at the herb beds.

'Oh?' I tried to sound politely interested but had no idea why I should be, and was, in fact, fighting an urge to join Ollie down the back of the compost storage.

'How can we help you, Mr Welbury?' Zeb came forward, wiping his hands down his legs and his presumption jerked me from my taken aback status and back to full management potential.

'Yes.' I threw Zeb a stern look for overstepping. 'What can we do for you?'

Simon Welbury looked at me again, in my tatty working trousers, my T-shirt speckled with shed nepeta petals and the smell of elderly and impatient cat which arose from my bundled flowers.

'Er,' he said. It was clearly the sort of day that bred confusion.

Zeb came further forward. I had to admit that he looked more managerial than me, or, at least his jeans were still clean and his shirt didn't look as though the Flower Fairies had staged a hit-and-run. 'You said "the band"?' he asked.

Simon turned to Zeb now and I could see his bafflement. How could the young woman – well, young*ish*, and definitely young compared to Simon – be the owner of this place and not the slightly smarter-dressed man who was approaching with confidence and not trying to hide behind a stinky bouquet? The dissonance was clearly written all over his face. 'Yes,' he said, trying to spread his words between us so he didn't have to commit to speaking to either one of us definitively. 'The band. The Goshawk Traders.'

He regarded us hopefully and with a proud expression, like a father revealing his offspring's Prize For Good Work.

'Wow,' said Zeb, faintly and his gaze flicked up to take in the variegated clothing of the people wandering around outside the shop, staring at buckets and picking up packs of dried herbs. 'The Goshawk Traders. Wow.'

I looked at both men and flourished my bundle of foliage. 'Who are they, then?' I asked.

Now they stared at me. In fact, the whip of the surprised ponytail nearly had my eye out. 'You've never heard of The Goshawk Traders?' Zeb asked. Simon just boggled. 'Best-selling band? Most downloaded albums? Headlining all the festivals this year?'

'Um,' I said, feeling stupid. 'I don't get a lot of time for stuff like that.' The only music I ever heard these days was the stuff we played in the shop, which was far more on the Peruvian Nose Flute end of the spectrum.

Simon clearly took pity on me. 'We're folk rock meets prog meets acid psychedelia,' he said. 'NME describes our music as the offspring of Mumford and Sons and Genesis delivered by The Grateful Dead.'

This did not enlighten me as much as he apparently thought it would. 'Are accordions involved?' I asked.

'Sometimes.'

'Oh dear.'

'Look, what can we help you with, Mr Welbury?' Zeb gave me a wide-eyed 'what the hell are you doing?' look. 'If you want to buy herbs...'

'Ah. No. Well, not quite. It's more *involved* than that.' Simon was talking to Zeb now, but that was fine. As long as nobody tried to send me to make tea, in which case I would, most certainly, play the 'this is my herb farm' card. But otherwise, I'd just stand here and listen. 'We'd like to film here.'

The multicoloured-clothed fraternity were still mooching around outside the shop, as though they were afraid to go too far from the minibus, like cats on a caravanning holiday.

'Film,' I said, trying the word out. 'Here.'

'Yes. We'd like to make some of the video for the new album here. We were driving past and Mika – that's Mika over there, viola and washboard – noticed your sign.'

Viola and washboard? I briefly wondered at the random words, then the phrase 'folk rock' echoed in the back of my head. Oh no, it was worse than I'd thought. Not just accordions, but washboards too.

Zeb was giving me increasingly desperate looks as though I were expected to say something but the only thing that occurred was the prevalent, 'Err.'

'You'd like to film a music video? Here?' He asked, eventually.

'Sizing the place up obviously, first, but, yes. If you'll have us.' The ponytail whipped again as Simon looked over his shoulder towards the band. 'Over here, lads!'

'Well, that's...' I began.

'How much?' Zeb waded in. 'I mean, obviously, you'd want exclusive use of the garden and parking, so there would be substantial costs to the business.' He gave me another wide-eyed look.

'We'll talk about that.' Simon smiled at the space somewhere between Zeb and me, clearly still uncertain as to who really *was* in charge and not wanting to offend the real boss. 'If the guys approve the place. We'll just have a bit of a walk around, size the surroundings up, that sort of thing. If that's all right?' he added to the air around my left ear.

I could feel another 'err' coming on, so was glad when Zeb said, 'I'm sure that's fine. It's fine, isn't it... Tallie?' Then he nudged me with his elbow.

The six band members wandered over in a leisurely fashion, four men and two women, or rather – I checked my presumption – four people in loose cotton trousers and two people in skirts. Lots of hair, some beards, piercings, a swirly tattoo and an overall air of patchouli; they were practically a caricature of a folk-rock band. 'This is Genevra, Will, Loke, Tessa, Vinnie and Mika.' Simon nodded towards each person; some of them waved rather sheepishly. 'The Goshawk Traders.'

I could see a couple of customers over in the yard, pointing and gabbling between themselves; one had pulled out a phone and was filming, and I was pretty sure it wasn't the delightful layout of the herb beds that was proving appealing.

'It's a gorgeous place you've got here.' This was Mika, a man with lavish dark hair swept back over the shoulders of a tailored jacket, an image of urbane male ruined by the baggy harem pants he was wearing. 'Oh yes.' Now he looked at me directly and I felt suddenly scruffier, smaller, hotter and as though I'd gained about four stone whilst standing here. 'You're the owner, right?'

He had very bright eyes, I noticed. Very bright and very dark, with long eyelashes that looked as though they were coated in mascara, which of course they very well might be. He smiled and I got hotter.

'Yes,' I said, vocabulary battling in my throat to force back the 'umm' that was struggling to get out, and making my voice higher-pitched than usual. 'Yes, that's me.'

He plays the washboard, the sensible part of my mind said. The *washboard*. But the non-sensible part of my mind, the part that was busy reacting to the knowing eyes and the high cheekbones, was shouting louder. This man was beautiful and he was talking to *me*.

'Amazing,' said the amazing man, and then the whole troupe, followed by Simon, set off for a wander around the perimeter walls, exclaiming and touching and sniffing, hems scraping gravel as they went and depositing little backwashes of grit in their wake.

'What is *wrong* with you?' Zeb said.

I tore my eyes away from the passage of the group and turned to him. 'Me? What's wrong with *me*? You've been here five minutes, I haven't even filled the forms in yet, and you're coming over all Earl of Grantham? You are here to do some part-time weeding and you think you can tell me…' I tailed off. Zeb was shaking his head.

'I'm sorry,' he said, hustling me by the elbow until we stood in the shelter of the Malva sylvestris. 'I told you a bit of a fib earlier. I'm not here for a part-time job.'

Some of the generalised irritation I'd been working up towards my mother evaporated. For once, this didn't look as though I could quietly lay blame at her door. 'Which is just as well because, as I told you, I didn't advertise one.' Zeb continued to stare at me as though it was supposed to be obvious why he'd come and I just wasn't getting it. 'Okay. So, why *are* you here, and if it's anything to do with HMRC I can tell you now that my tax returns are regular and squeaky clean.'

Zeb, with his floppy, half-spiked hair, who did not look like anyone the tax office would send on an investigation, gave me a pursed-lips look. 'That remains to be seen,' he said darkly. 'No. I actually run a business consultancy agency. Still quite small but I'm picking up business, and some of the business I picked up... is yours.'

My mind was freewheeling. Over in the car park I could see more cars pouring in and I felt a momentary lift of the spirits until I noted that all the occupants were training their attention on the band members, now standing at the junction of the radiating paths where a small bog garden was green and lush. It was also full of froglets, but they didn't seem to have noticed these, because there was a certain amount of posing going on.

I took a deep breath. 'My mother,' I said flatly.

'I don't know about that. But I've been hired for a month by a Mrs Amanda Fisher to raise the profile and turnover of the business.'

I stared over to where The Goshawk Traders were being stalked around the garden by a mob of phone-wielding people, and wondered whether my mother had influence in surprising spheres.

'And this sort of thing is exactly what you should be going for!' Zeb continued. 'Opening up to a wider marketing opportunity.'

Above us the mallow shook its leaves in a shiver of breeze. There was a sudden puff of scent, carried on the same breeze, from the lavender and thyme which were flowering nearby. A soft scent, one which carried memory: of helping my grandmother to cut herbs, the smell of the sheets on my bed rinsed in lavender water to help me sleep...

'I bought her out,' I said. 'She still draws a small amount of money from the business, but overall it's mine. She doesn't get a say in the marketing or anything else for that matter.'

'None of that is anything to do with me.' Zeb raised his head to watch the tight knot of people moving slowly along the paths. One or two had taken their attention away from the band to look at the herbs. 'But what *is* my concern is maximising your returns from this right now.'

'They don't want herbs! Everyone has just rolled in to see the – whatever they call themselves. It's hardly a huge sales opportunity, is it, unless you can conjure up about a hundred copies of whatever their last album is called for the shop.'

'Oh, good idea.' Zeb pulled his phone out and made a note. 'But of *course* this is a sales opportunity! You've got people through the door, that's the hard part. Now your job is to make them want to buy herbs.' He looked at my face. 'Isn't it? You haven't got a secret team of red-hot salespeople over there already?'

'It's just me and Ollie,' I muttered. He was right, of course he was.

'Oh dear.' Zeb made another note. 'It's worse than I thought. No sales assistance at all.'

We stood and looked at the band and Simon, who were gazing around at the layout and at the bunch of people following them at a small distance, phones outstretched, in silence for a moment.

'So you lied to me,' I said, watching with irritation as one of the women stripped flower heads from the foxgloves thoughtlessly with her fingers.

'I wanted a chance to see your set-up.'

'By lying. You could have just *said*.'

'I like to get a feel for businesses first. No point wading in with tips for improvement if you're already doing everything you can. I need to meet the workforce, see what's feasible for you, so it made sense to come in and work for a bit.' He sounded as though he were quoting from a manual. 'This' – he motioned towards the crowd in the middle of my garden – 'has just precipitated matters somewhat. And, to be fair, you didn't really ask, you pretty much accepted my story which was a touch on the thin side, to be honest.'

My mother. My *bloody* mother. Interfering again with a business that was nothing to do with her, other than her receiving a percentage of the profits, which was what we'd agreed when I'd bought her out. 'Just to keep my bank balance propped up, Natalie, darling,' she'd drawled. 'I need a little bit extra, you know that. You know how my health is, these days, I have so little…'

'I don't want marketing advice,' I said, sounding surprisingly firm. 'The business is ticking over nicely. I don't care what my mother said, or how she got you to agree to this, but I don't need you. Please go away.'

Overhead, the swifts shrieked as they played non-contact tag through the air. I could see Mika, taller than the rest of his bandmates, trailing a hand through the lemon balm bed and bending to sniff the resultant citrussy puff. He really was incredibly good looking, with his dark flop of hair and those intense eyes. It was a shame about the washboard.

Mika looked towards where Zeb and I were standing amid the falling mallow blossoms, almost as though we were trying to blend into the background. Even from two acres away I could feel his eyes on me. I didn't know whether it was best to turn away and pretend not to see him or keep looking in his direction but pretend not to be *able* to see him.

It was too late to do either. He grinned broadly and made an open-handed gesture, a kind of 'it's not up to me' movement that somehow managed to hint that if it *had* been up to him, the group would even now be setting up equipment and paying me large amounts of money.

'I suppose,' I added grudgingly, 'it would be a good earning opportunity if they filmed here.'

Zeb flicked me a look I saw out of the corner of my eye. I hoped he couldn't tell that I was watching Mika walk along the final path, only half my mind on the empty patch where Ollie had recently dug out some parsley that had bolted. The seed heads were hanging in my kitchen now with paper bags collecting the falling seed, and we'd meant to fill the gap with more mint, but hadn't got around to it yet.

'You're fired,' I said, almost dreamily to Zeb, and then wandered off across to the shop to serve any potential customers that might result from this incursion. It was just incidental that it would give me a better view of the band – *Mika especially*, my treacherous brain whispered – getting back on their bus.

3

The cottage was quiet. That was one thing you could say about it. It was also tiny, inconveniently laid out, prone to leaks and ridiculously creaky in high winds. But definitely quiet. Particularly after dark, when the gates were locked and I could sit in my kitchen alone, smelling the summer scents of the herbs beyond the open door, and listening to the scuffle in the beams above that I was very afraid might be mice.

I sat in the battered old armchair that had been Granny's, slumped over my knees with my head in my hands. I was supposed to be working, supposed to be filling in forms and checking out seed catalogues, but my laptop was on the floor beside the chair, its screen blank.

I kept coming back to Mother. Thinking she could hire me a marketing person without even mentioning it to me. I knew what she'd say though. 'Oh, Natalie, you know I'd love to be more involved with the business, but my health won't let me, so I thought I could help you out this way!'

There was no point in even raising it with her. No point in asking anything, or telling her that the business was mine now, that she had no right to interfere, even if she thought she was being helpful. There was absolutely no point. She'd laugh, brush me off, ask me to make her a cup of tea or pop to the shop for her. She'd avoid, deny, only talk about superficial things all the way through a conversation until I lost the desire to find answers. Or she'd be upset, seemingly appalled at my treachery at not wanting her help, and she'd take to her bed for a fortnight.

I rocked forwards over my knees a bit further. 'Granny, what do I *do*?' I said aloud. As usual, the shade of my grandmother remained silent on the subject, unless she was making her views known through the furtive rustling of rodent feet along the beams, and I couldn't decipher anything meaningful from that, other than that I probably ought to put the biscuits in tins rather than leave the packets on the worktop.

A car rattled along the lane past the gardens, slowed, and began the half-turn in through the gateway, arrested when it came up against the locked main gate. Well, what did they expect? It was half past nine and dark; how many pick-your-own herb places would still be open at this time of night? And how desperate would you have to be for a bunch of rosemary for your Sunday roast lamb to come all the way down our lane at this time of night?

I continued to stare, unfocused, at my knees. The evening air was doing its job of ironing out the stresses of the day with wind-borne wafts from the lavender bed undercut with the astringent smell from the fennel which hadn't recovered from the earlier pig attack and was going to need patching up. Tomorrow. I could do it tomorrow. Today was over and all that remained was a hot shower and to tip into my bed in the little back room upstairs. Yes. As soon as I could muster the energy, I'd get up and go to bed.

As I tried to persuade myself to get out of the chair and head upstairs, there was a rattle at the gate. Thieves? I jerked my head up. The shop was locked up, the till empty, and the hefty padlocks around the place were normally enough to deter casual snatchers. Unless someone was *really* desperate to gussy up their roast, nobody would come over the gate among the herbs, not in the dark.

But someone was. That sound was the weight of a person climbing the gate into the garden. One advantage of having grown up here was knowing every individual squeak and jingle it could make, and *that* noise was very definitely the gate dipping on its hinges as someone climbed up, followed by the squeal of rusty iron as the gate rebounded. They'd come right over. Any second now – yes, there was the slight crunch of the gravel beneath footsteps. There was no way to approach the cottage silently, unless you came directly over the herbs and that was asking for a broken ankle and some embarrassing questions when you were found face down and groaning in the sage bed.

I stood up and threw the switch by the back door. Instantly, the whole garden was flooded with enough light to read small print by. Every flower head stood stark against the darkness, every leaf arrested as though the light was glue, sticking them to the night. Big Pig snorted, her sleep disturbed up in the barn, and some of the guinea pigs squeaked hopefully, in case this had been a sudden dawn.

In the middle of the garden, one leg raised in the act of picking his way forward, was Zebedee McAuley-Wilson. He'd thrown his arm up over his eyes to shield his vision from the blinding levels of light and was also fixed in place by the sudden illumination. He looked like a scarecrow that couldn't look a rook in the eye.

I stood by the open door and watched him cautiously drop his arm, blink a few times, and then, adjusting to the light levels, see me.

'Can you turn it off?'

'I can, but I'm not going to,' I replied, folding my arms in what I hoped was a matter-of-fact way. I didn't go quite so far as to lean nonchalantly against the door behind me though, I wasn't quite that good an actor and my heart was still pounding at the sight of someone in the garden after dark.

'Okay.' Cautiously, because he was presumably still blinded by the floodlights, Zeb began to pick his way forwards, squinting down at his feet and blinking ferociously. I waited until he'd got all the way before I turned off the light and watched him shake his head and screw up his eyes, adjusting back to the more normal level of light from the kitchen bulb.

He stopped when he got to the door. 'May I come in?'

'What for?'

He looked past me into the kitchen. 'To talk about what we do next.'

I reached out and pulled the door closed, so its solidity was at my back. 'There is no "next". I fired you, remember?'

He'd been gone when I'd returned from selling a few bunches of herbs to some guilty-looking customers who'd obviously only turned up to see The Goshawk Traders. At least they'd bought something; the band had just got back onto the bus and gone. My eager eyes had sought out Mika, but he didn't look back at me as they drove away. He'd been involved in conversation with someone I couldn't see and I'd been flustered and overheated and forgotten the price of the sprayed angelica heads. But at least the contrast had been nice and quiet, and, once Ollie had been persuaded out from the compost corner, it had been a pleasant remainder of the day.

'You can't fire me. You didn't employ me.'

'But I don't want you here.'

'Then I suggest you tell that to the person who *did* employ me? Your mother, I think you said?'

I looked over at the distant outlines of the ivy that clambered enthusiastically over the far wall and muttered that she wouldn't listen.

'She's paying me, you know. For a month's worth of marketing advice,' Zeb went on.

'More fool her,' I replied tartly.

'No, I just meant, if she's paying me, then where's the harm in letting me stay on? You might not want me, but I could be useful.'

'Useful, how?'

He didn't speak for a moment. The silence rattled with seed heads in a passing breeze and an owl hooted atmospherically. The air was warm and heavy with scent but it was so familiar as to hardly register. 'Look,' Zeb said finally, and there was an urgency to his voice that took my attention away from the gently swaying ivy back to him. 'My business is new. I need some testimonials to put on my website and your mother has promised some extravagant praise if I can just turn this business around. I need the work, and you...' he tailed off to stare pointedly at the chamomile bed. 'You need some proper marketing,' he finished. 'We could help each other. Plus, it's already paid for.'

He was only half-lit in the amber light that came past me through the window from the kitchen lamp. He was hunched, the silhouette of his hair almost trembling with eagerness against the sky and there was something about his keen slender shape, bent forwards with the desire to stay employed, that reminded me of Ollie.

The owl hooted again and then flew, a ragged, torn-paper outline across the air of the garden.

'Oh, for heaven's sake, come inside,' I snapped. 'It's ridiculous trying to talk to you when you're grovelling in the dark.'

I opened the door and went into the kitchen, not looking to see if he followed, but I could hear his feet on the brick floor as he came in. I put the kettle on.

'It really is lovely here,' he said. His tone was humble.

'Stop it.' I fetched the mugs. I had to dig for a spare; Ollie would know if someone had used his mug and he wouldn't like it, so I found an ancient bone china cup at the back of the cupboard. 'I've been working here since I could toddle, there's nothing you can tell me about the business.'

There was a furtive squeak from somewhere in the rafters. I hoped he hadn't heard it.

'All right. Maybe you don't need help with the day-to-day stuff. But what about The Goshawk Traders? If Simon decides that they do want to film here, you could do with someone to help manage that. You'll want to publicise the fact that the gardens were used in their video, maximise visitor numbers for as long as possible afterwards. And what are you going to charge? You'll have to close the gardens while they're here, so you need to allow for...'

'Yes, I know!' In truth I felt a bit stupid, which was making me snappy. Stupid that I'd fallen for his 'looking for a part-time job' spiel. If I'd hustled him out there and then with the truth that there was no job, none of this current exchange would be happening, and I wouldn't be wanting to murder my mother. No, scrap that, I'd still be wanting to murder her, but it would be for some other reason. 'Sorry. I do know. I just – well. I haven't thought that far in advance yet; after all, they may decide not to film here at all.'

There was another silence into which the kettle boiled. It was clear that neither of us knew what to say from here on. I knew what I wanted to say – something about him being here under false pretences and my mother having no right to force her way into my life – but we'd covered that and I would only be digging over old ground.

'I used to be a chef,' Zeb said suddenly and surprisingly from behind me. I kept my eye on the kettle, unsure as to whether this was an unasked-for confidence or whether he was following some mental train of thought obvious only to him. When you worked with Ollie for a while you learned that only about twenty per cent of words actually got said by some people, and sometimes entire conversations with you went on without you even being aware that you'd spoken.

'A chef,' I echoed and poured water onto teabags because it gave me something to do with my hands and a reason for not turning around to face him, only to embarrass myself further.

'Yes.'

Good grief, this was painful. 'I still don't know what you're doing here at this time of night.' I turned around and caught him stroking his thumbnail along one of the cracks in the old table, his head bent and his hair flopping so that he now looked like David Tennant's sad younger brother. 'You presumably have a home to go to.'

'A flat.' He took the mug I held out. 'In Pickering. Over a takeaway.'

'Well, that's...'

'I had a house. A lovely house and a wife.' He spoke very quickly now, as though he wanted to get the words out. 'But being a chef can be dreadful hours and split shifts. We wanted to start a family but I was never home and she didn't know when I'd be coming back half the time.' He wasn't looking at me, he was keeping his eyes firmly fixed on the riven surface of the table. 'So we split up and I retrained and I'm having to start again.'

I had no idea why he was telling me this, and no idea how I was meant to react. 'I'm sure that was all very painful.' I sat back down in the slouchy chair. It had kept Granny's imprint so well, after the sixty or so years of her having sat in it, that I had to form myself into the shape of an eighty-five-year-old woman just to get comfortable.

'So I need this job.' Zeb slumped further forward until he was sitting almost by accident on one of the stools. 'I've lost everything and I have to start again, and your mother is willing to give me a shot. I'm hoping that telling you this will appeal to your better nature and stop you slinging me out of the door.'

'Ah. You want me to pity you.' His confessions made more sense now.

'No!' Now he sat upright and looked more like the assertive Zeb who had talked to Simon about payment this afternoon. 'I'm trying to explain why I'm here. Why I want you to give this a go, just for the month. What have you got to lose, after all?'

I sat back in the chair, cupping my hands around my steaming mug and looking at him, his elbows on the table and an urgent expression on his thin, dark face. What did I have to lose? My autonomy. My independence from my mother, hard won after years of fighting and a continuation of border skirmishes. I mean, I understood her need to keep me close, of course I did. Her life hadn't been easy, filled with losses and fear, and I was all she had. But even so...

Then I thought of the band, traipsing around our carefully laid out acres, those casual hands scooping at flowers and fingers snatching at leaves, releasing scents to the air and a confetti of petals strewn in their wake. The dark eyes of Mika, watching me, and I realised how desperately I wanted them to come and film here.

'Do you know how to get in touch with The Goshawk Traders?' I asked.

Zeb sat straighter again and put his mug down on the table. 'Simon gave me his details.'

'Then I think you should do that. Tell them we'd be delighted to have them film their video here. Lay it on a bit thick about how much we'd do for them – make the whole place available for as long as they wanted, close to the public, all that.'

'Payment?'

'Think of something. Not so much as to put them off, but enough to compensate for being closed while they're here.'

Zeb was scrabbling through his pockets. He finally pulled out his phone and started tapping in notes. 'That's great.'

'And you are not to tell my mother anything.'

He paused, fingers mid-tap. 'When you say *"anything"*...?'

'I mean about this place. No inside information, nothing about the band filming here or our turnover, what we're doing, what we're planning. Nothing. You can just about tell her what day it is, because she's always a bit hazy on that one. Did she ask for regular reports?'

'No, she...'

'She will. And I know she's the one paying you, but *I'm* the one who will kick you out on your ear if I find out that you're spying for her, okay?'

He looked at me steadily, as though he were reading the subtext in my words. 'You and your mother...' he began, carefully.

'If I use the phrase "it's complicated", that doesn't even touch the sides. She's paying you but I'm the boss and if you want your testimonials and some pictures for your website, then I'm the one you have to stay on the right side of.'

The steady look continued. It was as though the apologetic Zeb, the Zeb who'd been telling me about his past life, had flown out of the door like a sprite, and here I was, left with the businessman. But I'd seen the vulnerability, that half-closed expression when he'd told me about his life. Zeb had offered me something that not many others had, an insight into life outside this little valley, an intimacy that tingled at the edges of my brain. Very few people treated me as though I were worth talking to, but he had.

After a moment or two Zeb said, 'That sounds remarkably Mafia-like for someone who runs a herb farm.' I didn't reply and eventually he sighed. 'Right. I'm paid by her but I'm working for you, got it.'

'You never know, perhaps the Goshawk people might put some work your way too, if you play your cards right.'

I got a sudden smile for that, a brightening that lit his eyes. 'Never thought of that, good call.'

'But you absolutely and totally *do not tell my mother anything*.' I gave the words such heavy emphasis that he frowned.

'Right. Got it.'

'Especially about the pig.'

'The pig?'

I sighed. 'The pig in the kitchen. The pets' corner was my idea and my mother thinks – look, never mind.'

'Pig silence will be maintained.'

'Better be.'

We drank our tea in a slightly more comfortable silence, whilst outside the owls continued their haunted conversation across the garden.

4

'Do you need me to get you any shopping, Mum?'

It was the next morning, time for my scheduled visit although there would often be phone calls summoning me to an emergency – which could range from her tripping over in the kitchen to a moth on the bedroom curtains – in between times. I'd left Ollie sorting out the bald spot in the parsley bed and Zeb keeping an eye on the shop. Usually I had to close when I visited my mother, so at least he was coming in handy for something.

'No, it's fine, darling, I'm going in later myself. When I feel up to it.'

My mother was currently a duvet-swathed form in the middle of her bed. She'd suffered from poor health since before I was born, something that her doctors didn't seem to know what to do with or how to treat.

'All right. Shall I open the curtains and get some air in?'

The duvet shuddered. 'I need the darkness, Natalie, you know how I get.'

Alongside her, unasked questions also shuddered. All

those things I wanted to say, all those things I wanted to ask. She was carefully not mentioning Zeb, and I was, equally carefully, not saying that I had even met him. There was no way I could phrase my disapproval at her actions and no point in my even trying. She would spin the situation to make everything sound reasonable with a 'but I'm just *interested*, darling'.

If it ever came to a passive-aggressive-off, we'd probably tie for first place.

'Right. Well then. I'd better get back.'

My mother struggled up onto her elbows. 'Have you still got that weird kid working for you? Oliver Twist, or whatever his name is?'

'Ollie Boniface, Mum. Yes. Ollie's still there.'

I didn't know why she was asking. I'd employed Ollie when I'd fully taken over the business four years ago, he was nothing to do with her.

'But you don't really need him, do you? Can't he get a job somewhere else?'

She looked older today, I thought, seeing her face properly now she'd half sat up against the ridiculous number of pillows she insisted having on her bed. She was fifty-two but today her cheeks were sunken and her wrinkles were prominent. She looked far older than her years, but she'd had a traumatic life, and stress aged you dreadfully. It was when I looked at my mother's face that I felt the most pity for her, but if she was going to diss Ollie, that pity was in short supply.

'He's not good with people,' I said shortly. 'But he *is* great with herbs, so he's staying.'

'But you're *paying* him, darling, and he doesn't do much more than dig, does he? You could fire him and save his wages.'

I thought of Ollie, his joy at working with the plants,

helping out with the animals. 'No, Mum. I need another pair of hands around the place.'

'I'm sure you could manage,' she muttered from beneath the duvet foothills. 'It's only digging and weeding and suchlike, and you could do that in the evenings.'

I sighed, but inwardly. Despite having herself been brought up at Drycott, my mother could be surprisingly obtuse about the sheer amount of work involved. 'I have to do the paperwork in the evenings, Mum. I wouldn't have time. Or the forms and the tax stuff wouldn't be done properly, and I can't risk that.'

Mother sank back, like a tanker going down in the Atlantic. 'Hmm,' she said. 'Anyway. I need a sleep now, Natalie darling, so I'll see you later, all right?'

There was nothing I could say to this. I was there because she summoned me, then behaved as though my arrival was all my own idea and she couldn't possibly *think* why I kept popping round all the time. I left the musky, stuffy bedroom with the tightly drawn curtains and drove back to the wonderful reassurance of the herb farm.

Which was in a state of uproar.

'You have to keep the rabbits off the herb beds!' I could hear Ollie yelling as I parked outside the stables. 'Else they eat everything!'

'I'm more worried about that damn pig!' Zeb was bellowing back. The pair of them were communicating as though they had a mountain between them rather than a couple of acres of planting, and when I got out of the car I could see Zeb, armed with the ubiquitous broom, chasing rabbits around the parsley while Ollie poked ineffectually at the bulk of the pig who was snorting her way happily into the earth near the moss garden.

'What on earth has happened?' I climbed over the gate, so as not to give the pig any chance to get out into the car park and plopped down in the middle of a small guinea pig family gathering, to much squeaky dismay.

'Got out,' Ollie said shortly. 'All of them.'

Three black rabbits hopped merrily through the thyme. I had brief Mr McGregor thoughts. 'Get the pig back first,' I said briskly, trying to stifle the panic that was rising at the state of my herbs. 'She can do the most damage. We'll round up the others afterwards.'

Ollie and Zeb, armed with the broom, began rather ineffectually to try to sweep the pig back towards the barn, with vague 'shoo shoo' cries.

I picked up a bucket, one of the rubberised ones we used to carry stuff up and down the garden, put a handful of gravel from the path in it, and shook it. 'Come on, pig, dinner!'

The sow raised her head hopefully and began to trot towards me, surprisingly dainty on her spreading trotters, but with increasing pace. I ran towards the barn and into the penned half where she had her quarters, with the pig behind me, and as soon as she got between the gates that contained her I slammed the pen shut and whipped myself and the bucket out of reach. Disappointed snorting resulted, and she stuck her head into her feed trough as though she firmly believed there must be *something* there, even if she couldn't see it.

I fetched a scoop of pig feed from the locked bin and tipped it into the feeder. I got a damp cough of acknowledgement and a piggy snout instantly started to hoover up the feed, one small eye rotating upwards to watch me, presumably in case of more miracle dinner.

'I'm only feeding you because otherwise you won't come back to the bucket,' I muttered.

Snort. This time it sounded derisory and I deserved it. I couldn't even stand porcine disappointment. I was not only a people-pleaser, I was a pig-pleaser too. I sighed. My mother had trained me well.

Ollie came into the barn with an armful of rabbits gathered to his chest. Our rabbits were pretty tame. They had to be when they were petted on a daily basis by children, and they tended not to run too far and were easy to handle, so they were flopped in a relaxed way between Ollie's arms. One was chewing lightly at his collar.

'Got 'em,' he announced cheerfully.

'How did they get out?' I looked at the catches on the doors. The rabbits shared a pen with the guinea pigs in the opposite corner to the Big Pig, which meant that not only their pen gates but the big barn gate had to be left open in order for everything to escape.

Ollie looked puzzled as though it had only just occurred to him. 'Dunno.' He plopped the rabbity bundle over the wire wall into their enclosure. 'I fed them all when I got here and I haven't done the mucking out yet.'

'You shut the gates after feeding?' I don't know why I asked. Ollie was assiduous to the point of obsession about checking things like that.

'Yes,' was all he said. There was no point in saying 'are you sure?' because Ollie was *always* sure. It was how his mind worked.

Behind us, Zeb came into the barn. He'd got a bucket of guinea pigs making squeakily disgruntled noises from the bottom of the container. 'How many should there be?' he asked. He looked rather ruffled and his knees were muddy. 'Because they're sneaky little buggers. I caught one trying to blend in to the rosemary back there, and it's not as if they're green or anything.'

'Nine,' Ollie said definitively. 'There's nine of them.'

'I've got seven.' Zeb peered into the bucket. 'I think. They move about a lot. There might be nine, if the big ones are sitting on some little ones.'

I found that I was looking at him sideways. *Someone* was opening gates. *Someone* was letting the animals out, and whilst the rabbits and guinea pigs were annoying, unless they were out for hours they couldn't do *that* much damage to the herbs. The pig, on the other hand…

'Have you got any idea how they escaped?' I asked quickly, watching his face.

'Not a scooby.' He shrugged and the movement made his bucket start squeaking again. 'Just heard Ollie shout, ran up from the kitchen and then you arrived. I'm not really used to animals, except in oven-ready pieces.'

He looked and sounded innocent. Thin, dark and intense, but innocent.

I looked around the barn. Pig was snuffling her way through her straw bedding now in search of any dropped food. Her gate was firmly fastened, the sliding bolt fully in place. The rabbits' pen had the same gate arrangement, but inside their actual accommodation was a metal fenced run which sat on the concrete floor to stop them from digging out, with a cosy house at one end. The rabbits were bouncing around their perimeter, like prisoners of war checking out the guards' timetable.

'Can we all make sure we double-check the gates?' I tried to sound firm. 'Someone must be… not quite fastening them properly.'

I couldn't accuse Ollie, because whilst I could possibly consider him leaving one gate open accidentally once, which would have accounted for the pig's kitchen adventure yesterday, I absolutely would not believe that he could do it twice in a row.

Ollie was detail-orientated. Leaving *two* gates open was just beyond him.

Which meant it was Zeb. And, given his irritation at having to round up the animals, it seemed unlikely that he was doing this with any good intent. Anyway, why *would* he? He was here to help us with marketing, not destroy the business. A tiny, pernicious voice inside my head whispered, *That's why he said he was here. It might not be true, you know. Perhaps Mum is paying him to discredit Ollie,* but I dismissed it. I had to accept what he said, what else could I do?

The two men muttered affirmatives, both sounding slightly annoyed.

'Right.' I watched Zeb decant his furry passengers into the pen and then come back out, bolting the gate in an almost pointed way. 'Let's get on, shall we? Ollie, we could do with some more mint varieties in the shop, if you could cut some bunches and put them on display?'

I had no idea why I phrased it as a question. I was the boss here, after all. Ollie brushed down the front of his shirt, gave me a beaming smile and set out for the shed where his herb-harvesting equipment lived.

'What about me?' Zeb was still holding the bucket, but relieved of its contents it swung at the end of his arm and I could see the bones in his shoulder moving under his T-shirt. He was too thin and too edgy for a herb gardener. Just the sight of him irritated me, and that was without the consideration of him letting out the animals. He reminded me of my mother, that was why. Not physically, obviously, he was tall and skinny for a start and not notably wrapped in a duvet, but his presence was her fault. Her responsibility. And the fact that neither she nor I had mentioned him earlier made my nerves feel as though someone was running a metal comb over their exposed endings.

'Are you still pretending that you're here to help with the garden?' My tone was sharp, accusatory, although I hadn't really meant it to be, and the glance he gave me told me it might have been too pointed.

'I can find out more about how the business is run and how best to promote it if I do a few hours here and there as part of the workforce.' His voice was very level. 'But I'd like a look at the turnover and your books too, some time.'

'Not going to happen,' I said firmly. The business was mine and my responsibility, but also not going quite as well as I'd hoped. Large local supermarkets were selling cut herbs, and they were open 24/7 so we'd lost a lot of the culinary business, and 'herbs as décor' was strictly a luxury market. The cost-of-living crisis had meant cut backs for everyone, and festooning your living room with bouquets of flowering herbs had become just a little bit less of a necessity. Thanks to the fact that Granny had owned the house and land outright and I had no mortgage, we were just about managing, but I'd had to take a loan to buy Mother out of the business, which was a drain on resources.

Zeb's mouth twisted. 'Right.' He sounded nearly as pointed as me now. 'If you don't need financial advice then I'll stick to the advertising end, shall I?'

He put the guinea pig transporting bucket down very carefully in the corner of the barn and went out with his back very straight. His whole posture screamed that he'd been insulted to the extent that it was very nearly a flounce, but I didn't know why. I was putting up with him as a favour and because he'd already been paid, but it didn't mean I had to like it.

'You do that. Have you got in touch with the band people yet to ask if they've made a decision about using us as a location?' I made my voice a little more conciliatory now, although I had to call out through the big barn door so that he could hear, and volume, plus the smell of pig, may have taken some of the smoothness out of my words.

I saw his step hesitate, as though he half considered just walking away without answering. Then he turned and came back.

'Yes. Simon said he'd try to get over again today to talk to you.'

I felt an immediate lift somewhere above my stomach. They were seriously considering it; that would be a boost to the business. A tiny fizz in the midst of that lift reminded me of Mika: dark interested eyes and a smile that sent little shivers down my spine.

'I suppose... you should be there when I talk to him.' I had no idea why I was offering this concession to Zeb. *I* could talk to Simon, of course I could. I knew how business was done – extract the maximum amount of money for the minimum amount of effort – and if the band were as well-known as everyone apart from me seemed to think, they'd have a budget for this sort of thing. But the thought that Zeb might report my business dealings back to my mother still rattled around in the back of my head. My people-pleasing was at war with my desire to tell her nothing about my business affairs; this way I could keep Zeb happy and he could tell Mother that we were diversifying and earning money into the bargain.

Zeb came up to the barn door and looked at me. 'You really want me there?' he asked, pushing his hands into the front pockets of his jeans, which made his elbows stick out at awkward angles. There was something endearing about his stance, something that made him look vulnerable; at odds with the business-minded individual he was portraying himself as.

'You might think of things I forget to ask.' It was all I could think of to say but we both seemed to have softened a little. He'd stopped flouncing and I'd stopped sounding as though I were ordering a flunky to sweep the yard. Treating him more like an equal.

'That could be a good idea,' Zeb said thoughtfully to the gravel flooring. 'Plus I might get some fabulous contacts from Simon, for the business.'

'I don't think folk-rock bands are going to be all that up on herbs.' I sounded acidic again and tried to cover my acerbity by coming out of the barn and joining Zeb in the sunshine. Behind me the pig grunted; she'd presumably been hoping for more food. 'Apart from the ones you can smoke, and there's none of that here.'

Zeb looked sideways at me from under a flopping curtain of hair. 'I actually meant *my* business,' he said dryly.

'Oh.' My ears heated up with embarrassment and I covered myself. 'Okay, well, we'd better get on if we're going to be in a meeting later. If you could keep an eye on the shop and help Ollie with the mint arrangements, I'm going to check on the damage the animals have done to the plants and work out whether we need to replace any.'

'Fine.' But he'd taken his hands out of his pockets now and dropped his shoulders. I was good at body language; when you lived with Mother for any length of time you learned to read subliminal signals because overt signals were hard to come by, and I knew that the olive branch of including him in the meeting with Simon had worked.

As I wandered over to the most badly beaten section of the garden I pondered on why I cared so much? Why would it matter if Zeb didn't like me and was in a state of permanent anger towards me? He was only here for a month, and *that* was on my sufferance. I could kick him out at any time and any financial restitution would be between him and my mother and none of my business. I didn't want *her* interfering and I didn't want *him* poking about in my affairs.

So why didn't I just say so?

The rosemary, being fairly resistant to damage, had fared better than the parsley. That poor plant was looking trampled and there were distinct nibble marks, plus the smell of crushed salad garnish wafted over the entire area. I knelt down and began trimming off the worst of the broken stalks and battered leaves. Luckily there was plenty to go round, so some judicious pruning soon made the bed look presentable, although the same couldn't be said for the fennel. Some of that looked as though it had been sat on, and there was already a big bald patch where yesterday's damage had been removed. I sighed.

'I hope we've got enough left to plant out,' I muttered. That was the problem with the tall herbs, they showed any slight impact so much more than the low-growing types. One good gale could level the most attractive plants, which was why this completely walled and sheltered spot was so ideal for my business. Granny had known what she was doing when she set it up, I mused, kicking gravel back onto the path from where it had been liberally redistributed onto the planting by pig and folk band activity. Drycott Herbs had been her baby. Well, my mother had been her baby, but Granny had always seemed rather fonder of the herb nursery than of raising children, which was probably why Mother was an only child; that and she'd turned out to be an experiment that Granny hadn't wanted to risk repeating.

The sun, high now above us and only slightly filtered through the tracery of the birch trees that formed a small copse in the field over the wall, soothed me. It settled on my head like a warm hat and slid down my back into my tired limbs, soft as a kiss. I inhaled deeply, getting a good waft from the variety of different leaves and flowers that variously needled or coiled around my legs as I stood in the middle of the bedding. This was where I belonged. *My* herb farm, *my* business, and Mother and her machinations could just fuck off.

It was just a shame that Granny wasn't still here to affirm my decision. But then, if she had still been here, Drycott would still belong to her, I'd probably be living now with my mother in her suffocating little house in the village and I'd be... what would I be? What would I ever have become if Granny hadn't taken me under her wing and taught me about herbs. Growing them, planting them. The right times to harvest. How to make arrangements that looked better than conventional flower bouquets, how to use them in cooking.

Without Granny, would I just have been a carer for my mother?

Ollie gave me a beaming smile, heading towards the mint beds wielding his best secateurs, and I bit my lip. *No*. I had to stop thinking that way. Some people just needed a bit more looking after than others. It wasn't Ollie's fault that he couldn't cope with strangers and that he was detail-orientated. And it wasn't my Mother's fault that she was so ill and needed help. It wasn't her fault that her life had gone so wrong after I was born, that it had caused her such trauma she now found it hard to function.

Nobody's fault. But it did mean that the end result was pieces that needed to be picked up, and I'd learned how to do that without asking why from an early age.

I stretched myself under the sun's warmth again and let myself relax. A bee, heading for the lavender bushes, bounced off my forehead, adjusted its flight path and lurched downwards to join its hive mates poking around the pale flowers at knee level. I bent to pick a bee-free stem and let the scent soothe me. Good old lavender. Reliable, perpetual, attractive – if occasionally tending to scruffiness, it didn't need much looking after and would do its thing year after year with the minimum of care.

I pulled the flower head between my fingers and wondered whether I'd been thinking of lavender or myself when that description had come to mind. There were an extraordinary number of similarities, although I was marginally less attractive to bees and probably – I looked down at my worn jeans and untucked shirt – less fragrant. The pale purple petals fluttered from my hands, torn and spoiled, to decorate the gravel as though fairy confetti had been liberally thrown at a fae wedding.

I had to stop this. Introspection was all very well, but it wouldn't get the fennel bed patched or the mallows tied in to their decorative supports. Self-analysis was self-indulgent. I was me, Natalie, Tallie to my friends, Fisher. Owner of Drycott Herbs and… well, all right, not very much else, but I had my own business and that was enough. The total lack of social life and any appreciable kind of romance was a side effect of having to work so hard, that was all. I tried really hard not to add to myself that having a mother who needed me on call 24/7 didn't help either of these things much, because hadn't I already agreed with myself that none of this could be helped? She hadn't chosen to be physically frail and mentally non-resilient, had she?

What she *had* done, though, was land me with Zeb McAuley-Whatsit, who was currently drifting around outside the shop, rearranging buckets and ignoring the fact that a car had pulled in and there were people who actively needed to be sold things wandering around the stable yard.

I watched him tweak a few buckets into place and then straighten up to greet the potential customers. He looked a lot more personable at a distance; he had that tall, long-limbed thing going on that made every gesture into something big, and his hair wasn't so objectionably floppy from back here. He looked like just another worker, the irritating questions and intrusive behaviour being too far off to bother me. I tried to ignore the tiny tug that I felt somewhere deep inside when I thought of his offer of help; the way he looked as though life had hit him very hard around the head and then expected him to get up and carry on. There was just *something* about Zeb, and I wasn't sure if that tug was fellow feeling or a desire to bury him under the mint bed.

While I was looking at him, Zeb looked up and across the acres and met my eye. It was too late to switch focus and pretend I'd really been checking the line of the fencing or assessing the distant marigolds; he'd clearly caught me staring at him because he raised his eyebrows. I didn't know whether he was questioning my stare, expressing surprise that I was even looking his way or raising a problem with a customer, but to cover my confusion at being caught out, I set off towards him. I had to work on a reason for going over, so I focused on the customers, a young couple, who might have questions. After all, it wasn't unreasonable for me to want to be there, selling things. I *ought* to be there and actively selling, in fact. Just so that he was in absolutely no doubt that this was *my* place.

I didn't let myself think about my suspicions regarding letting the animals out. There was no time now to wonder whether Zeb, whatever his reasons, was trying to sabotage my business.

5

It was mid-afternoon before Simon arrived, sweeping into the car park with a flourish of scattered gravel in a sporty little Audi. My heart did a tiny swoop at his arrival and then a dive when I realised that he hadn't brought any members of the band with him. That he hadn't brought *Mika* with him, to be precise. It felt a bit like visiting the Louvre only for the *Mona Lisa* to be away for cleaning that day.

I greeted him at the gate, where I had fortuitously been weeding the car park and not at all waiting for his arrival.

'Come on through to the cottage.' I led Simon through the gardens, slowly, to give him a chance to appreciate the lazy wave of stems in the faint breeze and the way the tree shadows threw a jigsaw of darkness across the walls. It was all looking very photogenic and lovely, which was fabulous. We needed the money that filming would bring in, and seeing the place under a grey cushion of cloud with everything hanging soggily heavy and accessorised with disgruntled damp pig smells might have put him off.

I tried to suppress my disappointment at the lack of Mika. There was absolutely no reason for the band to have come with Simon, but... damn it, I had little enough to look forward to. Did the universe really have to grudge me this tiny spark? Evidently it did.

I motioned Simon into the cottage kitchen, and he bent his head to come in under the low lintel. I had carefully swept the floor, wiped all the sides and put pots of herbs on almost all the flat surfaces to conjure the atmosphere of 'herb garden'. As I followed him in, however, I realised that it looked overdone. As though I were shouting 'this is a *garden*' in his ear; too desperate. And the light shining through the pots on the windowsill gave the room an underwater feel, too reedy and dim, which I hadn't noticed when I'd carefully and artfully distributed them earlier this morning. Once I was in the kitchen I swooped up some of the pots into a bundle at one end of the worktop.

'I've been potting up,' I said, to explain the Kew Gardens Glasshouse ambience.

Simon sat at the table and looked around. He seemed happy enough.

Zeb was now looming in the doorway. He had stalked down the long path, following us at a distance, but he hesitated at the door. 'Are you going to talk about – you know? The band filming?' he asked, standing on the threshold with one leg raised to step inside.

I widened my eyes. 'Well I don't think he's here to discuss buying industrial quantities of dill, is he?' I hissed back, then relented. 'Come on. You might as well earn whatever my mother is paying you,' I said, straining the words through a smile directed at Simon, who was looking around at the masses of greenery, and me, with an amiable expression.

'I shall do my best.' The foot came over the doorstep and Zeb greeted Simon. 'Hello.'

The men shook hands. Nobody had shaken hands with me, I thought, snarling inwardly. But then, I hadn't offered to shake hands with Simon. Should I have offered? When had I last shaken hands with anyone? I rearranged more pots to give myself something to do. There was now a veritable forest jammed up under the old dresser top, giving the kitchen – which always had a slightly olde worlde air from the beams and the flagstones and the ancient wooden furniture – a distinct tinge of the alchemist's basement.

Simon looked around the room and I watched him notice the herbs, scan the big beams and give the scratched old table a small smile. His ponytail looked less ridiculous indoors, somehow, or maybe he'd just brushed his hair better, because it sat neatly on the collar of his linen jacket. Still a little bit try-hard, as though Simon wanted to be younger, to fit in with his band, but not quite as out of place as the long hair had looked yesterday in the unforgiving daylight and the hint of bald spot.

'You've got a lovely location,' he said. 'We've talked about it, and the band are very keen to film here, if you think you can put up with us.'

I tried to lean nonchalantly against the Aga, despite the fact that it was so hot it was scorching my bum. 'How long would you need to be here?' I asked, working out what to do with my arms. Zeb gave me a nod of approval.

'Maybe a week?'

'A *week*?' I sounded horrified. I *was* horrified, I'd been thinking an afternoon, maybe a day at worst.

'Yes, it can take a while to get the right shots. And the band like to get involved, if you see what I mean; they need to settle into an area.'

'Why here?' This was Zeb, with the first interesting question I'd heard him ask. 'Why Drycott?'

Simon rested his elbows on the table and chewed at a nail. He'd stopped looking at us now and seemed to be focusing on a flapping variegated sage which waved cheerfully in a draught from the worktop. 'I love this part of the world,' he said.

'I rather mean, what attracted you to our gardens?' Zeb went on. 'If you saw an advertisement or something – we're trying to maximise our reach, you see.'

I sat down hard on the urge to say '*my* gardens'.

'The band and I were on our way back from a short-notice gig, over at Whitby,' Simon continued. He was speaking slowly, as though constructing the sentences word by word, not sure the syllables would fit together, like fake Lego. 'We're staying in York at the moment, playing some impromptu gigs to advertise the new album and I thought this looked like a picturesque route to drive. As we came past, Mika saw your sign and persuaded everyone to stop off.' Now the words flowed more easily. 'And when we saw the location, they all said it would be a great place to film for the new album. Put some videos up on YouTube – the band has its own channel, you know – some shots on Insta, start getting the word out.' He ran a hand over the top of his head, smoothing back stray wisps that were escaping the ponytail. 'The new album is out in November.'

'Oh,' was all I could think to say. They were just passing. I supposed that explained their desire to look around the gardens first. I had been hoping that they'd seen one of my adverts in the local free press – I needed some evidence that those were paying for themselves – but 'just passing' would do.

'So, I was thinking, perhaps we could book the garden out for this week?' Simon smiled a smile that seemed completely unconcerned that this was extremely short notice, that I'd have to close up completely, that I'd wanted to paint the back fence while the weather was nice, and what the hell did I do with Ollie?

'That sounds fine.' Zeb didn't even look at me. 'What's the budget?'

They talked money. I carried on staring at them, heads bent together as they negotiated amounts that I could only dream of. I had to admit Zeb was very good at this bit. He pointed out the costs to the gardens of being closed to the public and that we would have to lay off staff temporarily. I was bloody certain Ollie was going to get paid, even if he just hid behind the compost for a week. He emphasised that work would still have to be done, just around filming, which might be inconvenient. I would never have considered the practicalities of trying to weed, cut and make up bouquets very early in the morning before filming started, and of keeping the shop open even though the garden itself was closed. I would just have visualised vast amounts of money and nodded to all Simon's suggestions.

Perhaps my mother had been right. She'd always said I was more of a gardener than a businesswoman. In some small way my continuing to keep Drycott Herbs running and in profit must cause her a degree of dissonance.

In my pocket, my phone jingled and I excused myself to step outside into the smell of mint from Ollie's machinations, to find my mother on my phone.

'Natalie, could you pop over to the chemist and pick up some of my pills?'

I gazed around at the peace and tranquillity of my garden, where the sun was just beginning its setting slide behind the hills, streaking the clouds with a blood-in-water effect of pink, and bit down on the irritation.

'Mum, I was over this morning and you said you didn't need anything.'

A pause. The irritation had come out in my voice and I knew how wrong that was. She couldn't help being ill; it wasn't her fault and it wouldn't cost me anything – apart from fuel, time, and involvement in the business – to drop in at the chemist and take her pills over.

'*Darling.*' The word was drawled, tired and pain filled, the syllables broken. 'I'm in *such agony* and I didn't realise I was out of tablets until I looked in my handbag. It's only five minutes.'

I pictured her, still swaddled in the duvet despite the heat of the day and that stifling bedroom. 'All right. I'll be over soon.' Again, that emotion that I kept well tamped down. A smouldering ember of exasperation that experience had taught me it was pointless to give the oxygen of articulation. 'But it will have to wait, I'm in a meeting.'

'That's good.' Mollified now, her voice took on a more cheery note. 'But you'll have to hurry, the chemist closes at six tonight, don't forget.' And she hung up.

Damn, she was right. It was, a quick glance at the sky told me, getting on for six now.

'I have to dash out for a minute,' I said to the men who were still deep in conversation. 'My mother needs something.'

Zeb startled back away from his stance bent over the table, drawing with one finger on its cracked surface as though outlining a journey on an invisible map. Simon had been nodding along. 'But this is a business meeting.'

I'd already palmed my car keys and drawn on a jacket against the chill that inevitably resulted once the day had vanished below the far line of hills. 'I won't be long.'

Zeb and Simon looked at me, then at each other. Zeb looked aghast. 'But…'

'Won't be long.' I hesitated. I wanted to say something along the lines of 'don't come to any arrangements until I get back', or 'I know this is stupid but she needs her pills', but instead, I galloped over to my car, parked outside the cottage in the miniscule driveway, and hurtled off to the village, where I caught the chemist just about to lock the door and pleaded my way in for a packet of Mother's pills.

'We do a delivery service.' The pharmacist gave my dishevelled jacket and obviously rushed air a sympathetic smile. 'She could ring us direct and we'd take them over.'

'You know what she's like.'

Of course they did. This pharmacy had been dealing with Amanda Fisher since she was tiny. The little village, in this scoop of moorland which contained the houses, the few shops and Drycott Herbs, hadn't changed much since William I had blasted it into bleakness during the Harrying of the North. Drycott hadn't just been Harried, it had been Petered too, and now it was as though the population had made a collective decision never to move again. The chemist had been a chemist since 1932.

'Yes, but you can try telling her.' Again, another sympathetic look. 'You shouldn't have to dash out.' A wave of a hand as she ushered me from the premises, indicating the lateness of the hour and the fluster of my arrival.

I tried to imagine telling my mother that she 'ought' to do anything, and couldn't. When not struggling under the weight of her illness, Mother had the personality force of a heavy goods vehicle. You attempted to deflect it at your peril and the resultant injury, although never physical, was the type of scar that throbbed whenever it rained.

I drove ferociously to her house with my car tyres making impressive screeching sounds as I cornered, drew up in a fume of brakes, and hurled myself in through the front door, surprising my mother in the kitchen.

'Hello, darling. That was quick.'

She was making herself tea. She was also dressed, and evidently functional.

'I'm in the middle of a meeting.' I dropped the pills on the table. 'And I have to get back.'

'Oh.' Her face fell. She was still pale, I noticed, and hadn't done her make-up. Well, that would explain why she hadn't gone to the chemist's herself; she hated to be seen outside without her 'face' on, as though she imagined people wouldn't recognise her without her features being carefully outlined in whatever the latest range being advertised on TikTok was. 'I thought you'd stay for tea.'

Again that tug of guilt that bound me to her. I was her daughter, her only child, was it really too much to ask that I sat and ate with her, as though I were still that seven-year-old home from school, asking when I could go out into the garden to help Granny? But then I remembered that I'd left Zeb in charge of a meeting that could make or break my finances this year.

'Sorry, no, I have to go and negotiate. It's work, Mum, honestly.'

A sigh and her hand closed around the two packs of her pills. 'All right then. But I was going to make us something nice.'

'I'll come by tomorrow.' I dropped a quick kiss on her cheek. 'To make sure you're feeling better.'

Then I swept out to breathe deeply as the last of the day crept away beyond the hills. I'd had a narrow escape. She often cried if I said I couldn't stay, but this time she'd seemed almost resigned. Perhaps she was learning that I really *did* have to work? Ahaha – the laughter was hollow. Despite her having grown up on the herb farm, despite her having taken it over when her own mother died, my mother seemed to regard my job as just a cosmetic thing I did to fill in time. Specifically, to fill in time between doing bits and pieces for her.

I threw the car down the lanes in a way that would have been counted extremely unsafe somewhere more populous, and arrived back at the gardens just in time to pass Simon driving away. He gave me a toot of the horn and a blithe little wave as we inched past one another in the gateway, and then a blast of engine noise as he sped off, leaving me with Zeb in the car park.

'You let him go! Without talking to me!' I launched myself out of the car and Zeb put a galvanised bucket of valerian stems between himself and my ire.

'You weren't here,' he countered in a reasonable tone.

'You should have waited. I wasn't going to be long, and this is *my* business. I hope nothing legal got signed without me.'

'You weren't here,' Zeb repeated, his tone still smooth enough to level concrete. 'And Simon's coming back tomorrow to sort the paperwork – if you can manage to stick around for long enough.'

Now *that* was barbed. Although he hadn't dropped his gaze from my face, he'd picked up the bucket and was fussing the flower heads into a more orderly arrangement, as though he were worried that he might have to use the container as a shield.

'My mother needed me to fetch her prescription,' I snapped. I carefully didn't mention that the pills were over-the-counter ones and that she had been up and about and perfectly capable of fetching them herself. She would have had her reasons for not going, and I hadn't had time to have them listed out for me.

'Yes, but we were in a meeting.' He shuffled the bucket again, then bent to sniff the valerian which, as it smelled, as many of the decorative herbs did, of elderly cat, was clearly a ruse to avoid looking at me. 'It was business, and you walked out.'

'I did not walk out, I told you where I was going. And it's nothing to do with you where, when and why I do things,' I said, becoming more aware with each word I uttered that, in his position of self-appointed PR guru, it actually *was* his concern where, when and why I did things. Although it did give me a tiny inner smile that, should he report my inadequacies as the head of the business back to my mother, he was going to have to put a spin on 'having to attend to my mother' that would be worthy of a first-class bowler before she agreed it to be a black mark against me.

'Does this happen often?' Zeb's tone was different now, less accusatory and a little softer. 'Do you have to care for your mother?'

'Define "care",' I said and sighed. 'No. No, of course it doesn't. Today was an emergency.' I tried not to think of Mother, up and about in the kitchen and just not bothered about going to pick up her own pills. 'But I do like to help her out when I can. She's ill. Didn't she mention any of this when she recruited you for this job?'

'Er no, we didn't meet, not in person. Everything was done via Zoom and email.' Zeb looked slightly ashamed. 'I didn't think that our not meeting might be due to her being ill, I just thought it was a privacy thing.'

I nodded. If he hadn't met her in the flesh, then he wouldn't know. How could he? And without the rest of the story, without knowing what lay behind the complicated relationship I shared with my parent, I had to admit that it all looked dodgy – as though I were some kind of Girl Friday at my mother's disposal. 'It's complicated,' I said.

'That's what people say online when they mean they're in a relationship they aren't sure about.' He smiled at me now and I had to admit, his was a nice smile. 'Or when they don't think the other person is committed.'

'Oh, no, not like that,' I hastened in. 'It's more...' I tailed off. The story of my background wasn't anything to do with him and yet I felt an odd kind of urge to explain myself. It must have been the way he was looking at me; his expression mixed curiosity with unwarranted pity, which didn't sit well on his kind of face.

'I think,' he said after we'd been standing mired in our lack of conversation for a while, 'that we ought to have a chat.'

I panicked and snatched the bucket of valerian from him, the heads swinging from side to side as though they were trying to keep track of who was speaking. 'No, it's all good. I'll tell Mother that she can't interrupt meetings and I won't go over when we're busy anyway.' I spoke very fast, heading off his questions at the pass. 'She just likes to feel she's still involved, I think, I mean, she doesn't have much else in her life apart from me and Drycott and she wasn't really keen to hand it over to me but...'

His expression had switched to a raised-eyebrow impatience for me to stop talking which stifled my justifications.

'I meant, we need to talk about what Simon wants to do next week and how we're going to manage things,' he said, rather too evenly for my liking.

'Oh.'

'He's had some good ideas, but we really should discuss them tomorrow morning, before he arrives.'

'Oh.'

'Your mother...' He stopped and turned away, seemingly to watch the feather of birch branches that traced their way across the far fence, swept in a passing breeze. 'Your mother is your problem.'

Great. As if I didn't know that. 'I see,' I said, meaninglessly.

'I'm off now. I sent Ollie home early too, so you might want to close up and get the place tidy for tomorrow. I think Simon is bringing the band over to plan out the video?'

He made it a question. Why had he made it a question? Presumably he wasn't questioning the absent Simon as to why it was necessary for The Goshawk Traders to personally be on site, when they'd have a team of professionals who would script, set up equipment and work out shooting angles. Unless – I felt my collar tighten and become hot as a wash of embarrassment crept up the back of my neck – unless he'd seen my reaction to Mika and knew how much I'd anticipated his return.

My mouth flapped.

'Er,' I said, a feature of a lot of my conversations with Zeb.

He raised an eyebrow, turned smartly and walked over to his car. 'Tomorrow, then,' he said, getting in with a cheery, and to me dismissive, wave of his hand. He folded himself into the driver's seat and drove off with no further acknowledgement of my presence and I threw the bucket of valerian onto the gravel.

'Bastard,' I said. 'The utter turd.'

Swifts shrieked through the air above me and the pig snorted a reminder that it was feeding time in the barn. Everything else was silent. Even the herbs were still now, the breeze blown off to somewhere where its gentle passing would be remarked on with words like zephyr and caress, rather than followed by someone with string who muttered about having to stake the mallow. I sighed and began picking up the sprawled valerian, whose pale stems now feathered across the gravel like exhausted brides.

'This is *my* business,' I muttered, vindictively ramming the flower stems into the bucket so hard that they buckled. 'Zebedee can just boing off and do one.'

The bitter tinge of mint gave my words an extra edge and, pleased with myself for managing to get angry, I set about my garden work.

6

I dressed carefully the next morning. I'd got up early to allow myself time for a bath and to wash and plait my hair, turn out a clean white linen shirt and some slightly better-fitting jeans than my usual work ones. *Mika's coming over.* The thought gave me a pleasant buzz through my body, a little burst of energy that was unusual at this time in the morning, when the sun was barely clambering over the wall and the dew still lay its pearls along the feathery edges of the yarrow.

While I didn't allow myself to consider that Mika would do any more than smile my way, that was more than I could usually expect from a day. I had to take my little hints of pleasure where and when I could, and the thought of a handsome musician smiling in my direction gave me a warmth in my stomach that even tea couldn't compete with. I carefully ignored the mental image of Mika playing the washboard, replacing it with a more romantic vision of a viola tucked under his firm chin and those sparkling eyes smiling and long fingers drawing low, soulful music from a skilfully wielded bow over strings.

It was a pretty picture. And, as my love life resided entirely

Once Upon a Thyme 59

in my head these days, it kept me going sufficiently to take all the potted herbs that had added ambience yesterday back outside where I ranged them against the cottage wall. It was supposed to give the area the look as though the cottage had grown up amongst the plants, ethereal and other-worldly, but actually gave it more of a medieval peasant vibe. I rearranged the pots to leave the path free and was surprised by the arrival of Zeb, who must have climbed the gate without my hearing him.

'Good morning,' I trilled with the incipient arrival of Mika making me cheerful.

Zeb eyed me suspiciously. 'You look...' He stopped and was obviously raking carefully through his vocabulary. 'Clean,' he finished.

'Making a good impression for when the band arrive,' I said, perkily. 'Could you go and feed the pig, please?'

Zeb's mouth twisted. 'Can't you do it? I have a difficult relationship with the pig. She tries to knock me over.'

I became a little less buoyant. 'She tries to knock *everyone* over, you aren't special. And I'm clean, as you so charmingly pointed out. Plus, you're an employee, I'm the boss, so you are on trough duty for today.' His obvious reluctance made me add, 'And I have to go and cut some herbs for the buckets by the shop, before we have to close off the gardens.'

'I could do that?' His nervous glances towards the barn made me wonder if he knew I suspected him of being the one to leave the gates open on purpose. Was he assessing his chances of getting away with it again, when there was clearly only him and me here?

'You don't know what we need. And anyway, as you said yourself, you don't know much about herbs apart from having been a chef.'

'Which is not making me an ideal carer for Big Pig either,' he pointed out. 'She's just a collection of animated chops and rashers as far as I am concerned.'

'I'm sure she'll forgive you.' I nodded towards the barn. 'And you can throw some of the ruined parsley cuttings in for the rabbits and guinea pigs; Ollie left it all piled near the shed.'

I didn't give him a chance to demur any further, and took myself off to start filling the buckets. We were going to keep the shop open, even though the gardens themselves were closed. There was plenty of stock and people would just have to be cheated of the chance to cut their own herbs for a week; we needed the income.

Mallow and vervain, melissa and verbena, tall fronds of each stood fragrant and floral, their smudgy green foliage attractive against the bright silver of the buckets and the mellow old stone of the converted stable. I was very pleased with the effect as I tied each bundle into loose bunches with agricultural twine, so that they sprawled louchely in their containers, like drunken old men in a club. Over in the barn I could hear Big Pig starting her day with a good snorting honk in Zeb's direction, the rattle of the feed bin lid and the whistle-squeak of the guinea pigs, alert to the fact that their food would be next.

It was all rather lovely. Zeb was doing my bidding, the band would soon be here to start filming and both I and my herbs were looking their best. The weather was good and my mother... well, she'd been visited yesterday. I'd be able to admire Mika from afar while I manned the shop and generally tried to stop people trampling over newly established plant beds.

Today was going to be a good day and it wasn't often that I could think that. I was far more used to getting out of bed and staring out of my window across the neatly portioned acres wondering what would go wrong.

On occasion, I had even caught myself thinking that taking over Drycott had been a mistake. After Granny had died, when my mother had been in overall charge, I'd had the benefit of her buffering me from the worst of the effects of seasonal dips in sales. She had the knack of never seeming to worry about anything, and, I'd been able to concentrate on digging and planting and working out what was likely to be the most profitable seeds to put in for next year. Now Drycott was all mine, and so was the worry.

But nothing could go wrong today. I leaned against the warm stone blocks of the shopfront and felt the second-hand warmth seep into my bones. A brief concern about hubris made itself known. Something could *always* go wrong, there was never a day that passed without a minor catastrophe, but I bit my lip and squashed the feeling that doom was only ever minutes away. No. It would all be lovely. Of course it would.

I watched Zeb conscientiously double-checking the bolts on the barn gates as he came out with his bucket swinging, and bit my lip again. He would know I was watching. Even he wouldn't be daft enough to fail to fasten those gates when he was the only person who could be blamed for letting Big Pig escape, and while I was actually staring at him. Would he?

I watched him put the bucket back and stand, scanning the garden. *Would he?* Perhaps Zeb didn't want this job as much as he pretended; perhaps he was sabotaging things in order to be fired? He could say goodbye to any references that didn't contain the words *ruined the business,* but maybe he had reasons of his own for not wanting to continue. I didn't, after all, know very much about Zeb McAuley-Wilson, other than that he'd changed career and seemed diligent about his new one. I should really think about that.

On the other hand, I thought, as Zeb stared around again, I knew more about him than I wanted to. He'd changed his entire life. Lost his wife to divorce because of an over-demanding job, moved to a small flat – over a takeaway, if I remembered rightly – in Pickering. But I didn't know how he *felt* about anything. That mobile, large-eyed face didn't give much away, other than a general sense of anxiety and a desire to make the best of things that made me feel slightly guilty. He seemed nice: pleasant, kind, and he was good with the animals despite his lack of experience.

Behind me came the sound of vehicles on the road beyond the gate, the heavy growl of big engines rolling carefully down the gradient and the whine of brakes being judiciously applied. Why was I wasting time thinking about Zeb and his general air of sad disappointment in life, when Mika… when the band were about to arrive? I leaped to open the main gates – they were early, it was barely eight o'clock and I'd wanted to sweep the yard and finish cutting more herbs before they arrived, but here they were, two large lorries and the minibus pulling into the car park.

I had also wanted to park them at the far end, against the fencing to the garden to allow more room for passing customers to pull straight in, but they all arranged themselves by the entrance. They filled the entire car park, leaving barely a corridor, so any passing trade would have to drive between the two lorries to get in, which was almost guaranteed to put off any casual customers. I snarled inwardly. I hadn't realised that 'filming a video' would involve an entire team and quite so much heavy equipment. The shop could stay open for now, but we'd have to close completely when actual filming started.

Then the minibus drew up next to the door of the shop and I hurried to look busy and engaged in case Mika was looking out of the window. The buckets got another rearrangement and the herbs an unnecessary amount of fluffing and sorting, so I was crouching over the willowy spikes of the vervain as the band came slowly down the steps. Simon jumped from the driver's seat, and I watched him land on the gravel, wince and lean quickly against the side of the bus with a quick glance at the band members to see if they had noticed his less-than-athletic exit. He needn't have worried, they all seemed preoccupied with the task of getting out of the bus, talking amongst themselves over shoulders and shaking skirts and re-lacing boots.

There was Mika, last off the bus, resplendent in a wine-coloured jacket and bow tie, skinny black jeans and knee-high Dr Marten boots. He looked exotic, with his dark hair blowing in the newly risen breeze, bright eyes sparking with mischief and his stubbled cheeks highlighting slanted cheekbones. I found myself staring, peeping from between the spires of herb stems like a mortal watching the arrival of the gods from Mount Olympus.

'I've fed the pig.' Zeb's voice, prosaic in tone and content, made me swing around and nearly tip my display into a riot of broken stalks and puddles.

'Oh! You made me jump.' I excused myself for my overblown response. I hadn't heard him coming, so bound up in staring at Mika that even the crunch of Zeb's arrival over the gravel hadn't registered.

'Well,' Zeb said dryly, 'I do work here. For now. Would you like me to liaise with Simon while they sort out what they're doing and you keep an eye on… the shop?'

He meant Mika and he meant me to know he meant Mika.

He'd even angled his eyebrows in such a way that his sarcasm was evident on his face, which was a neat trick.

'I need to know where they want to film, so that I can make sure there's no damage to the herbs,' I said defensively, as though I'd really been checking out the band's disembarkation in case they'd been about to trample merrily through the herb beds. 'This *is* my business.'

'Well done,' Zeb said, still dry and sarcastic. 'I'm glad you can remember that when it's appropriate.'

'*You* don't have to be here at all,' I hissed, annoyance finally getting the upper hand.

'And if I hadn't been, they wouldn't be filming here. You had to leave during the vital meeting, remember? *I* set this up with Simon, while you attended to your mother.'

I opened my mouth to spit a well-crafted reply, but couldn't think of one. He was absolutely right. Left to my own devices, I'd have blown the opportunity. Wouldn't I? Or would I have ignored my mother's pleas and sorted details with Simon, while my phone blew up with accusatory messages?

I knew the answer to that, of course I did. I would have gone to the chemist, shrugged my shoulders at the lost chance to have a famous band filming in my garden, and plodded along on passing trade and the occasional advert that we could afford in the local paper.

I was my mother's daughter. She and I both knew it.

'Well, all right. But make sure they keep to the paths.' I looked away from my precarious bouquets and back over to the band, who were milling around and talking to the team of men that the lorries had brought, while Simon manhandled instrument cases out of the minibus.

'Will do, boss.' Zeb stepped smartly away. I narrowed my eyes in his direction, which brought Mika back into my eyeline again. God, he was gorgeous. The other three male band members, one in a plain white T-shirt and artfully torn jeans, one in dungaree overalls and the other in a pair of harem pants so loose as to almost be a skirt, faded into insignificance beside Mika. All their careful facial hair and assorted dreadlocks were mere background to Mika's slow smile and elegant movement.

I shook my head and went to unlock the shop. This was ridiculous. *I* was ridiculous. Until the other day I hadn't even heard of The Goshawk Traders. I had nothing in common with any of them, other than an apparent desire to be around herbs and knowing what a washboard was, and Mika was nothing more to me than a pleasant backdrop for a few hours. He was a passing distraction, that was all.

Nothing in this world would drag from me the admission that I had looked him up online, read all the articles I could find and checked out all his pictures. I knew that he was the same age as me, his star sign was Aquarius, he'd been born in Sussex, had a younger brother and parents who were classically trained musicians. He'd dated a famous pop star, featured in a lifestyle magazine in his tastefully decorated London home, and had given long, impassioned interviews on the state of the world and how humans could best help themselves and their environment.

I didn't know why I'd read the articles which had only left me feeling more inadequate and even more in awe of the man. When I'd thought he was just an attractive member of a band I'd never heard of, admiring him from a distance had been doable. Now I knew his parents' names, the name of his dog and what colour his kitchen was, professional detachment was a lot harder. Even though I knew those articles were carefully curated for their readership, the knowledge gave me a strange sense of second-hand intimacy, almost as though I personally had been invited into his converted chapel home to admire the monk's bench seating and the double height glass window in the bedroom.

When I looked over at where the band were now sorting themselves out, taking instruments out and checking them over, and Mika glanced up, saw me looking and gave me a big grin and a small wave with a viola bow, I found myself staggering, weak-kneed, back into the shelter of the shop.

This was *ridiculous*.

I rearranged the soapwort to give myself something to do. I could hide in here, pretend that manning the shop was important enough to keep myself out of the way.

'Tallie!' Zeb was waving from outside. I could see him, broken into fragments by the wobbly old glass which had probably been in the window since before the First World War. 'You're wanted!'

Oh bugger. I tried to pretend extreme busyness, but Zeb kept waving.

'All right, what's the matter?' I emerged to Zeb fidgeting on the gravel of the yard while men unspooled cables and erected a lighting system that could have illuminated a stadium. The sun was shining and I had no idea why they would need fifty million watts of competition for it.

'Simon wants to talk to you about where they can set up. They're looking at a static piece with the band playing and then shots of them walking around. Or something. He'll explain it to you, but I thought you'd be the one to know where they'd do least damage.'

There was no sarcasm or apology in his tone. He sounded friendly, open and professional, even though he was standing slightly hunched and with his hair flopping into one eye.

'So *now* I'm in charge?' I asked.

One eyebrow raised and vanished into the lock of hair now threatening to obscure his vision. 'If you can spare the time.'

Now *that* was sarcastic. I felt better immediately. Zeb unsettled me. He was a constant reminder that my mother still had an involvement in my business. I didn't want to like him because I didn't entirely know where his loyalty lay, and when he was being slightly unpleasant to me everything felt better. I could dislike him with reason.

'I'd better come and talk to Simon then, before you let them stomp all over the new fennel beds.'

I came out of the shop and almost walked directly into Mika, who was carrying something across the yard from the minibus.

'Hey, steady there!' He put out a hand to catch me as I tried to stop dead, failed, and slithered on the loose gravel. 'Slow down, you'll do yourself an injury.'

His hand was on my shoulder, half supporting me and half preventing me from crashing into him. He wore silver rings on every finger, smelled of musky scent and peppermint and his expression was of dark concern. I was instantly fifteen again. I could see Zeb, behind Mika's shoulder, giving me a look built entirely of evils.

'I... err... no, sorry, I mean, I... sorry, I was just...' I blushed, performed a move that was somewhere between a curtsy and a weak-kneed 'gathering of self', and dashed across the yard. Away from Zeb and his pointed statements about my work, but most of all away from Mika and his inordinate amount of sex appeal.

He'd actually *touched me*! I regressed further, from fifteen to about twelve, when I'd had an all-encompassing crush on a TV gardener, for which I blamed Granny's addiction to his weekly programme. I'd had pictures of him in my room, spent the money I earned from weeding and planting and bringing on seedlings for Granny on his books, and endured my mother's comments about his way of dressing and his accent with only the occasional bite-back on his behalf.

It was like that, only worse, because Mika was right here in front of me. Well, behind me now, as I fled through the gate and towards where the stolid figure of Simon was perching on the edge of the pond, looking uncomfortable.

'You needed to talk to me?' I panted on arrival, hoping that my cheeks had cooled sufficiently for me not to compete with the brilliant scarlet of the poppies which had self-seeded amongst the artemisia, and which were waving their bright flags of petal recklessly in the breeze.

'Just wondering where is off-limits, and whether we could set up here in front of the pond for the static shots? We've decided to start filming today, while the weather is good, striking whilst the iron is hot and all that. Have the band playing with the garden behind them?' Simon waved a hand, indicating the pond and the half of the garden that lay towards the shop.

'Of course. Maybe facing this way?' I inched myself around so that I had my back to the road. 'Then the backdrop is the garden and the wall out to the fields beyond, rather than the shop, which might get busy later? I thought you were only looking the place over today, so I haven't closed up.' *And please pay extra for the disruption,* I didn't add.

Simon nodded slowly. 'Yeah. That would be good.' Then he looked down at his feet, patting the mossy side of the pond as though distracting himself. 'It's a really lovely setting you've got here. Have you owned Drycott for long?'

At least talking to Simon meant I wasn't having to contend with Zeb, or tiptoe around Mika. He was nice and normal and not at all intimidating. He looked a little as though he should be wearing steel-rimmed glasses and standing behind a double bass in a jazz band.

'It was my grandparents' business,' I said, sitting beside him and trailing a hand in the water. 'They bought it when it was the local coal distribution yard and turned it into this. Grandad died before I was born and Granny carried on – it was more of a market garden back then of course. She moved into herbs later. My mum grew up here, in the cottage and only moved out to the village when she got married and had me. Then... then things happened, we moved back here to help Granny, Mum took over the business when Granny died, and I bought her out four years ago, so now it's mine.'

'Nice.' Simon was still looking at his feet, scuffing little piles of gravel into heaps with his trainered toes. 'It's a beautiful setting.'

He was clearly making conversation because he wasn't even looking at the 'beautiful setting', unless he had some kind of visual obsession with pea shingle and the wispy feathers of chamomile which grew over the edges of its bed to smooth the periphery of the path with fragrant greenery.

'I like it,' I said. 'Mind you, it's a bit less lovely in the winter months. We have some hardy plants and we try to make sure there's year-round interest, but it's hard in January when there's a couple of feet of snow on the ground.'

'How do you keep ticking over?'

I had no idea why Simon was so interested in the business. He was here to film, so it's here-and-now attractiveness was more of a concern, surely? 'We sell dried herbs and bouquets, and we have playgroups and toddler groups on educational visits and to play with the animals. We do birthday parties too.'

This had been a recent innovation and I was quite proud of

it. I was even considering a Shetland pony, for diversification, although I'd had one as a child and it had bitten, kicked and been very reluctant to be ridden, so I was still thinking it over. Big Pig was enough of a challenge for now.

Simon was nodding, still seemingly lost in his own thoughts. 'That's good,' he said vaguely. Then his eyes snapped up from the ground and he turned to look at me with an intensity that was startling. 'You seem happy. Are you happy here?'

The question was one that I often asked myself, late at night when I was exhausted and should be sleeping. *Was* I happy? I worked hard, I had my own business; it was creative and I could do what I wanted. I had my cottage, Ollie as workforce and cute, cuddly animals depending on me. But truly, was I *happy?*

'Mostly,' I said, the surprise at the question forcing honesty out of me. 'I mean, it's hard work and it can get lonely out here. But I do love it, really.'

Simon smiled. 'Best in summer though, eh?'

I thought of the acres under snow. Smooth and clean, with only the seed heads of the tallest plants bobbing above the field of whiteness. Birds flocking in to peck at them, the quiet of the deserted roads and the warm, composty fug of the kitchen where I'd spend the hours potting up seedlings and going through my herb books.

'It's not so bad in winter either,' I said. Then, with more strength to my words, 'I love it here.'

Simon smiled another vague smile, as though he were somewhere else. 'Good,' he murmured. 'That's good.' He seemed to be thinking of something other than a simple acknowledgement of my general content at living at Drycott, because he shook his head, coming up for air. 'You said your mother sold the place to you. Is she still around?'

'Oh, yes, she lives in the village.'

'You've no other family? No... brothers or sisters?'

I looked around again. Simon's questioning, while impersonal and seemingly just out of interest, made me uncomfortable. I never talked about my family, or lack of it, that was probably why. 'No. There's nobody else at all, just me and Mum.'

'That must be nice for you, to have her so close, then.'

I side-eyed him, but there was no sarcasm in his tone. But then, of course Simon had never met my mother. 'Yes,' I said loyally and stood up. 'Do you want to get set up now? Zeb and I can get out of your way so you have free run of the place; we'll sit up here in the shop in case of passing trade.'

Various men were trundling up and down the paths carrying pieces of equipment and behind them the band members sauntered about, poised and self-assured. I tried not to look at Mika.

'Hmm.' Simon was now focused somewhere in the distance towards the cottage, where I'd left the kitchen blind drawn after an early start. There was an expression on his face that I couldn't understand; he looked lost in a memory.

'Simon? We'll leave you to it?'

Simon jerked back to himself. I didn't know where he had been but it had made his brows crease together and his mouth had gained two brackets of tension. 'Oh! Yes, sorry, of course. We'll crack on while we have the light; catering will be up at eleven so we can break then. Yes. Of course.' He stood up and saw me evidently trying not to gaze at the band. 'Er, Tallie...' Now he sounded awkward.

'What?'

Simon leaned in a little closer. In front of us a frog plopped into the water from the mossy surround of the pond, a small, domestic sort of sound which made me smile. 'Mika,' Simon said. 'Just – be careful. I mean, he's a lovely lad, but he can be a bit...'

I felt instantly embarrassed and also defensive. I'd obviously been, well, obvious in my staring, but then I would defy any straight woman to look in Mika's direction and not feel their temperature rise and their eyes widen. He was a fever on legs. 'He's just one of the band,' I said, lying through my teeth. 'And I don't think he's even noticed me.'

'Oh, he's noticed,' Simon said darkly. 'Be careful, that's all.'

I had to admit to assuming a grace I hadn't pretended to up until then, as I turned away from Simon and headed back towards the shop, passing The Goshawk Traders carrying their instruments down to the centre of the garden with a flirty little smile. Simon thought Mika had noticed me, to the extent of trying to warn me off! Not that I needed warning, obviously, I had no more intention of provoking a famous musician than I did of seducing Zeb or Ollie, but it gave me a warm, solid sort of feeling in my chest. I had been noticed.

It did wonders for my self-esteem and I may have pranced a little as I went into the shop to surprise Zeb sniffing a dried herb posy.

'These are stale,' he announced. But it would take more than his depressing levels of down-to-earth to bring me off my fluffy cloud of gorgeousness. *Mika* had noticed *me*.

'We'll make up some new ones,' I practically trilled. 'Thanks for noticing.' Yep, I was riding that waft of joy all the way into being nice to Zeb territory. 'We can move those over into the decoration slot. If we're closing the shop from tomorrow we'll have plenty of time to restock.'

Zeb gave me a curious look, not unnaturally because I'd been sharp to the point of cutting with him up until now. Expressing gratitude when he'd told me, essentially, that I wasn't running the place properly, was always going to arouse suspicion. 'Okay,' he said and replaced the posy carefully on its shelf. 'So, what did Simon want?'

He wanted me to know that Mika has noticed me. 'Just some questions about where to film. And to chat about the place generally.' In unwarranted detail, now I came to think about it. Why on earth would it matter to Simon whether I was happy or not or how the business was going? 'I told him we'd stay over here, handy for manning the shop and out of the way while they film.'

Zeb was still looking at me as though he suspected that I'd had some kind of enlightenment whilst Simon and I had chatted. To be honest, it felt a little that way. The thought that Mika was watching me, that he had seen something in me *worth* watching, had made me lose about a stone in weight and gain an assurance of movement that only deportment lessons and a million pounds could have given me before. 'Don't you want to make sure that they aren't trampling the fennel beds?' Zeb asked, and the slight note of sarcasm brought me out of my tiny private dream in which Mika showed me his home and introduced me to his parents. Of course, that was what I'd half-accused him of doing earlier, wasn't it?

'Sorry,' I said, obviously surprising him again. 'I know you wouldn't have done that really.'

'Wow.' It was an under-the-breath mutter. 'Chatting about this place has cheered you up no end.'

I wasn't about to tell him the real reason for my cheerfulness, so instead I replied, 'It's not often anyone asks how I came to be here. People just sort of – accept me running the place, nobody asks how I can afford it or whether I enjoy it or anything. It's like nobody is really interested in *me*.' I stopped talking suddenly, aware that the ebullience currently bobbing me around in the stratosphere was causing me to be too talkative. Particularly considering this was Zeb, who might be an agent for my mother.

'So how *did* you come to be running Drycott?' Zeb leaned back against the counter. Outside, two of the lorry guys were arguing about something electrical, with much flourishing of wires.

'What?'

'You said nobody ever asks, so I'm asking.' He swung himself up to sit on the reclaimed wood counter that I'd made out of some of the old beams from the stable. 'Go on. We've got time to kill.'

I was taken aback. Did Zeb think that, now I'd been nice to him once or twice, he could dig into my background? My perplexity must have shown on my face, because he gave me a small grin and dangled his legs. 'After all, you know about me. Ex-chef, broken marriage, new career, blah-di-blah. Your turn.'

So, for the second time in ten minutes, I found myself reciting my life story. It had sounded matter-of-fact when I'd told Simon but suddenly here, in the shop which smelled almost antiseptically of dried thyme and mint, it sounded thin. As though life had dropped into my lap with a private education, fortuitous cottage and acres of land, and I was playing at running a business because I didn't know what else to do.

Which, when I thought about it critically, was close to the truth.

When I stopped talking, Zeb was still sitting swinging his legs, his head up so that he could see out of the window. I wondered what he was looking at. The view was almost entirely of the car park, and lorries were filling most of that.

'What about your dad?' he asked. 'You haven't mentioned him.'

This was the bit I always tried to avoid. 'He died,' I said shortly. 'When I was tiny. I never knew him.'

Now Zeb looked away from the bright square set high in the wall of the dark little shop. His gaze roamed the packets and jars of herbs for a second and then came to rest on my face. 'Ah,' he said. 'Sorry.'

I shook my head and went to the apothecary cupboard which stored samples of the culinary herbs, each in its own little drawer, carefully labelled. 'It's fine,' I said, fiddling with the marjoram. 'Like I said, I never missed him because I don't remember him being about at all. It was hard on Mum though. She had to come back here to live with Granny.'

'Do you know what happened?'

I could feel Zeb watching me, over my shoulder. This was all wrong. It was too dark in here, too musty and old. All the furniture was old, either reclaimed from when the shop had been the stable belonging to the cottage, which had been the local coal yard years ago, or bought from flea markets. Too old, too dark, and the smell of herbs was no longer the reassuring background perfume I'd known all my life – now it was ancient and dry, the smell of the graveyard.

'I don't like talking about it,' I said, sliding the marjoram drawer shut and adjusting the label.

'Does it feel a bit like it all happened to someone else?' Zeb asked, surprising me enough that I turned around. 'That's how I feel. About my life before all – this.' He waved a hand, hit a bunch of meadowsweet hanging head down above the counter, and caused a rain of dried flowers, which caught in his hair. 'I sometimes feel that I had a dream about getting married and being a chef, and I'm only now starting to wake up to real life.'

'No, I'm sorry, that's weird.' I saw him dust himself down, the white fronded petals trailing down like scented dandruff. 'Life changes. Doesn't mean it didn't happen.'

'What do you *do* with this stuff?' He knocked the last of the meadowsweet onto the counter and stared at it.

'Meadowsweet? Lots. You can make dye from it, use it for scent; it contains the active ingredient of aspirin too, so you can make a mild painkiller from the flower buds.' I ran my hand over one of the hanging bunches so that the trailing mare's tail tickled my palm.

'You could probably kill someone with herbs, if you wanted to,' he observed.

'I could, but I wouldn't. I don't grow any of the really dangerous plants, the nightshades and the hemlocks and all that, even though they can be useful medicinally.' I glanced up and caught his eye. 'Too easy for accidents to happen when you've got a pick-your-own farm and I'd never forgive myself.'

'No, you wouldn't, would you?'

It sounded personal, not like a general observation. His whole attitude was making me uncomfortable now, as though the questions had a point to them that he was trying to obfuscate behind a pretended interest.

'If you're trying to find out whether my dad died of poisoning, no, he didn't. It was a car crash, and, no, I didn't cause it, I was only a year old.'

Now there was a darkness to his expression, almost as though it had absorbed some of the astringency from the air. Not quite bitter, but curled around at the edges, dry and hard, like leaves that had been put away damp. 'I wasn't thinking any such thing, Tallie,' he said quietly.

'Well, good.'

'So you never knew him? That must have been difficult for your mother.'

I thought of my mother. Rattling around her cottage in the village, huddled up in the dark of her oppressively warm bedroom, sending me out for her pills. 'Yes. Her life has been hard. Bringing me up on her own, losing her husband so young and being ill.'

'And that's why you do so much for her?' Zeb had his head tilted so he could see my face. There was too much shadow in here.

'Yes,' I said slowly. I hoped he was going to change the subject soon. Talking about my mother and how and why we behaved the way we did around one another always made me feel – disloyal. As though I was prying into a relationship that was none of my business, which was downright peculiar, because as far as I was aware you can't pry into your *own* relationships. 'I like to try to make life easier for her, if I can.'

'Hence putting up with me, I suppose.' Zeb slithered down off the counter, a mixture of movement and limbs that made him look suddenly like an accident in action. But the change of subject was reassuring, now we were moving away from the topic of my mother. 'Maybe we should see how things are going outside?'

He flung open the door and instantly the cool darkness of the shop, with its sombre wood and rows of jars and drawers and hanging herbs, was flooded with light and noise and warmth. The incoming breeze made everything oscillate, filling the air with loose petals and the smell of summer.

There was something uncomfortable in the transition. It was jarring and Zeb seemed to feel it too, because he didn't immediately rush out into the light and noise, but stood in the liminal zone of the doorway, half in shade. 'Or maybe they're getting on just fine without us.'

I could hear voices, laughing, and I was almost sure that one of them was Mika. Tinny weak notes of music flared momentarily through the air. 'They'll have to play louder than that,' I said, meaninglessly, filling the space with words.

Zeb gave me a pitying look. 'They put the music on afterwards, in edits. They only have to look as though they are playing for the video.'

I didn't often feel stupid other than when I was with my mother. Out here, with the plants and the practical work, I was in my element, so the feeling that I'd said something daft made my cheeks heat up and my neck prickle. 'Oh. Yes, of course.'

'It's all fake, Tallie,' Zeb said, looking out across the yard now. I was glad he'd stopped looking at me because it meant I could cool down and regain my non-sweaty composure. I fanned my shirt, pulling it away from my body to get some cool air to help. 'Everything out there, it's fake.'

'The herbs are real,' I said, injecting a robust tone to pretend that I'd only been joking about the music. 'And the pond.'

'Oh yes. All your things are real. It's them that are fake.' He nodded towards the little knot of people swirling down the path towards a lighting set-up that could have rivalled a Hollywood production. 'Don't you think?'

Mika's not fake, I just stopped myself from blurting. 'They're doing their job, Zeb. Just like we are,' I added, although neither Zeb nor I were doing anything more than standing around chatting. 'I don't think they're any more fake than any other band.'

'I didn't really mean that.' Zeb still stood in the doorway, sliced by the shadow of the shop and the blaze of the sun. 'More that – here they are, pretending that it's all about the outdoors and that they're close to nature and yet they've got a catering bus on the way and they're surrounded by make-up and lights and stuff to make them look better. They could just be... normal.'

'Film themselves playing a song on their phones, and eat sandwiches, you mean?' I said, past the noise of one of the lorries revving its engine. 'I think The Goshawk Traders might be a bit past that level now.'

'But no one should have to *be* "past that level".' Zeb sounded angry, and I wasn't used to anger from him. 'Why can't everyone be on a level playing field? Why does money have to equal "better"? They get all the promotion and the advertising and all that, when there are other people out there working just as hard, harder probably, and scratching around for little scraps of public attention and money?'

He'd spun round in the doorway to give me the full benefit of his ire, shoulders hunched and his hair punctuating each sentence with a little forward nod from the impetus of his annoyance. It was, curiously, reassuring for me to see him lose his cool. It made me feel less inferior – and the realisation that I had felt inferior at all, just because he seemed to be together and a little disapproving of my life choices, made me purse my lips at him.

'You might be taking this all a bit personally,' I said. 'The band is successful. Of course they're going to have resources poured into them. A lot of people will have money riding on them carrying on being successful, don't you think?'

There was a moment of quiet. Coincidentally, the noise outside stopped too; the lorry had done whatever it needed to and the background voices receded to a murmur and the occasional musical twang. Zeb suddenly slithered down the door frame to sit on the step with his legs jutting out into the yard and his head in his hands.

'Sorry,' he said, his voice muffled and his punctuating hair scraped back beneath his fingers. 'Sorry. It's just that it sometimes seems so unfair, don't you think?'

It felt wrong to be standing behind him at my full height while he was obviously undergoing some conflict, so I went over to sit next to him on the pleasantly warm stone of the shop step. This squeezed us together in the doorway, our shoulders touching, but it was infinitely preferable to towering over him.

'Like I said, sounds personal. Anything you want to tell me?'

There was a pause. He seemed to be thinking. 'Guy I worked with,' Zeb said, eventually, still indistinct through hands and hair. 'We trained together. He was very... I don't know how you'd describe it. Personable? Good looking? And pushy, very pushy. He had money behind him, wealthy dad and money seems to equal confidence. Got himself a job working for a TV chef and now he's got his own programme on Sunday morning TV, cooking for the masses.' The hands lowered and Zeb looked at me sideways. 'Wanker.'

'Ah, professional jealousy. That's always a good one.' I smiled. Zeb's sudden flash of anger made me sympathetic. I'd felt the same way myself when more successful and high-profile herb farms featured in the glossy magazines. 'Was that when you decided to stop cheffing?'

Zeb breathed a deep sigh that rocked his entire body. 'Partly. Seeing him popping up every week and my wife asking me why I didn't do that – make a fortune being a celebrity while I explained that he had a team of people behind him making him look good, that it was all fake and not really what being a chef ought to be like – I started to realise that she really didn't have the faintest idea.' Another sigh. 'That she didn't really know me at all.'

A burst of sudden laughter rose from the garden and I looked between the parked vehicles and through the fence to see the band laughing among themselves, Mika in the centre looking pleased with himself. They all held their instruments casually as though they were extensions of their bodies. One of the girls was sitting on the edge of the pond, Simon I could see behind the lights, waving a hand. Getting The Goshawk Traders into a position to start filming looked like trying to bottle clouds.

In my pocket my phone beeped a text. It would be my mother, stuck in the era of texting. I'd only just got her to stop phoning me every time a thought crossed her mind. I pulled the phone out and looked at my screen.

> Natalie, darling, would you pop over? I'm feeling quite dreadful and not up to cooking, could you perhaps make me a sandwich?

There was a horrible contraction somewhere near my heart. She needed me. But here I was, watching Mika – who had 'noticed' me – and supervising the filming to prevent anything dreadful happening.

'Your mother again?' Zeb looked down at my phone screen too. Normally I would have felt annoyed, spied on, but for some reason this time I didn't.

'Yes.' I held out the phone so he could read the message.

'And you don't want to go?' He pushed gently at my hand, turning the phone back away and onto my lap. I saw him look towards the band.

'I don't want to, no. But she's not well.'

'Well enough to feel hungry, evidently.' Zeb raised an eyebrow.

'She doesn't eat much.' I could hear the apologetic tone in my own voice, the justification dripping like lemon juice from every syllable, sour and tongue-shrivelling.

'I could go.'

I stared at him. 'But... but you don't know her.'

Zeb gave me another hair-bouncing smile. 'We've met. Over Zoom, when she recruited me. Maybe it's time I met her in person and told her that I'm only staying for the month on sufferance?'

'But she wants a sandwich,' I said weakly.

'I'm a bloody chef, I think I can knock up a cheese and pickle without too much trauma. Besides...' He stopped so suddenly that the unsaid words made a little gulp in his throat, as though he was swallowing them rather than letting them out.

'Besides, what?' I asked, when it became evident that he wasn't going to finish under his own steam.

'Besides, it might be good for her to know that you can't always drop everything and run when she calls,' Zeb muttered, leaning forward so he was talking to his outstretched knees. 'I can talk up how important it is that you're here, keeping an eye on what's going on.'

'You wouldn't mind?'

It might have been my imagination, but Zeb seemed to look from his jeaned legs up out across to where Mika was holding court, making the rest of the band laugh uproariously again. It was only a flick of a look, and he might really have been checking to see where Simon was, or that Big Pig hadn't chanced another excursion across the borders, but to me it seemed he was looking at Mika. 'No problem,' Zeb said. 'It doesn't really need two of us to sit here and ogle them, does it?'

'I'm not ogling,' I said, offended.

'Of course you're not.' Zeb started to get to his feet. 'Anyway. Would you like me to go and make your mother a sandwich? It might be best if you text her back and warn her that I'm coming though, otherwise I'm just a random strange bloke turning up at her door.'

'You aren't random and strange,' I said, without thinking.

Zeb paused, halfway up the door frame, looking down on me where I still sat on the step. 'Thank you,' he said quietly. 'There was me thinking you thought I was…'

'She's already met you on Zoom,' I finished and his mouth dropped from the half-smile it had been wearing to look as though it had caught on his teeth.

'Oh, yes. Right.'

'I'm texting her now.'

'Okay. I'll head over. Which house am I aiming for?'

I had my head bent over the screen; it was hard to see the letters in this flame of white light. 'The first house next to the stream. The stepping stones cross right to her front garden gate.'

Zeb hesitated for a moment, but I was too busy sending the text to ask if he wanted anything else, then he was gone. I heard his car start and the spit of gravel as he turned out onto the lane.

I waited until he was safely out of sight. Then I got up to go and ogle the band and see how the filming was going.

7

It was chaos in my garden. At least, to me it looked like chaos. I had to admit that everyone present had probably done this many, many times and therefore knew exactly what they were doing, but it didn't seem that way.

A man with a camera was running around making beckoning and arm-gathering motions to anyone nearby; at the same time three men trundled behind him carrying heavy equipment as though they wanted to put it down but didn't know where. Simon was arguing earnestly with a lady with an iPad who kept trying to show him something on the screen while he shook his head and gestured frantically at the air. In the middle of it all and seemingly unconcerned, stood the band. Mika was still making everyone laugh.

The air smelled bitter: of crushed stems, of bruised and battered greenery, an apothecary's practice room.

I wandered down around the edge of the garden, across the furthest paths, trying to keep out of the way while making it clear that this was my patch and I was very much present, like a ghost that doesn't want to be seen but wants its presence to be felt.

When I drew level with the pond, Mika hailed me.

'Hi, Tallie! Don't worry, it's always like this at this stage.'

I froze, self-consciously trying to flatten myself against the climbing rose which clambered up the wall, and wondering if pretending to be pruning it would be a step too far. Mika, handing his viola to the most dreadlocked band member, came over. His feet didn't seem to touch the gravel, as though he made no noise approaching me. He must have done, but my heart was capering wildly in my ribcage and, as a result, drowning out any sounds quieter than that of the band's generator. I could swear I saw stars.

'Sorry, we seem to be making a bit of a mess,' Mika went on. 'It will all be put right before we go. Simon's very good at that sort of thing.'

He'd reached me now. I remembered, finally, that I was wearing a clean shirt and my most flattering jeans, and that this was *my* garden, and straightened from the slightly obsequious crouch that I'd fallen into. 'Er. Okay,' was all the witty repartee that I could come up with. I *wanted* to say that they were crushing the border edging, could they please stop walking on the beds, that it was a lovely day, wasn't it? That I hoped they had everything they needed, that everyone seemed very disorganised but I expected the filming would get done at some point and that I was delighted The Goshawk Traders had chosen Drycott Herbs to film at. But I was too afraid that what might fall out of my mouth was, 'You are the most gorgeous man I've ever seen,' so I kept it closed.

Mika tossed his head so that his dark curls spiralled around his head, and gave me a half-smile from brilliant eyes. 'Come on,' he said, 'I'll introduce you to the band properly.'

To my astonishment, he scooped up my hand and held it easily and loosely in his, tugging me gently forward until I stepped away from the rose and onto the gravel next to him. 'They don't bite,' he said, grinning in a way that made the word 'wolfish' spring into my mind, to be dismissed under a flurry of 'sexy twinkling, wow, tall, hot, leggy, stylish, *famous*' which was fighting to the forefront of my brain. 'Well, I can't vouch for Loke, but the others are fine.' Another grin, and a single raised eyebrow with the grin on that side rising alongside it; the resulting quirked expression took the perfection from his face and made him look arrestingly normal.

'Guys.' He addressed his fellow band members, who were grouped around the pond like a bunch of very convincing statuary. 'This is Tallie.'

As though they should know who I was. As though they should care.

A chorus of rather lacklustre 'hellos' followed. Mika still had hold of my hand and was now draped alongside me, so close that I could feel the rhythm of his breath against my arm. 'Tallie, this is Will.'

Will was the tall man in the tight T-shirt and black jeans, lots of piercings and a beard that you could have lost a Viking in. His arms were a mass of swirly tribal tattoos and he had a nose ring which reminded me that we'd meant to ring the pig and never got round to it.

'Vinnie and Genevra.'

This was the man in dungaree type overalls and a tie-dyed shirt and the girl in swirly skirts, who were sitting together, her on his knee. They waved.

'Loke. C'mon, man, give us a smile!'

Loke, who owned the dreadlocks and a beard that didn't really suit his round face, rolled his eyes with a hopeless kind of attitude as though he wanted to be a million miles away, and threw me a sheepish grin.

'And Tessa.'

Tessa was blonde and beautiful. All the band were beautiful in their own ways, but she was classically attractive, tall and slender with legs in washed-white jeans and a top that looked as though it was made of lots of layers of gauze laid over each other. She nodded, absorbed in tuning her guitar as it lay in her lap like an affectionate cat.

'That's us. The Goshawk Traders. Just a bunch of ordinary people who got lucky.' Mika looked down at me and I noticed his eyes were a pale brown, almost yellow colour. I gave him a small smile and didn't let on that I'd read up on the band and knew that they had met at a prestigious music school – there was nothing ordinary about any of them, they had all been selected for their places in that school because they were musically gifted.

I also didn't let on how much I knew about Mika. There was something in his confident air that made me think he would assume that I already knew all about him. I didn't want to think of him as arrogant enough to believe that I would have looked him up, so I kept quiet.

I wondered what my mother would say if she could see me. She wouldn't have known who The Goshawk Traders were, obviously. I conveniently forgot that I had never heard of The Goshawk Traders either until Simon had pitched up.

Then the familiar feeling of guilt at leaving her alone in her house, at letting Zeb go to her instead of going myself simply so I could hang out with a famous band overwhelmed me. I ought to have gone. I might not have *wanted* to, but I should have. I was her daughter.

'Could you excuse me, please?' I said, overcome with politeness right out of a 1950's etiquette handbook. 'There's a phone call I need to make.'

I backed away slowly as though the band were a dangerous animal that might fly for my throat. Mika seemed reluctant to let go of my hand and I had to tug at his arm before he would release my fingers.

'Come back after,' he suggested. 'We'll be playing soon.'

'I will. I just need...' And I fled with a Cinderella flourish, back along the gravel path to the dark coolness of the shop, where I draped myself, panting, over the counter, to the consternation of a pair of customers who had arrived while I'd been with the band.

I sold some herbs to them and it calmed me down. This, after all, was my area of expertise, advising on the herbs to use in any situation. These two had bought a new house and wanted to smudge it with sage before moving in, and needed to know *which* sage and in what form. We had a pleasant chat about houses and atmospheres, I sold them some sage sticks and they went away happy.

Then I remembered, with that familiar pang of guilt, that I'd meant to call my mother.

'Hi, Mum! Did Zeb find you all right?'

A clinking sort of pause, then, 'Oh, yes, darling, he's here now, we're having a lovely cup of tea and putting the world to rights.'

But, I thought, *you were feeling too ill to get up and make yourself some food, and now you're sitting having a cup of tea with Zeb...*

'That's nice,' I managed.

'Yes.' Another pause. More clinking. 'He says he told you that I brought him in to do some PR for the business. I hope you don't mind.' Not a question. I didn't know what to say to this without annoying her.

'He did.' Well, he had. It was an incontrovertible fact, nothing she could pick the bones out of to wrangle me over.

'It was meant to be a surprise.'

Ah. Right. She was going to frame it as 'doing me a favour'. That was fine, I knew how to approach it now, what angle to take.

'Yes. Thank you, but it wasn't necessary, honestly. I've got this, Mum. We're doing all right. I'm keeping him on for this month because you've already paid, but I won't need him after that. You can give him a glowing reference though, he's been...' I stopped, unsure. What exactly had Zeb been? 'He's liaised with this band and they're here now filming a music video, which is going to be great for business,' I finished.

'A *band*?' Lady Bracknell's 'a *handbag*?' could have been uttered in just such an appalled tone.

'Yes, you won't have heard of them, they're a bit modern for you.' My mother was stuck in the music of her childhood. There was still an A-ha poster upstairs in my cottage with little kiss marks all over Morten Harket's face. In my mind, my father had looked a bit like Morten Harket; in real life I wouldn't know. There were no pictures of him anywhere.

'Do they have guitars?'

'Well, yes, most bands have guitars, Mum. This lot are a bit posy and I'm not convinced on the washboard front but...' No. I wasn't going to mention Mika, not to my mother, who would instantly demand that he be taken round for her inspection.

'Someone plays the guitar?' Her voice had gone a bit faint and I could hear Zeb asking if she was all right.

'Yes. What's wrong with that?' There had been a note in her voice that had made my spine prickle, but there was absolutely no point of connection between my mother, sickly duvet-wrapped and hating the outdoors, and a bunch of late-twenties musical nomads. She clearly hadn't even heard of the band, so it was the musical genre that was making her sound so weird.

I heard her dismiss Zeb and then come back to me. 'Nothing, darling, of course. Guitar players tend to be so *fickle*, that's all. But I suppose you're just keeping an eye on the garden, as Zebedee says.'

Why did she have to use the full form of everyone's name all the time? Everyone, absolutely *everyone* called me Tallie, even the postman. My mother was the only person in the world to use Natalie and sometimes it made me feel as though I were someone else when I was with her, someone different to the person the rest of the world saw. She was at it with Zeb now too.

'Yes. I'm just making sure that nobody tramples anything too badly.'

'You don't have to… to *interact* with them?'

Too late I remembered that my father had played the guitar. It was one of the very few things I had ever been told about him – he'd been tall, and he'd played the guitar in a band. Nothing else; just as there were no pictures of him, there were no memories either, as though that car crash had wiped him from the face of the earth. But my mother had been traumatised by being left, ill and alone with a baby, while the man who had promised to love her forever had died so tragically; I could understand why none of it was talked about. Angela Fisher was fragile, easily damaged and needed protecting – we were poles apart in every way. Clearly she was now triggered by the mere mention of guitar players.

'No, Mum. Not really.' The thought of Mika rose again, like bubbles in a boiling liquid.

'Well, good. You stay away from people in bands, Natalie. They're no good.'

I was almost certain that not *everyone* in a band was going to profess lifelong love and then get themselves killed, it just wasn't statistically possible, but she was looking out for me and my future. My mother didn't want me hurt in the same way as she had been, that was all.

'I'll keep an eye from a distance, Mum. It's fine. They're only here for a week, filming this video, and then they're gone.'

'Why don't you take a holiday?' This was a surprising turn. My mother had never suggested that I might need a break from the herbs since I'd taken over the business. 'Maybe while Zebedee is here and the garden is closed? It might be a lovely time to go away somewhere – Italy is beautiful.' A momentary breath, during which I actually *did* consider a short-notice holiday to bask on a beach or wander the mountains. 'I could come with you.'

The vision of lying sun-drenched in a bikini or walking through picturesque markets with a raffia bag and enormous tomatoes, shrivelled and died. 'No thanks, Mum. I've got work to do. Big Pig made a real mess of the fennel beds and I want to get that put right and Ollie has the week off, you know how he is.'

I heard Zeb again, an amused tone in the background. My mother actually giggled, a sound I didn't think I'd ever heard her make before. 'Well, of course, you know best, Natalie.' She even managed to say my name without its usual sarcastic edge, which was a miracle. 'Oh, and Zebedee says he's heading back now, to' – another little giggle – 'to stop you from fraternising with any guitarists.'

We said our goodbyes and I slumped, exhausted, over the shop counter. Why did my mother have the effect on me of making me feel as though I'd spent a day in the company of forty thousand hyperactive toddlers? In fact, even a playgroup visiting to cuddle the rabbits, stroke the guinea pigs and feed turnip heads to Big Pig, with the concomitant risk assessments and enforced hand washing, was a breeze compared to a short conversation with my mother.

'Tallie?' It was Simon, appearing in the shop doorway. 'Has something happened? Are you all right?'

I straightened up. 'Yes, yes, all fine, I was just – polishing the counter.' To add veracity I dusted a corner with my sleeve. 'How are things going?'

'Mm, fine, fine.' Simon didn't sound totally convinced. 'The band want to do a few interior shots and I wondered if you'd mind if we used your kitchen.'

Interior shots? Was this a music video or a drama documentary? I hastily tried to remember whether I'd washed up last night's pots and pans and swabbed the toast crumbs off the work surface. 'Well, I...'

'It's Mika, you see.' Simon sighed heavily. 'He's got a "vision" apparently, for how the video ought to look. To make the band look approachable and ordinary. He thinks them making mugs of tea and chatting round a table might be just the thing.'

'I thought this was a video of them singing and playing?' I was confused. The garden was one thing, but when things started bleeding into my home life I wasn't sure. *But Mika...* whispered a treacherous little voice in my ear.

'We intercut. So the video runs the length of a few songs, and some of the time they're playing and singing and the rest of the time they're wandering about.' He sighed again. 'It's not like it was back in the old days when you sat behind a drum kit with a camera on the lead guitarist, and just tried not to sweat too much.'

'Maybe tomorrow?' It would give me a chance to make the kitchen look cutely cottagey and fit in with the band's aesthetic, whatever that was. I could look it up before morning. 'There's a few things I need to do in there today.'

Simon slumped into a relieved stance. 'Oh good. I hoped you weren't going to be difficult about it. Mika can be very... single-minded when he's got a vision.' Now he raised his eyebrows at me as though I were supposed to understand a subtext that I hadn't even known I ought to be looking out for.

I thought about Mika taking my hand and leading me over to introduce me to the band. He hadn't given me a chance to say, 'No, sorry, I've got things to do.' Was that a sign of his single-mindedness? A determination to make life go the way you wanted wasn't always a bad thing though. Hadn't I had to grit my teeth and make things happen, particularly in the early days of running the herb farm? I felt the memory of the pressure of his fingers around mine, the way the light had caught in his curls, his laughing eyes.

'Yes. Tomorrow,' I said again, firmly. 'That will be fine.'

Simon lingered, one hand on the top of the door frame. 'Well,' he said. 'That's good. I'll go and tell the band.' He didn't though. He stayed with the sun running along his back and his expression in the shadow of the shop. 'It's nice in here,' he said eventually.

'Yes, I think so.' I looked up at the beams where dried foliage hung, and around at the stone walls, dotted with bunches, bouquets and posies. 'I like it,' I said again, more quietly.

'Very organised. Tidy.'

'I try.' I wondered why he was still here. Then I had the awful feeling that he was going to warn me about Mika again, that he'd seen us hand in hand in the garden and taken things the wrong way. I didn't *want* to be warned off Mika. I wanted to be encouraged, and if not, then just left to admire him hopelessly from the sidelines, not given chapter and verse on whether he left his dirty socks on the sofa or slurped his soup. I wanted Mika to remain the impossible pinnacle of perfection.

'Right. I'd better get on. If you're filming round the pond, I can sort out that fennel.'

I advanced on Simon, who eventually had to move to one side and let me pass, and I kept on walking, giving him no chance to start another dark cautionary tale. Out in the sunshine I could see the band being filmed; a waft of distant music from speakers hit me with the scent of warm chamomile and I thought that from now on I'd always think of this moment when I brewed chamomile tea. That smell of hay meadows would forever bring me the image of Mika sitting on the edge of the pond looking soulful, with his viola pouring sweet notes into the air and a girl's voice raised in plaintive song, a tune like an old folktale snagging on modernity.

8

I hadn't got to bed until the early hours of the morning. After all, the curtains had needed a good wash anyway, and the windows needed cleaning; there were the wooden work surfaces to sand and oil – I couldn't get away with covering them in herb pots again. Fortunately for my sleep schedule I managed to stop myself short of painting the walls and cleaning out all the cupboards, but I fell into bed exhausted just before the sun began to tickle the tops of the far hills.

All of which meant I was woken by Zeb yelling up the stairs. 'Tallie? Are you here? Your curtains are closed, are you ill?'

He'd gone straight home after meeting my mother, so I hadn't been able to tell him about the arrangements for today; if I had, I would have been able to put him to work sweeping and polishing the floor tiles. Going home for a nice quiet lie down was the natural reaction to being in my mother's company for any length of time, so I couldn't even blame him for dipping out on an afternoon's hard work. He'd probably had a killer migraine and low-grade earache to sleep off. And at least he'd had the decency to text me and tell me he was 'working from home' rather than vanishing. But the result was I'd not told him that I'd be up late cleaning the cottage and preparing the kitchen for its starring role. It hadn't seemed the sort of thing I could text – *by the way, while you're not here I'm going to be martyring myself to the cause of housework in an attempt to undo six months of neglect so that Mika thinks I'm a domestic goddess.*

So when Zeb shouted me awake, I jerked upright with a confused 'blurgh?' to hear him coming cautiously up the stairs.

'Tallie? You sound...'

Before I knew it, Zeb was in my bedroom, looking startled at my bed hair in the morning light that filtered through the curtains at the tiny window.

'I'm fine.' I was performing a weird sitcom mime of clutching the covers to my chest as though I'd been caught naked, when, in fact, I was wearing T-shirt-and-shorts pyjamas. 'I had a late night, that's all.'

Zeb stood and stared into the room. 'Wow. Some of the things your mum said are beginning to make sense now.'

The urge to explain myself was so strong that I couldn't squash it down, even though this was Zeb not my mother. 'It's just – I spent some time doing research and studying.'

'I can see that.'

I wondered what he really *could* see. Obviously the absolutely factual, that my bedroom walls were covered in books and bookshelves, and where they were naked of shelving there were magazine articles and printouts stuck to the walls. Garden designs, yes, herbs and their uses, but also articles about people whose parents – one or both – had died or been killed when they were very young. Psychological works on 'Blame and the Child', pages of work on self-forgiveness; it all made my bedroom a bit like the office of a therapist with poor short-term memory.

'Did... err... did you learn anything?' Zeb swept out an arm. 'From all this?'

I looked at the walls. 'Mostly that Blu Tack isn't good enough to keep printer paper vertical and that nobody knows what they are talking about,' I said, trying to slide out of bed without him noticing. If I could get him out of the room and away from this shrine to self-improvement, then he may forget about it.

'Did you have therapy?' He walked over to where a corner of a newspaper article had come loose and was flopping and curling across its print. 'Because I think you may have needed it.'

I started to bridle at this unwanted and unwarranted observation, but then relaxed. Zeb was only saying what he saw, and even I had to admit that my wall coverings made me look as though I had issues. 'There was no point. I was a year old when my father died. I didn't really start to understand what was going on until I found out about the accident.'

'Which was when?' Zeb started squinting, reading the print. It was a bio piece about the actress Kate Beckinsale, describing how it felt to lose her father as a young child. I had identified in a probably rather over-the-top way, given that my similarities to Kate Beckinsale began and ended with 'female, lost male parent'.

'I was about ten. Until then I only knew that he'd died.'

'Oh, Tallie,' Zeb said softly. The words were swallowed by the half-light, weighted to the carpet under the dust motes that sank in the sun's rays.

'Oh, no, it's fine, honestly.' I hustled him out of the room, hoping he hadn't noticed the scatter of clothes on the floor on the other side of the bed, or the hedgehog nightlight. 'I'm interested, that's all.'

'Do you know what happened?' We'd only got as far as the tiny landing and Zeb stopped walking, so I ricocheted off his shoulder and against the banister. 'To your dad?'

'He...' I held the wooden rail firmly in one hand. The smell reminded me so much of Granny; old wood and lavender water had been her signature scent. 'He was coming home for my birthday party. He was driving too fast and he crashed into a tractor on one of the lanes near here.'

Zeb had gone very still. 'And that's why you think it was your fault?'

'No! I was one! I couldn't even feed myself, let alone ask him to make sure he was home in time for my party. Of course it wasn't my fault.'

But still, deep down, deep inside there was that tiny little voice that whispered to me sometimes, the sound of wind through leaves, *if it hadn't been your birthday, if he hadn't been hurrying...*

'Your mum told you that much, then.' He'd started moving again now, thankfully, edging his way down the desperately steep staircase. Granny used to let me slide down on her old tin tray, I remembered suddenly. I couldn't have been more than four. Where had Mum been? Bed probably, one of her poorly days.

'She had to, I needed to tell school. Something about filling in a Life Book, I don't really remember.'

'And that's it? That's all you know about him? I did notice there were no wedding pictures up at your mum's place.'

'I never felt I could ask. Granny used to let bits and pieces slip now and then, so I know he was tall, he had dark hair, but they'd both clam up if I asked anything directly. He played guitar in a band, I know that too. Mum was apparently so totally devastated when he died that she couldn't even bear to hear his name. I think she burned all the pictures of him, I've never seen one.'

'That's... harsh. He was your dad, surely you have a right to—'

'Mum and Granny brought me up very well, thank you,' I said stiffly. 'It wasn't easy for Mum, often being ill and then there was the time...' I stopped and swallowed my tongue.

'Something else happened?' We'd made our way to the kitchen now. It smelled of bleach and various cleaning products and I hadn't seen it sparkle this way since Granny died. It felt like a stranger's house.

'I...' I didn't know how to phrase it. 'When I was eighteen months old, a man tried to snatch me. Mum and I were shopping, in York I think, in a supermarket. She took her eye off me for a moment and...' The vague memory of a smell, smoke and aftershave, and the feeling of being lifted up and held against a soft shirt.

'Oh.' Zeb sat against the table. 'Did the police...'

'He was gone before they arrived. Apparently Mum screamed and he put me down and ran for it. But it's made her rather... *focused* where I am concerned.'

He nodded. 'I think I understand.'

It was weird. This was the first time I'd talked, really *talked* about my father and about the attempted abduction. It was the first time I'd had anyone to talk *to*, losing a dad being seen as slightly embarrassing when I'd been at the posh school where everyone seemed to gain parents as divorced mothers remarried and fathers acquired girlfriends. Friends had always been rather distant, and my life had revolved around the herb farm and Mum, so I hadn't had the confidantes that might have listened. Now it was all coming out in the face of Zeb's questioning and I wasn't quite sure how I felt about that.

'After that was when she moved back in with Granny, and she didn't like me being out without her. She'd put me on the school bus and fetch me from it at the end of the day and I wasn't allowed to go into town on my own, things like that. I think it frightened her, nearly losing me when her husband had died so recently.'

'I...' But Zeb didn't get any further before there was a commotion at the door and a rotating collection of people arrived. Simon was there, Tessa and Loke, two men with cameras – and Mika. All of them looking beautifully turned out, cool and achingly trendy, just as you might expect to see a band on TV, living their best lives. I just wished I hadn't agreed that they could live their best lives in my kitchen.

'Hey, Tallie.' Mika stepped inside. 'Nice gear. Very cute.'

Oh God, I was still in my pyjamas. Zeb had distracted me from the business of getting dressed, and oversleeping had meant that I hadn't slipped into the little dress I'd hung up in the bathroom ready, hadn't put on that carefully curated make-up that I'd been planning. It had been going to take me at least an hour to look natural and 'just got out of bed', and now here I was, natural and 'just got out of bed' for real. My skin went very tight and hot.

'We got talking.' Zeb sounded almost amused, but not in the same way Mika was. 'Everything's running a bit late today.'

'We'll go and do a bit more work outside.' Simon took pity on me, probably because my face had reached the same temperature as the sun. 'Come back in half an hour, when you've had chance to sort yourself out.'

He hustled everyone back outside, Mika trailing behind and giving me a cheeky wink as he left, which didn't help my overheating problem. I watched him go with my hands up to my betraying face and a state of horrified terror pulling my 'cute' pyjamas even tighter around me. They were an ancient little shorts set that Granny had bought me on a rare trip into town, and pre-dated me owning Drycott by quite a way. Actually, thinking about it, they may have pre-dated puberty by quite a way. There was a kitten on the front of my shirt.

Zeb nudged me. 'You were going to get dressed,' he said.

I couldn't make my body work. The dichotomy of talking about my father and Mika being in my house had made all my systems shut down and all I could do was lean rather feebly against the Aga, wondering if my legs were stubbly, if Mika had noticed and if he would care.

'I'm just a bit...' I said faintly.

'I can see that. Come on.' He gave me a firm push now. 'Upstairs. Clothes on. I'm working on a way to charge them extra to be in here, and you don't want to put me off, do you?' He gave me another nudge nudge with an elbow, until I stepped forward, found there was enough strength in my legs to walk, and tottered up to the bathroom to compose myself and get rid of the stupid kitten T-shirt.

* * *

I didn't bother with the make-up in the end. There didn't seem much point. I tried to tell myself that I looked better 'au naturelle' but the back of my mind echoed with some condemnatory phrases that my mother had used occasionally when I'd tried dressing up to go out, which might have contained words like 'pointless' and 'trying too hard'. And I didn't want to be seen as trying *at all*. I did put on the little dress though; short and swingy, it gave me confidence. My legs were good, if stubbly, and brown enough for the hair growth not to show, as I established with my magnifying mirror and a bright light in the bathroom.

So by the time the band returned, laughing and loud, to the kitchen, I was properly covered with my hair brushed and feeling far more able to face Mika's particular brand of self-confident flirtiness. Zeb had gone to feed the animals, the film unit had split in two – half to film in my kitchen with Loke, Tessa and Mika, and the other training cameras on Will, Vinnie and Genevra being beautiful among the gillyflowers. I was the awkward one, the odd one out, even though this was my damn farm. I didn't belong inside, where Mika and Loke were trading in jokes and pretending to make tea, or outside, where their bandmates posed against the high brick walls next to the crab apple trees which were full of small birds. All I could see was my saxifrage being stepped on and quite a lot of parsley getting bent.

I stood under the mallows, half-heartedly tying odd sprigs in and moving the supporting wire frames, trying to look busy and fully employed whilst feeling stupidly exposed in the dress and rather pathetic. Whoops of laughter came from the house and whenever I looked at Will and Genevra they were happily chatting whilst Vinnie submitted to being posed amid the greenery. I wasn't sure what was giving rise to this peculiar feeling of loneliness; after all, I worked on my own. Ollie did his thing but he wasn't company, he was a colleague. Everything I did, I did alone and it didn't bother me. Except that now it did.

Fed up with feeling as though absolutely everyone else had a role apart from me, I sought out Zeb in the barn. He was heaving a hay bale between the pens, preparing to fill the rabbits' rack and bed up the guinea pigs. I was pleased to note that he also looked out of place; his long frame and slender limbs were incongruous wrestling the bales, like a spider attacking a house brick.

He noticed me standing in the entrance. 'What?'

Big Pig, seeing me and hoping for more food, snorted up from her trough. 'Nothing.' I glanced back over my shoulder. Genevra and Will were heading to the cottage arm in arm while Vinnie trailed behind, snatching at stems and plucking leaves. The entire band was going to be all over my scrubbed pine and oiled oak. I hoped they weren't going to be laughing at the memory of me in my PJs or criticising my taste in mugs. Or, even worse, pulling leaves off the basil that I was bringing on in pots on the window ledge. 'Just feeling at a bit of a loose end.'

'Nothing to cut? No customers?' Zeb wrangled the bale down and cut the twine. The guinea pigs set up a squeaking that went from front to back in a tuneless chorus, seeing the hay about to descend, and he stepped over their fencing to shake it into their house, while they ran around his feet like animated toupees.

'Not really. No customers, anyway. I could cut some angelica heads, but the bucket is still quite full in the shop. I'm going to muck out the pig in a minute.' I leaned against the stone wall. The barn was the old-fashioned, open fronted kind, built as stalling for the horses when Drycott had been the coal yard. Big farm gates kept Big Pig in her half, more gating and low fencing separated the rabbits from the central food preparation area and a final gate kept everything closed off. It all looked a bit makeshift and cobbled together, but it worked, mostly. I leaned over and rattled the nearest gate, which seemed secure.

'What are the band up to?' Panting, Zeb distributed the hay and started coiling the twine to hang on the handy nail Ollie had driven into the barn wall, when our previous string arrangement had failed.

'Filming. Being beautiful. Laughing. That sort of thing.'

'Oooh.' Zeb straightened up, one hand in the small of his back. 'You sound jealous.'

'Do I? I'm not, not really. They just all seem so *together*, like they've got life sorted out.'

'They're famous. I think a lot of things are easy when you're famous. Doesn't mean they're any better than you or me though.'

'Very philosophical.' I remembered what he'd told me about his ex workmate who now had a TV slot, and his bitterness made sense. I took a slice of hay from the bale and half-heartedly shook it loose to put in the rabbits' rack.

'You've nothing to feel inferior about, Tallie.' Zeb sounded serious, but had hay in his hair. It was hard to be philosophised at by someone who looked like Wurzel Gummidge. 'You've got your own successful business, your own house, all this.' He threw his hands wide and more hay trailed from his grasp.

'"All this" being squeaky rodents and an enormous pig,' I said sullenly.

'Don't be obtuse. You've done okay, admit it. Growing up can't have been easy from what you've told me, but you came through.'

I stopped and thought, staring at the excited bundle of guinea pig circling around Zeb's feet like hyperactive mop heads. 'There wasn't much choice,' I said. 'School was tough – Mum sent me to the private school over in town rather than the local comp, so the locals called me "posh" and behaved as though I'd personally chosen not to go to school here, as if I thought I was too good for them, and the girls at school treated me like an oddity. I was a disappointment to my teachers because I wasn't interested in much apart from horticulture. I grew up knowing that I'd probably take over Drycott so I didn't exactly cover myself in glory on the academic front.'

My mother had been sharp about that too. On the one hand telling me that she was 'looking after' Drycott for me, once Granny died, and, on the other, telling me that I should study harder, take more exams, get better reports. My repeated questions as to why, when herbs weren't that bothered about A levels, as long as you got the soil depth right, were never answered.

'I hated school,' Zeb said surprisingly. He stepped over the rabbit's fence. 'Everybody was just so... *shouty*.'

'I'd have thought cheffing was pretty shouty too.'

'Different kind of shouty. I knew what to do there. School was everyone shouting at cross purposes, but when you're in a kitchen you've got one job to do and you ignore any shouting that isn't directed at you.' He replaced the remains of the bale on the hay stack and wiped his hands down his thighs. 'At least this job is quiet.'

'You're only here for a month,' I reminded him, possibly too pointedly. I could hear sounds that indicated that the band had left my kitchen and were milling around in the garden and I didn't want to turn around in case Mika caught my eye again.

'I meant *my* job,' Zeb said evenly. 'Targeted marketing. Going in to companies and businesses and finding out how best to increase their market reach within their chosen sphere.'

'Oh.' I thought for a second. 'What's a "market reach" anyway? Sounds like what the greengrocer does down in the village when he's trying to get the apples from the back of the stall.'

'I hoped that nobody would notice that.' He perched on the gate that led out into the garden, sitting hunched on the top bar like a multicoloured crow. 'The concept is sound though, go into businesses and help them make a profit.' He sighed. 'I just wish it wasn't so... *hard.*'

I leaned on the gate beside him, forced to look out across the herbs which were slowly nodding their fragrant heads as the weight of the day pressed them into somnolence. Part of my mind was appreciating the loveliness of the plants while another part dwelt on the back-breaking work that was necessary to keep them looking so gorgeous. The beauty on the surface was only there because of the hours and hours of physical labour that nobody saw.

'Ants in the parsley bed,' I said.

'What? Sorry, are there? Does that matter?' Zeb bent lower over his knees, closer to me, his hair bouncing in a worried fashion.

'Maybe. Possibly. But I was being philosophical.' I could smell the metallic tang of the galvanised gate and was keeping my mind focused on that, rather than the sight of Mika, with one arm around Tessa, as they danced for the camera in a flourish of waltz that kept squashing the loose edging of the border. 'Ants in the parsley. Everything looks fabulous on the surface, but underneath it's dark and nasty and sharp.'

'Your mother wants me to report back to her, you know,' Zeb said suddenly. 'She wants to know how successful Drycott is, how the turnover is looking.'

I jerked a look of surprised alarm at his face. He was carefully not looking at me, but staring out at where the band were pretending to sing for the cameras as far as I could tell from the abrupt snatches of chorus that competed with the blackbirds singing from high in the birch trees. 'She *what?*'

'Oh, I'm not going to.'

'Good.'

'Probably.' Now Zeb swung himself down from the gate so that he was on the other side, facing me. He blocked my view of the band now walking together into the centre of the garden and I had to move slightly sideways so I could keep on disapproving of what was happening amid my herbs. 'She was very logical, but I thought about what you said about you owning the place and her only having a small financial interest, so I thought I'd run it by you first before I told her anything. I've been trying to work out how to tell you – that's why I didn't come back yesterday afternoon.'

Now we were face to face I could see the accumulated lines of worry that crowded his eyes and pleated his mouth. Zeb had one of those faces that showed every emotion but indirectly, belated smiles preceded by a brightening of his eyes and frowns that came after everything else had drawn together. This all occurred to me in a rush, as though I were seeing him for the first time and it made me soften towards him a little.

'Did she say why?'

Seemingly encouraged by my not losing my temper at him, Zeb leaned in a little closer. 'No. She didn't. But I'd like a look at the paperwork for when you bought her out of Drycott, if you've got it. There's nothing in the small print about her being able to sell, is there?'

I could feel my eyes widening, the pupils becoming solid as pebbles. 'No! I mean, she doesn't have any control over the farm, not any more. It's mine, with a percentage of income going to her to help with living expenses like a small pension. It's what was agreed at the time because I bought it for less than it would have made on the open market.'

'Maybe she wants to increase her income then. By making

sure that you are earning as much as possible.' Zeb bit his lip. The action creased his cheeks.

'Or maybe she just wants me to do well.'

'There is that. But why would she want me to report to her? Why employ me to look into your marketing without telling you?'

'Tallie!'

I pulled back from Zeb, seeing Mika approaching, his clothes liberally dusted with pollen and the flecks of seed from where he'd danced through the planting scheme.

'Oh, hi, Mika.' I sounded breathless as if I was surprised to see him, which was ridiculous because he'd been around all morning. 'What's up? Do you need something?'

Mika looked from me to Zeb, one eyebrow doing the work of a whole lot of questions, and then he smiled broadly. 'We've stopped for a break. Wondered if you'd give me a tour of the garden. I'd like to know what you've got planted up in that shady corner – there's a patch in my place in London, I'm having trouble getting anything to establish.'

'Under the big oak tree?' I asked, and then kicked myself ferociously for knowing that his London garden *had* a big oak tree, and, even worse, for letting *him* know that I knew.

'Yeah.' Mika brushed it off, but I'd seen a knowing flash behind those dark eyes, and mentally kicked myself a bit harder.

'I'll let you get on then.' Zeb turned away but I hardly noticed him leaving because of the glory that was having Mika's attention turned on me. I did see Zeb pause as he headed out towards the shed, and look back over his shoulder as though there was more he wanted to say. There was certainly more I wanted to say, about why my mother was still so involved in Drycott, about how she'd been born and raised here and so of *course* she was interested in the business; how she only wanted me to be successful and profitable because she knew it was all I was really fit to do and the failure of Drycott could see me out of work and struggling.

But that chance had gone now and been replaced with Mika, his dark hair curling around his face and highlighting those laughing eyes. He held out a hand to me. 'Come on. While they won't miss us.'

Feeling inelegant and trying not to flaunt my legs, which suddenly seemed to be more stubbled than they had earlier, I climbed up the metal bars of the gate and Mika took my arm to help me down. His fingers were soft on my bare skin, although I could feel a slight roughness on his fingertips, presumably from playing the viola, and his grip was firmer than was necessary just to help me down from a gate I climbed at least twice every day. It almost felt as though he was afraid I would run away if he let go.

We wandered over to the shade beds, Mika keeping his hand on my elbow. His grasp felt warm, almost possessive, and I snuck a little look at his face as we meandered along the curved gravel paths past the majestic, sour valerian. Mika wasn't looking at me but he was still smiling. The small rising breeze lifted a few strands of his hair and played with it like a lover, rearranging it on the collar of his shirt until my fingers itched to smooth it down.

'This is our shade spot,' I said, somewhat breathlessly, pulling up abruptly as we reached the first of the mint beds. 'It's mostly mint at the front here, with foxgloves, chervil and woodruff, almost any woodland plant will thrive…'

Mika looked at my careful planting but as though his eyes weren't seeing it. He looked different here, away from the trappings of fame and in my territory, slightly plainer, a bit less twinkly. 'Yeah,' he said, dreamily. 'Yeah, very nice.'

I stopped talking. There wasn't much point in giving him planting information when he wasn't taking it in. My heart started to canter in my chest – had he brought me over here for some other reason than to discuss shade-loving plants? Did I *want* there to be any other reason? This was *Mika*, after all, famous and the subject of numerous magazine write-ups, whose picture probably graced many a phone and iPad screen, the idol of too many fantasies. What on earth could he have to say to *me*?

'It's cool here,' he said eventually, his fingers starting to feel a bit sweaty on my bare arm.

'Well, yes, it's the shade, that's why we put…'

'I mean this.' He swung his other handout to take in all the bedding along this side of the garden. 'Your place. Simon was right, it's a great location to film.'

Ah. The alternative meaning for 'cool'. Did anyone use that nowadays, wasn't it horribly old fashioned? Or had it come back into fashion again when I'd been busy polishing buckets and turning compost?

'I like it,' I said, simply. Somewhere behind us I could hear voices, Simon and a girl, Tessa maybe, slightly raised as though in disagreement.

Mika let go of me and turned around. It seemed to me as though he deliberately avoided looking where the voices were coming from, as though he were expecting to be summoned and didn't want to go. My heart increased its pace to an absolute gallop, but I stayed looking at the shady planting. Overhead the trees whispered and the dappled light moved with the breeze.

'You're cool too, Tallie.' Mika had lowered his voice a little and I got a quick flick of those dark eyes. 'We should grab some food sometime. I'd love to hear how you run this place.'

The practical part of me wanted to say that I ran this place just like anyone else ran a business: on hard work, not enough money, and desperation, but the thought that Mika... *Mika*... had almost asked me out on a date overrode everything else. I opened my mouth to say that this was a lovely idea, and then the mild disagreement going on behind me changed into shrieks.

'Oh,' said Mika, with mild interest. 'There's a pig in the garden.'

I whipped around now, so quickly that my dress spun a blurred print pattern round my legs. 'Big Pig? Oh, no! How the hell...?'

I was running already, leaving Mika, leaving that lovely, almost-suggested date and belting down the path to where Big Pig was happily trundling her bulk along the centre of the garden. Tessa had jumped onto the pond surround and was clutching her arms around herself as though the presence of a pig might cause her to shatter. Simon was sheltering behind an obelisk. The remaining band members had fled to the cottage, where they were clustering in the doorway with worried looks over their shoulders at the encroaching creature. Big Pig looked very satisfied with herself for making everyone panic, and stopped to stick her snout into the parsley bed for a good root.

I reached her at the same time as Zeb did. 'The gates were shut,' he said, out of breath. 'Definitely.'

'I thought they were.' I looked at him suspiciously. I knew *I* hadn't left a gate open.

'You were there. Did they look shut to you?'

We stood either side of Big Pig, who had now dug a little

trough all along the edge of the border, and was happily chewing something that made her dribble green.

'Get her bucket. We'll have to lure her back in.' I wasn't going to discuss how the gate got left open, not when sharp trotters were digging up the gravel and Simon was making little squeaky noises from behind the woven wire of the ornamental planter he was inadequately sheltering behind.

'She might just follow me.' Zeb slapped Big Pig on her ample rump. 'Come on, girl. This way.' He gave me a quick smile. 'She likes me,' he said, as the pig's head came up, ears a-tremble with anticipation of a better snack than parsley. 'Come on. Let's find you some proper food.'

He set off along the path and Big Pig, after a reluctant last mouthful, snorted and went after him, jogging along with her tail twitching in expectation of a bucket of pellets.

'That's *horrible*,' said Tessa, from on top of the pond wall.

Simon waited until we heard the clang of the gate closing before he emerged. 'It was rather disruptive,' he said, smoothing his hair back and trying to dislodge a bee, which was taking rather too close an interest in his floral shirt.

'Horrible,' repeated Tessa and flung herself at Mika, who came strolling towards us wearing a huge smile. 'Did you see? There was a *pig* loose!'

Mika scooped her into an embrace. 'I saw, Tessa. I don't think it was dangerous though.'

I was just relieved that Big Pig had gone after Zeb without complaint or reluctance. Maybe she was bored in her barn, all this activity going on out here while she languished in her straw?

'It's gone now,' Mika reassured Tessa. A momentary flare of jealousy spiked my heart rate; a few minutes ago he'd been almost asking me out, now he was here treating all this as entertainment, hugging his bandmate and smiling that unconcerned, amiable smile that was so attractive.

'Well.' Simon finally rid himself of the bee. 'Perhaps, if you'd all grab your lunch now and we can do some still shots afterwards, while the sun is shining? I want to get some stuff up online this evening, get the promo boys putting up the trailers.'

When Mika didn't suggest that I join them for lunch, I gathered what remaining dignity I had, and went back to my kitchen.

9

Unfortunately for my desire to sit around brooding and remembering Mika's touch and his suggestion of a meal together, the shop was busy that afternoon. Whether it was people wanting to come and catch a glimpse of The Goshawk Traders or whether they genuinely decided that herbs would be the perfect addition to their décor, I found myself advising on and selling copious bunches and posies and statement stems. None of the customers seemed disappointed at not being able to pick their own fresh herbs and there was a degree of loitering in the car park that led me to believe that herbs might not have been their main reason for travelling the dusty incline. I reminded myself to be grateful that they had arrived and were willing to spend money, and the band were largely invisible anyway, the lighting in the cottage meaning that they had decided to redo this morning's 'tea' shots when the sun shone full through the windows.

It was nice to be busy, to be able to forget Mika and his dark twinkling eyes, Zeb and Big Pig, my mother's sudden interest in my turnover and the mice in the cottage beams. Here, with a willing crowd actively wanting to spend money, I could be Tallie. I could educate, inform and, more importantly, ring cards through the till to the extent that I could envisage the bills being paid at the end of the month rather than wrapped around the year with little bits of money being thrown here and there. A good turnover day would mean a little extra money for Mum too which might be enough for her to lose interest in trying to improve my income. Her obsessions never usually lasted for long anyway. The only one which had, was me.

I watched the last couple leave the car park as the sun bent the shadows over the roof of the shop and laid them gently across the gravel, and enjoyed the sudden silence. There was nobody anywhere in evidence, all I could hear were the swifts peeping from their upturned bucket nests in the eaves outside and I could enjoy my acres without...

'Oh, there you are!'

'God, Zeb, you made me jump!' Zeb, who had been emptying the wheelbarrow, evidently having mucked out Big Pig, emerged from the shadows, barrow first. I'd been so far gone in my reverie of trailing hands through the herbs and the way Mika's curls bounced around his face, that I hadn't heard him coming. 'I've been in the shop. Working. Selling stuff. You know, doing what I'm supposed to.'

He nodded, gravely. There was straw all down his front. 'Good. How were the takings?'

'Excellent. And nobody got to see the band, so I suspect many of them will suddenly discover that they need more yarrow heads for their downstairs bathroom décor, and be back.'

'Lovely.' The barrow went down on its rest. The whole thing needed a good clean, I noticed, there were clumps of muck sticking to the base. I ought to take to it with the hosepipe.

Then I wondered why I was noticing the state of the wheelbarrow when I'd got a world-famous band in my kitchen and Zeb standing right in front of me. Was this my life now? Excitement breaking out all over and I was the one standing out here worrying about pig muck?

'You look very pensive.' Zeb's voice floated through my musing. 'Wondering how to spend today's takings? Because the handle on this is loose, look.' He wiggled the barrow handle, which was, indeed, loose. 'So I think that's a priority spend.'

'Ollie can fix it,' I said, still lost in my realisation that I was all about the quotidian and normality. ABBA and the Beatles could have been hosting an, all right extremely unlikely and probably quite spooky, get-together in the kitchen and I'd *still* be out here worrying about sluicing pig poo off a wheelbarrow. Why couldn't I get excited about what was happening instead of worrying about incipient rust? 'When this is over and he's back.'

'Ah yes, Ollie.' Zeb leaned comfortably against the fence. 'I know he's a good worker, but wouldn't you be better off with someone who can actually, you know, *talk* to customers? Serve in the shop when you're not here?'

That jerked me out of my self-study. 'What? No! Ollie's great. He knows every kind of herb, he knows where they grow best and he's a master of the compost. Just because he's a bit socially awkward, that doesn't make him a waste of space you know.'

I must have sounded fierce because Zeb looked startled. His eyebrows shot up to compete with his raggy hairline, which was bobbing about with an alarmed life of its own. 'Well, yes, I know that. It's just that you're paying him to work here but he can only do half a job. If you had someone who knew about herbs *and* could work in the shop then you wouldn't have to close whenever you needed to be somewhere else. Maximise profits, you see,' he finished, apologetically. 'Unless you and

Ollie have – history?' he added, in a tone of such disbelief that I almost laughed.

'No.' I had to shut down that line of reasoning. 'I took Ollie on because... because...' I stared across at the sleepily nodding herbs for inspiration. The weight of the sunlight was pressing down on everything now with its early evening heat, as though the day was nearly fully cooked. Time to close the shop.

Zeb followed me as I went to the A frame and began dragging it into the yard. 'Because?' he prompted. 'My imagination is working overtime here.'

'I'm certainly not paying extra for *that*,' I said, and he laughed.

'So. Ollie.' He took the bottom half of the big stand, which proclaimed Drycott Herbs pick your own farm and shop to be open and helped me carry it inside.

I sighed. 'Look, you mustn't breathe a word of this to Ol, all right? Not that it matters so much now that he's turned out to be so good, but I don't want him to think...'

'You have a secret desire for his body?' Zeb hauled the frame over the step and we both stopped, back inside the deep shade of the shop again, where it felt as though night had fallen suddenly.

'Don't laugh,' I said. 'Ollie is lovely. He just doesn't interview well, that's all. It's not his fault.'

Zeb tipped his head. The shadowing in the shop made him look sharper. It accentuated the planes and angles of his face and the line of stubble which drew his cheekbones in with a graphite smudge. The stalks of straw stuck to his shirt now made him look more natural, more as though he belonged here. 'Of course it's not his fault,' he said, and even his voice sounded different. More thoughtful.

'Ollie came just as I was taking over Drycott from Mum,' I

said. Without thinking I pulled a piece of straw from Zeb's front and began pleating it in my fingers. 'His mum knew we were looking for workers and she brought him over one day in February.'

I remembered the sheer terror on Ollie's face that day. He'd been almost green with fear, and his mother had had to spend several minutes persuading him out of the car, his hands clenched with tension on the edge of the seat.

'I took them both into the cottage and made them tea, and Ollie loosened up a bit when he saw all the herbs. Once he started talking to me it all seemed to get better for him, and we chatted about growing things for a while – he had his own garden at home and he'd been experimenting with – never mind.'

'Poor Ollie.' Zeb shifted and more straw fell off him. 'That must have been hard for him.'

'Then my mum came down. She'd been having one of her poorly days so she'd not been about much but she heard us talking and she came into the kitchen. Well, Ollie was off like a rabbit then, and I told his mum I'd be in touch, and once they'd gone, my mum started laughing. She wasn't... she wasn't very polite about him, put it that way. So I told her I was hiring him, starting next week, and it was one of the only times I've ever seen her speechless.'

I stopped. That was all he needed to know. Ollie had turned out to be a terrific asset to the business, and the fact I'd hired him in the first place to annoy my mother in one of the few, subtle ways that I could go against her shouldn't come into it now. I always reassured myself that at least I hadn't hired him because I felt sorry for him, because it was obvious he would struggle to get work anywhere else. It hadn't been pity, it had been the desire to show that this was *my* business now and Mother no longer had the last word.

'He's great with the animals too,' I said, twisting a barley head around the straw figure that my hands had made without thinking about it. 'Like you. Men seem to have an affinity with Big Pig.'

'Hm. That's damning with faint praise if ever I heard it.' He leaned back comfortably against the counter. 'Why is she called Big Pig?'

I rolled my eyes at him, although I didn't know why. He wouldn't be able to see in the gloom. 'Because the guinea pigs are small pigs, obviously.'

'But why not something worthy of her? Like Tallulah or... or... Gladys? Big Pig isn't a name, it's a description.'

'When she came she was only meant to be temporary,' I said, staring out of the window now towards the animal barn. 'She was a few weeks old and someone dumped her in the gateway. They'd probably bought a piglet as a pet and then realised how big they get. They're cute when they're small, but they only stay small for a fortnight, and whoever dropped her off must have known that I had a barn. I was going to pass her on to a farm, but I got fond of her.' I thought of the bulk of Big Pig and her seemingly perpetual desire to stand on me. '*Fairly* fond, anyway,' I added. 'So I made the best of it and we got the rabbits and the other pets and they see us through the winter with playgroup visits and suchlike.'

'She's an accidental pig?' Zeb started to laugh now. The movement made the straw fall from his shirt onto the shop floor and I narrowed my eyes at him.

'You're making a mess.'

Zeb looked around the shop, rather ostentatiously for my liking. He was making the point, and rather well I had to admit, that it wasn't exactly pristine in here. Seeds had dropped from some of the dried heads that hung from the rafters to condiment the floor, and various loose strands of stem and leaf fluttered back and forth across the stone floor in ankle-height draughts.

'What's your mum living off?' he asked, surprising me because I thought he'd been about to point out that he was hardly ruining the décor with two bits of loose straw in here. 'I mean, you're not keeping her afloat with her proportion of your takings, are you? And she doesn't work?'

'Well, no, she's ill.'

'So she's on some kind of disability payment?' Zeb was looking at me very intently now, his eyes dark in the shaded coolness of the shop.

'No, she can't get disability because the doctors don't know what's wrong with her.' There was a sting in my blood now, an increase in my heart rate as though Mika were coming through the doorway, which he definitely wasn't because I could hear the laughter billowing across from the cottage. The band were standing in my kitchen doorway and there seemed, from a quick glance out of the window, to be a lot of photography going on.

'Has she always been ill?'

This was more familiar territory. 'Yes. Even before I was born, apparently. She keeps going to the doctor and coming back saying they're going to do more tests, but it's been *years* and they haven't found anything. She'll be fine for a week or so and then suddenly she can't get out of bed for days. Everything hurts and she's sick and can't stand. Like migraines but worse.'

'Sounds rough.'

'Yes, Granny brought me up, more or less. I mean, Mum was

there, of course, but she often couldn't go out or help with the herbs because she had to stay in bed.'

'Hmm,' Zeb said.

I leaped to the defence of my family. 'Look, a long-term disability isn't anyone's fault. Like... like Ollie. Mum can't help the fact that she's often laid up for days, it's just how it is and it's all I've ever known. Granny was brilliant, she looked after me and taught me all about herbs and their uses and then when I took over I branched out into decorative bouquets and things...'

'And how did your mother feel about that?'

I recoiled at the question. Zeb was getting very personal all of a sudden with all this deep involvement in my family. It was, after all, none of his business.

'Look. You're here to maximise the profits and report back to Mother that the place is doing well, right? Not to prod about in my background – none of which is relevant to turnover.'

My hands had started to sweat and I picked up the crude straw figure that I'd woven from the counter to give me something to do with my fingers. Why did discussing my growing up make me feel so... so... *twitchy*? It was all very straightforward, I was hardly the first child to be brought up by their grandparent because of parental illness, so why did it make me feel so nervous? Or was it just the way that Zeb kept pushing, like the worst kind of counsellor, trying for a crack in my personality?

'So, anyway.' I cleared my throat and twisted the little straw man back into shape. I'd nearly pulled his head off. 'That's all you need to know. And thanks to the band filming and paying for the privilege, we'll be solvent for a bit longer.'

I went behind the counter and began tidying the drawers of my apothecary cabinet, neatening the labels and making sure that none of the plastic envelopes of dried herbs were protruding. It was probably the last job that needed doing, but there was something about Zeb's continued stillness and bouncing hair that made me feel vulnerable. Outside, the sounds of the band being raucously happy floated from the other side of the garden, like dust.

'Tallie,' Zeb said, steadily, 'what the hell happened to you?'

I slammed the dill drawer shut so fiercely that I caught my finger and yelped. 'Nothing happened to me.' The pain filled me with the spurt of anger I could have done with a few minutes ago. 'There's nothing. No secrets, nothing hidden. I'm as above board as... as...' I searched for something visually appropriate. 'As that dried angelica,' I finished. It wasn't 'above board' so much as 'above the counter', but it would have to do. 'I'm just someone who owns a business that they are trying to keep afloat,' I finished, definitively.

'Can I see the books then?' Zeb stepped towards me.

He got me by surprise. I was sucking my injured finger – that nail was going to go black, I just knew it – and almost doubling over with my urge to make him see that there were no huge secrets in my background. 'All right!' I snapped. 'If it's so important, I'll show you. Tonight, once we've got rid of that lot.' I jerked my head in the direction of the cottage, then had a momentary stab of 'what if Mika chooses tonight to ask me out to dinner?'

'Unless anything else comes up,' I amended.

Zeb jolted into life, as though forty thousand volts had shot through him. 'Good. Great,' he said, cheerily. 'Tell you what, once Mumford and Sons there have finished arsing about, I'll go and fetch us a takeaway and we can sit and go over the figures, how about that?'

I was taken aback again. 'Oh. I was just going to have a sandwich.' I hadn't even thought about food, or that inviting him over for the evening might involve eating.

'And now you're going to have a takeaway. I'll drive over to Pickering, pick one up. I'm presuming that nobody delivers out here?'

He didn't even wait for an answer. He was gone, back out into the acid-wash daylight. I heard Big Pig grunt a greeting as the barrow squeaked its way back into the barn, and the guinea pigs set up a rival squeak, ever hopeful of green goodies dropping from above.

I finished tidying the shop. Its interior was so familiar to me that I could do these day-to-day jobs without thinking, the jobs I'd done almost every day since I could walk, since Mum and I had come back to live with Granny. Check everything is put away, remove the till drawer, make sure nothing is left switched on and then lock the door. My body carried out the tasks without the involvement of my brain, which was busy whirling through Zeb's questioning. Why was he so interested in my past? There was nothing there for him to poke around in, nothing but an age-old tragedy and an impecunious upbringing. So what had he seen, what had he thought, that would make him conclude there was anything else there?

And why did his questions make me so anxious?

10

The garden felt quiet after the band had gone. To my disappointment Mika hadn't sought me out for any more tête-à-têtes. He'd been seemingly absorbed in the extended photography session, which had seen Tessa and Genevra change into dungarees and loiter attractively around Big Pig while the men pretended to pick apples from the crab apple tree in the hedge. I pointed out that the apples were in no way ripe and wouldn't be ready for harvest for at least another couple of months, but apparently this didn't matter. Which did not make me think kindly about the sort of people who bought their albums – I mean, surely anyone with half a brain could see that those apples were blatantly unripe and that the girls didn't have a pig board and weren't equipped to deal with a recalcitrant sow? But watching the band being photographed, constant poses interspersed with laughing and occasional bouts of singing or holding an instrument in a photogenic way, had led me to believe that visual veracity was a little thin on the ground in The Goshawk Traders life.

Zeb had finished the mucking out, fed the animals and

disappeared, presumably in search of the fabled takeaway. I sat in the cottage and relished the new silence. Apart from the whirr of the computer fan and a blackbird singing high in one of the birches, there was no sound.

I knew I should switch on the irrigation system and give the damp-loving plants a good drench now that the sun had gone from their corner, but I couldn't bring myself to move. Sitting here, in Granny's old chair, surrounded by the smell of aniseed and grass cuttings and feeling the residual heat that the sun had left behind I could relax. This was *my* garden. *My* business. It didn't really matter what Zeb might say or do, or even what he might tell my mother, this was me. Staying afloat, doing what I did best.

Sitting alone in a room.

I tapped at the keyboard once or twice. The accounts were all safe, all backed up and everything delineated and carefully tabulated. The tax office could have used me as an illustration of how to keep financial affairs clearly separated and accessible. Everything had headings, there were spreadsheets for everything. I was so squeaky clean that the screen almost smelled of detergent.

I tapped again. Then curiosity made me type in my father's name. Jonathon Fisher. I periodically searched for mentions of him, although thirty-year-old local car accidents were apparently not priority for digitisation and there had been nothing, up to now, about his death, online. That state of affairs continued and I felt a momentary prick of disappointment. It would have been nice to show Zeb an article, a death notice, anything that related to my father. Some proof that I was still trying to work on how I felt about his accident, and that all those articles on my bedroom wall were a part of something bigger, an actual investigation rather than the obsessions of an orphaned child.

Sometimes... sometimes it felt almost as though Dad had never existed. My mother, crippled with grief, couldn't utter his name. I only knew he'd been called Jonathon because Granny had occasionally slipped up and mentioned that I'd got his eyes or, more usually, some prejudicial element of my personality. He'd been expunged from our house as though he'd never been, and only I and a surname remained as a reminder that my mother and Jonathon Fisher had ever been joined in holy matrimony.

I scuffed the chair back a few centimetres, hearing the scrape of the old wooden legs against the brick floor, a sound so familiar that it was almost like my heartbeat. Granny had always dragged the legs when she'd moved her chair. I remembered my mother wincing at the noise, hand held dramatically to her forehead, more indications that she was having another of her 'unwell' days. Most of my childhood memories of my mother were of a swaddled figure in a bed, a darkened room, me carefully carrying a glass of water or a cup of tea up the steep narrow staircase to hear a faint 'thank you, darling' as I put it on the bedside table and crept away again.

I leaned my head against the dented padding of the chair back. Remembering those days gave me a little burst of heat in my heart, a tiny shot of fondness for my mother. I loved her utterly, of course I did. She'd kept me safe, kept me housed and fed and cared for in those dreadful dark days after the death of my father, and that couldn't have been easy for her. She loved me back, I knew it. My near-snatching by a stranger with who only knew what in mind in one of the places she should have been able to feel safe, a supermarket, must have hit hard too. No wonder she tried to keep me contained and herself isolated. Her illness, undefined so she couldn't even say 'I have...' whatever it was – and get practical help, support, the medication that might deal with symptoms, pulled her inwards. It made it hard for her to cope with me, so no wonder she'd moved back in with her mother. It also occasionally made her unable to see outside herself and her situation, to imagine how life might have been, might *still* be, for me.

It wasn't her fault.

I sighed and closed my eyes, feeling the worn leather of the chair against the back of my neck, almost like the fingers of a lover kneading my muscles. I had a brief flash of memory of the touch of Mika's hand, taking mine to lead me up among the tall flowering foxgloves and the summer-scented mints in the shaded garden. And then memory stretched to include his laughing with Tessa, his arm reassuring around her after the pig incident, his general easy affection with her.

Mika was not for me. Simon had warned me that Mika was – how had he put it? 'He can be a bit...' Simon had never actually finished that sentence. I remembered the whole of that time with Simon, his surprising questions about my situation and his dark almost-warning about Mika. How would he have finished? 'Mika can be a bit...' What? Over-excited? Over-affectionate? Over-dressed? Reckless, careless, casual with his affections?

I didn't really care. It had been so long since a man, any man had noticed me. I protected myself against casual incursions by cultivating an aura of obsessive busyness, always dashing around the place cutting or weeding or planting, so any man who came as a customer would have got the impression that I was far too absorbed in the garden to date. I could have slowed down, flirted lightly with some of the delivery men who brought the animal feed or the hay and straw. Service engineers who periodically came to poke at the Aga or the hot water system in the cottage or the irrigation unit had been chatty; surely I could have dropped my single status and an assumed availability for nights on the town to them?

But I had been raised on dreadful tales of how falling in love ended. Granny had, on some late winter nights when my mother had been confined to her bed and we'd sat around this table illuminated only by a single swinging bulb, been condemnatory about her daughter's choice of husband. No details had passed her lips, nothing I could winnow out for information about my father. Just vague, dark hints about meeting and marrying quickly – from her tone, I deduced that I had been 'on the way' and marriage had been hastily scrambled in order for my mother to remain respectable, which was ridiculously old fashioned even thirty years ago. This valley, on the edge of the moors, was still populated by families who had been here longer than most of the trees and before the rivers had settled in their current courses; old-fashioned courtesy and manners caused ridges and rifts out here like fingerprints of behaviour. Granny would have wanted to save face and not be seen to have a daughter who had succumbed to modern morality. Maybe she felt a twinge of guilt afterwards at forcing Mum to marry? Maybe things might have been less intense if I could have been born to an unashamed single mother with a perhaps less-than-present father? Forcing Mum and Dad into a relationship which might not otherwise have gone the distance with the concomitant awful ending, was really down to Granny.

Now, here I was, with a mother I couldn't imagine introducing to any potential partner because of her overt mistrust of any utterances of love or devotion – 'men will say anything, Natalie. Anything. And then they will leave you heartbroken' – and a herb garden which took so much of my time and energy that I didn't really have the opportunity to meet anyone anyway.

A mouse scraped along the beam and I allowed myself the briefest fantasy of introducing Mika to my mother. Surely he, with his sparkling self-confidence, wouldn't be daunted by her recurrent illness and her dark hints about relationships ending. He'd be wild and energetic, sweep her out of her long sadness and into glamour. He'd entice better doctors, specialists, into a proper diagnosis of her energy-sapping headaches, sickness and inability to function. She'd get the proper medication and re-emerge into the life she'd lost, back into fashion and modern hairstyles and, perhaps, a new man. She was still young, after all.

I tried to imagine my mother dating and my concentration switched back to the mouse on the beam. A tiny, hunched outline scurrying between the walls of the kitchen, it disappeared down inside a crack where the ceiling met the top of the wall and any visions of Mum being whisked off her feet by a dashing older man were swept away by new visions of an enormous nest of mice threatening to bulge my ancient walls and bursting onto the gardens in a mass of seed chewing and plant wreckage.

I pulled the table up against the wall and climbed up to try to peer down inside the wall, which was where Zeb found me, some minutes later.

'If you're trying to get rid of the evidence, may I suggest a bonfire?' He stood and looked at me for a minute, the parcel in his hands giving off a trail of steam and a fantastically enticing smell.

'What?' I banged my head against the ceiling, startled at his entrance.

'You know. Disposing of financial documents relating to dodgy dealings?'

'By hiding them in the walls? Where mice would be almost

certain to turn them into confetti within seconds?' I jumped down and the table rocked, clattering against the floor like wooden applause.

'Great disposal mechanism. Or you could feed them to Big Pig, she'd eat anything.' Zeb raised the paper-wrapped parcel. 'Talking of which, here's our food.'

Zeb irritated me, that's what it was, I thought as I fetched cutlery and dug some plates out of the back of the cupboard. Whatever he said, however it was phrased, it grated against my nerve endings and made me want to contradict him, to wipe away that air he had of *knowing best*. This was *my* business, I knew how to run it and how to maximise our profits. Zeb was only here because of my mother. His lanky presence in my kitchen was unwanted, even if he did come bearing delicious takeaways that scented the air with spices and hot oil.

He clearly saw my frown of annoyance as he laid the plates on the table, because he tilted his head at me until his fringe fell into one eye. 'Are you all right, Tallie?'

'Of course I am.' The aggravation made my tone sharp and the words sound as though they had been handpicked to hurt.

'Okay. Have you got the figures and everything there for me to look through?' He brushed off my rudeness as though he expected nothing less, which upset me slightly.

'Yes, the computer is ready for you when you finish eating.' Then, because he really had been kind to bring food, 'And thank you for the takeaway. I don't get to eat them very often, can't be bothered to trail into town. Mum usually gives me a sandwich or something at hers when I fly by in the evenings.'

Zeb didn't even pause in his careful laying out of the food. 'You go round there most days?'

'I like to check on her. She doesn't go out much and sometimes she's too ill to eat, so I make sure she's at least had a hot drink.'

'So she doesn't give you a sandwich, you make yourself one in her kitchen? She's got a lovely kitchen, by the way. As an ex-chef I appreciate a nicely laid out cooking area.' He looked at mine, rather pointedly: the Aga which was mostly used to heat the water; random units and surfaces which, thanks to my night spent sanding and oiling, looked amazing but were unsullied by food production. 'I take it that you don't cook much.'

The smells from the food parcels now in the middle of the table were making my stomach gurgle audibly. He'd even brought *chips*! 'I don't have a lot of time for cooking.' Now I sounded apologetic, what was wrong with me?

'So your life is running this place and taking care of your mum. What do you do for fun, Tallie?'

Zeb swirled himself into one of the chairs at the table and tore himself a portion of naan bread to dip in some sauce. I stayed where I was, standing by the wall. 'Is that a trick question? Are you trying to get me to admit to spending all the day's takings on wild nights out in town?'

'I'm trying to establish what opportunities there are for expansion or diversification. If you're already up to maximum capacity – i.e., no time for anything else outside this place, then it would mean hiring more help.' He eyeballed me through the fragrant steam. 'It's not personal.'

Now I was annoyed with him *again* for making me feel awkward. And also, I admitted to myself somewhere deep inside, a tiny bit disappointed, although I wasn't sure why. Perhaps because I enjoyed bickering lightly with Zeb? It was nice, in a vaguely masochistic way, having someone challenge me and say something other than Ollie's usual 'righty-ho!' when asked to do anything. Zeb forced me to have ideas, to think about Drycott rather than carrying out the same motions and actions as I had been for the last twenty years or so, when I'd taken over most of the physical work from Granny.

Zeb made me think. And, exasperating as he might be, I was finding that I rather enjoyed that level of challenge.

'By the time I've closed Drycott for the evening and sorted everything out for the morning, it's usually too late to go and do anything else. Plus, there's Mum to visit, and she sometimes needs me to do a few bits and pieces for her. My social life is limited to the customers and any sales people who might pop in. Which,' I added in a momentary blurt of honesty, 'isn't actually very many.'

Zeb paused, a bread-scoop of curry sauce half way to his mouth. 'My wife had an affair,' he said.

It was so out of context that I wasn't sure I'd heard him right. 'Your wife did what?'

'Come and have some of this food.' He waved a fork. 'There's loads. I may have overdone it slightly. The curry looks good, I think the battered sausage might have been a step too far though, but I don't know what you eat so I got a bit of everything that the takeaways in Pickering have to offer. You were just lucky that the pizza place was closed, or there would have been that too.'

He was weird, I decided, sitting opposite him and ladling portions of random food onto my plate, which formed a pattern more complicated than the flag of Turkmenistan. This was the second, or was it third, time that he'd talked about his life in this random, half-cautious way, as though it was a subject that slid away the closer he got to it.

'You said your wife did something?'

'Had an affair, yes. With that TV chef guy that I told you about, the one I trained with. I don't blame her in one way, I was never at home, but, seriously? With another *chef*? If she'd slept with some bloke who worked a nine to five, home in time for tea and TV every night, yes, I could have understood that. Reliable, sensible hours, consistent pay. But – another *chef*! That's like, I dunno, telling everyone you hate tattoos and then sleeping with Jason Momoa.'

We sat and stared silently at the battered sausage. 'Actually...' I started, but Zeb carried on.

'It wasn't her fault. I mean, it was, she didn't fall on his penis or anything, but I really wasn't a great husband. We weren't a marriage, we were an accident waiting to happen.'

Another moment of silent staring. The sausage stared back. 'Why are you telling me this?' I asked, at last, when the cracks in the batter had begun to look as though they wore a sympathetic expression.

Zeb shook his head and his fringe wobbled. 'I'm not altogether sure,' he said. 'Perhaps because you've been so honest with me about your past? I suppose I want you to know that I understand what it's like to be trapped and then to try to change things, only to find that it's too late? Maybe?'

'Only I'm not.' I dragged the computer forward on its desk and fired up the screen with one hand as the other was holding something that I was very afraid might be a kebab. 'Here are the figures for this financial year. If you go back a page you can see last year's.'

'Mika seems to like you.'

That surprised me into nearly pulling the monitor off the desk. 'What? Really? No, he's just being...' I remembered that hand cupping mine, those bright, mischievous eyes. 'Just being nice,' I finished.

'And you clearly fancy him.'

'This is this month's takings. You can see how they rise month on month from about April…'

'I think he's an utter dick, of course, but you flirting with him so outrageously is making sure that the band stick around to film as opposed to heading over to the coast or some stately home and garden.'

'…and we're about ten per cent up on the takings this year from the equivalent period last year, which is good,' I continued, resolutely not listening to him, although his words were seeping through my desire to distract his attention and reaching my 'desire to hit him with the battered sausage' layer.

We both stopped speaking at the same time. I turned away from my screen to see that he was looking at me over his plate, with a suspended popadom dipping dramatically under the weight of something orange. His expression was unreadable. There seemed to be some element of hope in there, and a question rearing its head under the slightly raised eyebrows.

'What the hell are you on about?' I shunted myself back to the table. Despite my desire to avoid any of his questions – about my mother, about Mika – the smell of the food lured me back to my plate.

'I like you.' Zeb's eyes had gone to the table now. 'And I don't think you deserve what's happening here.'

His tone held a weight, an import. Every syllable bent under the doom it contained, as though they meant something other than the simple message they were conveying.

'That's very… I mean…' Flustered, I tried to fork up a piece of something from the curry sauce, but it turned out not to be a piece of chicken as I'd expected, but something soft which fell apart on impact and left me scraping around to try to regather it. 'There really isn't anything "happening" here, you know, Zeb. I'm trying to keep the business together, that's all.'

'I'm not good at communicating.' He stood up so suddenly that I was almost sure I heard the surprised squeak of a startled mouse, chair sliding back from the table to give him room to start pacing. 'Another complaint from my wife and I seem to have got worse, side effect of a job where you poke through people's finances when they don't want you to. I thought it would be useful, come in to businesses and tell them what to do – but it turns out that nobody wants you there except for management. Everyone on the floor is already doing what they can and what they're told. No one has the authority to change anything except the top bods, and they don't really care, except for profitability, when sometimes that's not what it's about.'

He stopped talking and looked at me, his hair flopping with curtailed movement.

'Well you just managed to communicate all that without a problem,' I said tartly.

'It isn't what I thought it would be.' Zeb leaned against the door, restlessly. I wondered if he was allergic to the additives in the curry or something, because he was decidedly twitchy. 'I want to help people sort themselves out, but I'm beginning to realise that I need something more creative. I loved that, with the cooking, being able to dream up new dishes, new ingredients, and I thought I could translate it into showing people new ways to run their businesses. Turns out that everyone just wants more money for doing the same old stuff.' He sighed. 'I'm not cut out for this. I hate the whole "reduce expenses, advertise more", which is all my job really comes down to.'

'Again, not entirely sure why you are telling me this.' I watched him carefully. There was a fidgety impatience about him which made me wonder whether he might be about to launch into a meaningless tirade, start telling me that the moon landings were a hoax.

'To be honest, neither am I.'

Zeb came and sat down again and we ate some more of the random collection of food items in near silence. Eventually, because he was still looking anxious, I asked, 'So, what would be your dream job? If you could do anything in the world?'

His chewing slowed, and he looked thoughtfully into the curry, as though he could read his future in the bobbing chicken lumps and the orange sauce. 'Good question,' he said slowly.

'I thought so, yes.'

I began collecting the empty containers from the table to make more room, stacking them to one side to rinse out, and consolidating the leftovers onto a plate. The battered sausage rolled, solitary and unwanted, into the remaining rice.

'I don't know.'

Zeb's quiet answer made me look at him. He'd put his fork down and was staring across the kitchen, through the brightly lit circle that was the table and our plates full of food, through me, and on into the formless darkness of the far corners, as though he'd been asked to calculate the square root of forever. 'I don't know. I've been looking all my life. And that's terrifying.'

I sat down again. 'I've never had a choice,' I said. 'I was born to take over from Mum, who was always going to take over from Granny. I was an absolute nightmare at school, as I told you – I didn't need qualifications and careers days made me want to hide in the toilets. As long as you can tell parsley from hemlock, you're good in this job.'

Zeb's attention snapped back to my face, and he smiled. 'You and I are coming at things from the opposite direction, aren't we?' He picked up another popadom and broke off a section.

'As long as we aren't about to collide over my accounts.' I sounded brisk. Thinking about school, about my lack of interest in anything despite what my teachers had called 'an obvious ability', made me feel slightly guilty. I'd always been so sure of my future – take over Drycott and run it until I retired – I'd never even bothered to try. What might I have done with my life if I hadn't walked into the family firm? What might I have wanted to do, where might I have wanted to go? It was uncomfortable to think that I might have had an alternative future.

'I like Big Pig,' Zeb said, again seemingly apropos of nothing. 'And the small pigs.'

'Well, she hasn't eaten you yet, so I'm assuming the feeling is mutual.'

'I mean, maybe I could work with animals? I don't mind shovelling and feeding and all that, and it's nice to feel wanted by something that doesn't shout at you and is mildly affectionate. And the work is necessary unlike cooking for people who don't care, or trying to feign enthusiasm for raising profiles, again, for people who don't care. And, of course, there's no shouting. The shouting has really put me off most jobs, to be honest.'

'You clearly haven't been on the wrong side of a bucket when Big Pig is hungry,' I muttered.

'So, yes. I think I might like to work with animals.' Zeb poked at some yellow bits on his plate. 'Maybe you could take me on here to expand the small animal side of things? We could extend the barn, buy a piece of the field behind, turn it into an alternative income stream for winter – the car park is already there and the visitor facilities – and the animals could eat any leftover herbs. Plus the manure is good for the land, and you could pen chickens or pigs on unused sections to turn the ground over and fertilise it.'

My mouth dropped open and I felt my eyes widen. 'What the hell are you doing thinking about expanding the pets?' I asked when I'd regained control of my lower jaw. 'That is outside your remit, surely. My mother would go spare.'

'She took me on to maximise the turnover. Taking on some more animals, turning the barn into a proper pets' corner could be useful in those down months when the garden is bare.'

I stared at him. 'It *is* a proper pets' corner,' I said.

Zeb forked up another mouthful of curry and chewed, but looked as though his mind were elsewhere. 'But the animals keep escaping,' he said reasonably. 'What would happen if they escaped one night and vanished? Plus it's not very accessible for children with disabilities. You have to climb over that little fence to get in with the guinea pigs; it would be better if you could open the whole pen up.'

I carried on staring. My spine had begun to prickle and my scalp was tightening. *It was him. He was letting the animals out to try to get me to make a more permanent structure, to change their accommodation. Why? To teach me a lesson?* 'No,' I said.

'Why not? I mean, I haven't looked at the books yet, but you can't be doing more than just ticking over in the off season, and that will be – what? October to March? Six months of no real earnings.'

'We sell dried herbs and posies. We sell herb arrangements for interior décor,' I said sulkily and wished I'd turned off the computer. Our off-season earnings were, indeed, woeful, and he'd find that out the second he flipped to the winter pages of the spreadsheets.

'So, turn the barn into a proper animal enclosure. You could rescue some more cute squeaky things, advertise it as a real experience, employ someone to be in charge. We'd have to look into the additional insurance of course. Big Pig could do someone a proper menace if she wanted to.'

'I've got insurance.' I sounded so sulky now that I was only a whisker away from stomping up the stairs shouting 'You're not my mother!' and slamming some doors.

Zeb put down his fork and picked up his plate. 'Right. I need to go through these figures for a bit now. Do you want me to wash up first?'

I couldn't speak. The irritation I felt at his presumption had gone beyond just making my hair itch now. I wanted to hurl the plates at his head, stab him with the forks and I'd even have a go at causing bodily injury with the leftover naan bread if I stayed here.

'I'm going out,' I said, trying to sound cool and professional and not half an inch away from killing him with the comestibles. 'To check on the garden.'

'Fine, you do that.' Unconcerned, Zeb started to clear the table. 'That curry wasn't bad, actually. I'd have left out the coriander though.'

No, I couldn't stay in here. Despite the warm glow from the lamps and the appealingly domestic smell of food and whatever aftershave it was that Zeb was wearing that had the scent of the sea about it, I was not going to wait while he discovered that he was absolutely right about us needing to make more money in winter. I didn't think I could take his smug tap of the screen and turning to me to make that smiling-not-smiling face that I just knew he'd do.

The tosser.

I satisfied myself by jerking the door closed behind me as I went out. It caught, as it always did, on the tiles and refused to slam, but it made a wonderfully punctuating squeal as friction and speed of closure dragged it shut. Then I stood in the night beyond the illumination from the windows, and breathed.

Cool dark filled my lungs. The rosemary was flowering and scenting the air with a subtle tang. During the day, feet had crushed some of the chamomile and its medicinal aroma rose and fell with the breeze. Warm brick, cooling wood and a top note from the pig barn completed the olfactory bouquet of a summer night in the herb garden. It smelled peaceful and I felt my shoulders start to drop, the tension evaporating into the warm air. *Mine.* I knew every plant – I could identify them in the dark, just by the feel of their leaves. I'd raised most of them myself, from seed, from cuttings; grown them on in home-made compost, planted them out, watered them, brought them on. They were, in effect, my children. So I supposed my standing here, breathing in those unique scents, was almost the same as standing in my children's bedroom watching them sleep.

I sighed and wandered further along the main central path towards the pond, which was alive with the plops of froglets. I wondered if my mother had ever come into my room to watch me sleep when I'd been small. Granny had, I knew, because I'd sometimes woken up to see her standing by my bed or sitting in the little reading chair in the corner, or smoothing my cover. She'd whisper me back to sleep with her hushing and occasional mutters of 'poor child'. It suddenly struck me that Granny must have found it hard, having Mum come back home with a toddler in tow, just when she'd got used to having the place to herself. After all, the cottage was tiny, two sensible bedrooms and the weeny box room where my cot had just fitted, and Mum could take up an incredible amount of space when she wasn't confined to her bed. How had Granny *really* felt, taking back her widowed and traumatised daughter and her doted-upon but lively granddaughter? She'd never even hinted at any emotion other than gratitude that we were safe and well mixed with that undercurrent of irritation peculiar to the elderly, but... I looked around the peaceful quiet acres, straining to increase by stretching feathery arms through the fences. Surely she must have felt – what, cheated?

Or perhaps she had relished having our company. After all, she must have been lonely after Grandad died, and perhaps I was putting my feelings of being intruded upon and disturbed in my solitude onto her. I knew little else, other than the duty calls to my mother and quietly running this place, whilst Granny had known what it was like to have a husband and a child – noise and bustle and conversation.

I was lonely.

The knowledge came over me so suddenly that I took half a step back in astonishment, my feet rattling on the gravel until I felt the cushioning of damp moss beneath me. *Lonely*. It had never occurred to me before, but then I'd never had an irritating man washing up in my kitchen before. I'd never had that chatting over the kitchen table, a figure moving in the light of the swinging bulb indoors while I checked the watering system. It had always been just me. Except for Granny's last few years, after Mum had moved back to the village, when it had been just me and Granny here, rattling around Drycott. By then she'd been arthritic and mostly confined to the cottage and her chair. I'd worked out here alone and come indoors to a still-warm teapot and Granny upstairs in the room that was now mine, trying to get comfortable and watching eternal repeats of *All Creatures Great and Small* on the little TV at the end of her bed.

Now my life consisted of just me and my mother. My mother to whom duty tied me as tightly as this bindweed clung to the mallow. Whom I loved and resented and my heart ached with the duality of feelings.

To distract myself – after all, how could I resent a woman who was so ill that she'd had to leave most of the raising of her daughter to her own mother? – I wandered over to the animal barn, creeping quietly through the dark so as not to disturb sleeping rabbits.

Big Pig was on her feet. She'd got her nose under the gate opening and was lifting and dropping the entire gate very gently. I stood in the shadow and watched as she shook the fastening loose, then leaned against the metal of the gate until it swung open. With a quick glance over her shoulder, Big Pig stepped delicately out of her pen and across the barn to the small, fenced area of guinea pig and rabbit. While I watched, she carefully nosed open their gate in the same way and trod down the mesh fencing until it was ground level, allowing a couple of the guinea pigs and an alert rabbit to scamper over, whereupon she briskly opened the main barn gate and led her little band out into the garden.

'What do you think you are doing?'

My voice made her stop, with a sudden, surprised snort that made her ears flap. I could almost see her thinking, wondering whether she could turn around and head back to her pen and pretend never to have left, to have no piggy idea how to jolt the gates open or how to push down the fencing to let the other animals out. For a moment we stood opposite one another on the path, Big Pig and I, and I restrained the urge to laugh. It *wasn't* Zeb letting them out for reasons of his own. It wasn't Ollie, being unimaginably careless. It wasn't the band or any of their associated film crew. No human was involved and I couldn't believe the overwhelming sensation of relief.

'Get back in that pen,' I tried. Big Pig remained on the path, eyeing me up, her ears stiffly erect and her tail outstretched, as though she were trying to make herself look bigger which, as she outweighed me about five times, was ridiculous. She didn't move, despite the two guinea pigs who sprinted between her legs and made a dash for the parsley.

'Zeb!' Calling him was all I could think of to do. I daren't move for fear that Big Pig would take this as licence to run amok around the garden again. We'd only just got the fennel bed straight after last time, and the chewing power of the guinea pigs and the rabbits could do almost as much damage as a rampant sow. 'Zeb!'

I could hear the sound of running feet on the gravel and Zeb arrived at my elbow. 'Are you all... oh. I see.'

He'd got his sleeves rolled up and for some reason this made something inside me which had previously been solid, go melty at the edges.

'We have to get them back. The band need the place to look consistent for filming and if she tramples half the beds they won't be able to finish the video.' I kept my voice level and my eyes locked with the little blue orbs of the pig. The tufts on her ears trembled, but otherwise she didn't move.

'What do you need me to do?'

'I don't want to move. I'm keeping my eye on her and tracking where all the small squeaky beasts are heading, so we can bring them all in. If I go and get the bucket she can rampage around half the garden before I'm back. And she likes you, she'll follow you back inside.'

Like a hypnosis practitioner and subject, Big Pig and I stood, eyes fixed on one another. I didn't even turn to look at Zeb.

He took a deep breath. 'If I get her back in, can I come and work here?'

I broke the porcine-human stare-off. 'That's blackmail! She could destroy my business!'

'But I'm good with her and she'll follow me. Isn't that worth it?'

'Zeb!'

In front of me, Big Pig took a careful, and almost calculated to insult, step forward. I didn't move but I did quickly work out how much damage I would sustain if she just charged me. She could flatten me on the path and trample over me without even noticing.

'Zeb!'

Big Pig snorted.

'Can I come and work here?'

He'd come up beside me now and the pig was looking from me to him and back again. I threw him a desperate look. 'You'd rather wrangle pigs and muck out barns than carry on working in the clean and indoor world of promotion and finance?'

'Yes.' Zeb's voice was very level. 'And help plant herbs and learn to make up bouquets and sell things in the shop. To be honest, I'd rather personally hose Big Pig clean every day and polish her little trotters than carry on doing what I have been.'

'This is still blackmail.' I chanced a look at him now and Big Pig took advantage of my distracted attention to advance another step. Somewhere behind me, two guinea pigs and a rabbit were playing hide and seek among some caraway in the culinary section. They'd already caused some damage, I could smell the rich, aniseedy scent from crushed stems.

'I know. But you really could do with another pair of hands.'

'I've got Ollie. Zeb!' I added his name urgently, as Big Pig, clearly fed up with the ongoing impasse, began to advance slowly towards us, as though playing the world's worst game of Grandmother's Footsteps.

'Ollie's brilliant at the herbs but he can't deal with customers. I can. And I'm pretty sure I can look at the figures and work out a way to increase your takings by more than the salary you'd pay me.'

Big Pig had almost reached my knees now and I'd either have to jump aside or risk being ploughed into my own garden.

'All right, all right! On a trial basis, six months, and if you can pay for yourself over that time, you can stay. Now, work your pig magic, *please*.'

'Thank you.' Zeb sounded cheerfully perky. 'Right, Pig, come on, let's have you back in the barn.' He strolled casually around and slapped her on her mighty rump whereupon, to my surprise, she turned a neat circle and followed him happily back to her pen.

I watched them go, shaking my head with astonishment. How did he *do* that? Maybe he and the pig shared some fellow feeling at being oppressed by me? I could hear him pouring pig feed into her trough, but surely she wasn't sufficiently certain that he would feed her, when she could have had the freedom of the garden. If I hadn't spotted her letting herself out just now, she'd have been out there all night and I dreaded to think what The Goshawk Traders would have turned up to see in the morning if the pig and the small rodents had been scoffing and rooting for hours.

My heart rose into my throat at the thought. A few minutes ago my biggest worry had been feeling a bit lonely and hard done by, now I was realising that my inattention to the detail of gate closing mechanisms could have cost me my business – or, at least, the large chunk of money that the band were paying to use the premises, plus most of the summer's earnings.

I felt my blood sting with the what-might-have-beens. I'd been lucky. Lucky that the pig had only just worked out how to let herself out, and lucky that she'd been recaptured before too much damage had been done. Perhaps Zeb, damn him, was right and I did need another pair of hands. Someone else to check things, someone else to man the shop, someone to talk over planting plans and layout details, so it wasn't all my responsibility. All those things I could have talked to Mum about, but didn't dare, because I didn't want her advice shaping my business and my life. Not any more.

But did it have to be Zeb? With his lanky limbs that looked as though they might snap if he lifted heavy weights and his strange fringe, his big dark eyes and his sudden switches of conversation from the practical to the emotional. Was he really the best person to take some of the pressure off me?

I tried to avoid the mental image of Mika working here. That was fantasy. I knew of course that there was no way that a famous musician would give up a life on the road to plant parsley and stir compost. Zeb was offering and he was right about me needing help. 'Tie her gate up with string!' I called across to the barn. 'She's opening the gates herself.'

Zeb called back something I couldn't hear and faded off to become a shadow in the distance and rattling metal. I set off after the elusive guinea pigs, combing through the taller growing herbs in search of the whistling bundles, swearing under my breath about how I'd been backed into a corner by a long-limbed farmer-wannabe and a Big Pig.

11

Zeb was early next morning. The dew had barely settled itself on the edges of the ferny yarrow when he was climbing over the gate and arriving in my kitchen.

'Thought I'd start my employment as I mean to go on,' he said brightly, watching me make tea and wrinkle my nose at the smell of last night's curry still lingering in the furnishings.

'You were already employed here,' I said. 'Remember? You're here in both capacities for the rest of the month, and after that the jury is out.'

'Well. I'll just have to make sure I earn my keep then, won't I? Pig wrangling and looking into the options for more animals, plus giving a bit of advice on the financials.' He leaned against the door frame, still watching me. 'Any chance of a cup? I left before I had breakfast.'

I grunted, which he took as assent, claiming the half-empty kettle and the pack of tea bags with alacrity and the kind of smile I'd more normally associate with a primary school teacher introducing the school play. I flopped down in Granny's chair and watched him through the steam of my own cup; he was moving with a new deftness as though he had a new routine to establish and was going for it all guns blazing.

'I looked through your accounts,' he said finally, lifting his mug to me in a kind of toast. 'After I'd put Big Pig back, while you were still rounding up the small squeakies. They're in pretty good shape, I have to say.'

'You make it sound as though you expected everything to have been written on the back of used envelopes in pencil.'

'Not at all.' The infant teacher smile was turned on again. 'I had every faith in your rigour and attention to detail. And you're right, your mum isn't drawing that much money from the herb farming, is she? A couple of hundred pounds a month at most.'

I grunted again. A couple of hundred pounds would be a *very* good earning month, but I wasn't about to point that out.

'So what does she live on?' Zeb dragged out the chair from the table that was nearest where I sat, and slid himself onto it. 'She's too young to be getting any kind of pension, and even if she *is* getting benefits, they'd never pay for that house of hers.'

I shook my head. 'I always thought my dad must have left her some kind of insurance policies or something. She's never worked, so there wouldn't be any pensions, apart from the state one, and she's got a good fifteen years before she can get that. Plus, I think Granny helped her out here and there.'

'Hmm.' Zeb frowned into his mug. 'She owns the house in the village? Or does she rent?'

'Owns it, I think.' I put my tea down on the arm of the chair, the hot ring on the leather adding to the thousands that already decorated it.

'You aren't curious about how your mother is managing to keep body and soul together?' He lifted the frown to my face now.

I sighed and let my head flop back. 'You don't understand. I was brought up not to ask questions. Believe me, I tried. When I was younger I used to ask about Dad, what he was like, whether he looked like me, whether there were pictures. Or about how Mum came to meet him, when they fell in love, how he asked her to marry him – I was full of questions.'

I heard Zeb take an extra-large mouthful of tea and gurgle 'ow' at the heat, then gulp it down.

'But asking Mum anything would send her to bed for a fortnight. She'd get huffy and go to her room and then she'd be ill and Granny would get cross with me for making Mum upset. There would be *an atmosphere*.' I remembered those days, Granny barely speaking to me, Mum not speaking to anyone – existing only as a series of thumps overhead and a blanketed swaddle in her bed. I'd learned early not to rock the boat.

'So they taught you not to ask questions? That explains how easily you accepted that I'd come for a job that didn't exist. Although it clearly does, now,' Zeb added hastily. 'You were trained.'

I thought about this. The hand not holding my tea tightened on the slippery leather of the chair as I dug my fingers into the fabric, which felt uncomfortably like a human arm. 'I didn't want to upset Granny, she was teaching me about the herbs, and it was horrible here when she wouldn't talk to me. I had to trail along behind her as if I didn't exist.'

'So not upsetting them became more important than you knowing about your own father?' Zeb sounded angry and I opened my eyes, straightened up to see him blazing a dark look at me across the kitchen. 'Seriously?'

'It...' I tried to think how I'd felt. 'If I asked about Dad, or about the past in general, it made things... I don't know, sort of *worse*. And it didn't matter, not to me, not really. Dad was just this person who once existed, like Napoleon or Henry the Eighth.'

In my pocket my phone buzzed a text. I didn't look. I knew who it would be from and most likely what it would say. Zeb refocussed that dark stare which was becoming uncomfortable.

'But neither Napoleon nor Henry make up half your DNA,' he said quietly. 'You have a right to be curious.'

'But it doesn't *matter*.' I slithered out of Granny's chair. 'I'm me and I live and work here. I know who *I* am, Zeb, and that's the only thing that's important.'

I hoped he wouldn't point out all that research and all those printouts that decorated my bedroom walls. My knowing of myself had so obviously been made up from a lot of piecemeal reading and other people's experiences that I knew more about than I knew about my own. Now, to distract myself from the way his eyes were flickering over my face, I pulled my phone out of my pocket. As I'd thought, Mum.

> Natalie, darling, could you pop over? I've nothing in the cupboard and I can't go out today, I'm feeling too ill. I went shopping yesterday but I seem to have forgotten bread and potatoes and I'd like some of that lovely soup they do in the shop.

She didn't sign it or leave a kiss, but that was typical. When Mum was ill she could barely summon the energy to type, other than to list what she wanted.

'Your mother?' Zeb raised an eyebrow.

'Yes. I'd better get over there. Well, I'll go via the shop, she needs a few things.'

'Finish your tea first.' Zeb moved out of his chair and lifted my mug into my hand.

'Oh, but...'

Once Upon a Thyme

'She's not going to get worse if you stop and drink your tea.' His voice was firm. 'You should take better care of yourself, Tallie. What's the saying, "put on your own oxygen mask before you help others with theirs"?'

In the crowded shadow of my little kitchen, still smelling of last night's food, Zeb sounded more serious than I'd ever known him.

'I *do* take care of myself,' I muttered.

'You ate last night as though you hadn't seen solid food for weeks. I've only ever seen you make yourself toast, and you're out in the garden from dawn 'til dusk. You're too thin, your clothes are hanging off you and – forgive me for this – you don't look as though you've had a proper haircut for years,' Zeb said, then added, 'Sorry,' as though he realised how much his words would sting.

'I...' I began, then realised I couldn't refute any of this. To launch into an explanation of how hard it was to eat when the shop was busy and I was the only one available to man the till, how my hands were usually too full of planting or weeding to make it worthwhile making a sandwich, how I hadn't had a chance to do any clothes shopping for ages or to get to the hairdresser and anyway I couldn't really afford it would take too long and I needed to get some shopping over to Mum. 'I'm going out,' was all I said, putting my half-drunk tea on the table now. 'To get Mum her food.'

'I'll come with you.' Zeb put his tea down, equally as definitely.

'What? No! You stay here, the band will be arriving soon.'

The thought of Zeb following me around the shop and then over to Mum's house and wandering around her kitchen while I checked she had everything she needed, filled me with horror.

'The band will do their thing, they don't need anyone here.

And I've been to your mother's before, remember? She likes me. I might perk her up a bit.'

'You might drive her into a relapse.'

'Ah, come on, if I'm going to work for you I'm going to have to help out with chores for your mother.' Zeb patted my shoulder. It reminded me, uncomfortably, of the way he'd slapped Big Pig's rump last night. More gentle, obviously, but still.

'You're coming to work with the animals.' I sounded mutinous, as though I was thrown back to my questioning teenage self, trying to ask why I wasn't allowed to go into town, why I couldn't go to the local school, why I had to go all the way to the private school two towns over. Why I was so *isolated*.

Questions I'd only dared to mutter in the silence of my bedroom. Asking them out loud would have been to invite Mum's illness to take over our lives again, and for Granny to alternate worrying with censure. Zeb was company. He was annoying and pushy and he pried into areas of my life that even *I* didn't look at, but he was *there*.

'All right.'

'I'll drop Simon a message so they don't worry when we're not here. I think they're doing some pick-up shots today, joining bits together and maybe filming a couple of tracks.' Zeb seemed to take my acquiescence as a given and trotted alongside me as I closed up the cottage, went through to the front and got in my car.

'She's not well,' I said, steering us out into the narrow lane.

'I know, you've said. Do you know where your dad died? Where the crash was, I mean?' Zeb turned his head from side to side as though the narrow innocence of the flower-crowded hedge banks were about to close in on us and squeeze us to death, like a horror film, and replay those tragic events.

'No. Somewhere near the village.'

'And his car hit a tractor?'

I concentrated on driving.

* * *

The little farm shop on the outskirts of the village had already put its raised tables out, and I left Zeb in the car so I could pick up the bread, soup and potatoes for Mum, plus a pint of milk as she'd almost certainly have forgotten that too. After a second's thought, I threw a packet of biscuits, some butter, a couple of tins of beans and some fresh veg in too. Mum could be surprisingly unfocused when she shopped, and I'd got used to turning up to almost empty cupboards after she'd supposedly done a 'big shop'.

Driving further on we met The Goshawk Traders' mini cavalcade coming the other way and I had to stop in a gateway to allow them through, with much waving and mugging out of windows on their part. Mika was sitting next to Tessa I noticed. I also noticed him blow me an exaggerated kiss as our vehicles slid past each other, unnaturally squashed into proximity by walls of bramble and exuberant dog roses. There was the bitter smell of torn Herb Robert too.

'He's such a tit,' Zeb observed mildly.

I thought of Mika's dark concentration when he looked at my face and the way my heart galloped into my throat when I had his attention. Of his casual, easy affection when he draped himself over me and his assurance that we should have lunch and he should show me his garden. Part of me wanted to agree with Zeb – some of that casual affection came dangerously close to unwanted physical touch, and it was easy for him to hint at future meetings that he never intended to carry out. But always in the background was that *possibility*, that small treacherous feeling that maybe Mika saw me as more than a gardener. Perhaps he saw through this chrysalis of dirty jeans and messy hair and duty to the – what? The bright social butterfly who would travel, live out of suitcases, unbothered and unfazed by the weirdnesses of life on the road? Ha!

'He's all right really.' I steered the tight corner that led to the bridge. 'He's just... effusive.'

The car bucked its way over the high rise of the single span bridge and down into the village. I parked beside the road and we got out to cross the stones that were the most direct way to my mother's front door. When the water was high, I had to go around the long way, back over the bridge and down the little lane, but I liked it best when I could step over the four solid flags. They were mossed and their edges trailed weed into the water, but they were securely fixed and pleasantly spongey underfoot.

'Is this where you grew up?' Zeb angled his head, looking up at the little house, with its deep eaves which gave it a look of slight puzzlement as they frowned over leaded windows.

'No. Mum and Dad actually started out in one of those houses down there.' I pointed to the terrace of farmworkers' cottages which fronted the road further down. 'I was born in the middle one, apparently. When Mum wanted to move back to the village, she bought this place.' I put my hand on the gate.

'Bit of a step up,' Zeb observed, pulling at the *Gertrude Jekyll* rose which was supposed to grow over the archway into the front garden, but was currently untidily sprawling its way down through the hedge.

I didn't reply and we walked up the narrow brick path – which, I noticed, also needed weeding. I'd have to come down with my tools one day soon – and in through the unlocked front door.

'Mum! I'm here, I brought the shopping!' I called down the hallway. Only dust answered me, hanging in curtains in the light that came through from the bright kitchen at the back. 'How are you feeling?'

A bump from above.

'Zeb's come with me,' I called again, just to forestall any intent she may have to appear on the staircase, *deshabille* and dishevelled, dragged from her bed by a desire to see what I'd brought.

'Lovely, darling,' came the drawled reply. 'I won't come down, I'm really unwell today.'

'But are you all right?' I asked, in one of those peculiar ironic statements that seem to run in families. 'Do you need me to call the doctor or anything?'

'No, no.' Her voice was faint. 'I'll be all right if I can have a good sleep. Thank you for the shopping, darling.'

I paused at the bottom of the staircase. Part of me knew I should go up. But equally, part of me wanted to stay down here, with Zeb, and not have to face my mother's shrouded form in that hot fusty little room.

'Leave her to sleep.' Zeb put his hand on my arm. 'It will probably be better for her.'

'You're an expert in my mum's illness now, are you?' His certainty annoyed me. 'She might need something.'

'She knows you're here and she can ask if she does,' he said, reasonably. 'Who will it help if you go up?'

Me, I wanted to say. I could see that she was safely tucked up and reassure myself that she was still alive – although her calling out to us had pretty well removed that fear that today would be the day I'd find her cold and still, swathed in duvet and the room already smelling of death.

'Let's get this stuff put away.' He was moving through into

the kitchen, opening and closing cupboard doors. 'Does anyone else live here? It seems a big place for just one person.'

'No, it's just Mum.' When I went through, he had his head in the under-sink cupboard.

'What on earth are you doing in there?'

'Nothing.' His head came out again. 'Thought I'd find some kitchen spray, that's all. Sink could do with a clean.'

'That's the chef in you coming out.' I hauled the bag of shopping onto the table. 'It looks fine to me.'

'You, Tallie, are hardly fit to talk. Your kitchen looks as though a *Country Living* designer had a breakdown.'

'I'm too busy for housework.' He was annoying me again. 'If you are going to be obsessed with cleanliness and tidiness, you really aren't the right person to be working with animals.'

He grinned broadly at me. 'I was thinking of a donkey. Kids like donkeys and they are just so daft looking, with those ears. And maybe ducks? We'd need some more land, of course. Hens, to clear land and get rid of slugs and stuff, plus we could sell the eggs.'

Competently he unpacked the bag, putting potatoes, milk and veg away while I stood with a half-pound of butter in my hand and stared at him. 'You've thought it through? Already? I mean...'

Zeb came across the kitchen, took the butter from my hand and slipped it into the fridge which, as I had known it would be, was almost empty. Mother had probably bought nothing but industrial quantities of coffee and peanut butter which was what she seemed to exist on. 'Of course. I told you, Tallie, I think working with animals might be the vocation I've been looking for. I loved being a chef, but it was too stressful, and I hate the financial advice thing. It was prompted by my dad's career, he was something in banking, and I thought there may be a genetic component.'

This was the first time Zeb had mentioned anything about family, other than his wife. I didn't know why he'd chosen now to introduce the topic, other than to distract me from the fact that he seemed very concerned with the contents of my mother's kitchen cupboards.

'Where are your parents now?' There was a lump of very old cheese at the back of the fridge. I threw it away.

'Oh, Dad died some years back, and Mum lives with my sister in Wrexham.'

That seemed to kill that avenue of conversation. Zeb carried on peering in cupboards. 'Are you looking for damp, or something? Why are you so worried about the cupboards?'

Almost guiltily he straightened up, catching his head on the underside of the kitchen countertop as he did so. 'Er, nothing. I'm just curious.'

'You aren't going to suddenly drop the idea of working with animals and decide to go into kitchen design and construction, are you?'

Ruefully he rubbed his head and twisted his mouth at me. 'Sadly for you, no. Look, Tallie, I can do this, I know I can. I can grow the pets' zone into something we can use to be financially solvent during the times that the garden is at its leanest. We can make use of the facilities that are already there, the parking and the shop, the handwashing station, and expand those toddler and playgroup visits that you have into proper events.' His eyes were shining now. He looked as though he'd already run the pros and cons in his head and come up with plans. 'You can leave it to me, you concentrate on the herb garden, growing and selling and all that, and we can run things as almost two separate businesses. Probably beneficial tax wise too.'

I sighed and led the way back into the hall. 'We're off now, Mum!' I called. 'Sure there's nothing else you want?'

'Mmmm? No, darling. I'll ring you if there is.'

Zeb raised an eyebrow at me.

'Fine then. Bye.' I'd never really noticed the relief I felt on leaving Mum's house before. Maybe it was the way Zeb stared around the overgrown square of the front garden that made me see that I much preferred being outdoors. The hedges that separated the house from its only neighbour were adolescent with leggy growth, pale shoots that had sprouted in the last week or so, and adorned with convolvulus trumpets and thistle flowers. 'I ought to come over and do some work,' I said, hands on hips. 'It's getting out of control.'

'Your mum can't garden? Or employ a gardener?' Zeb pulled at a dandelion which was forcing its way up between the paving bricks, a touch of bright gold optimism among the damp weeds.

'She does garden.' I felt ridiculously defensive. 'When she's well. Plus, you know, it's my job and everything.'

'It's not your job to care for your mother though, is it? I mean, if she could get to the bottom of her illness then maybe she could get help? As it is, she seems to rely on you and not be too bothered about how her illness impacts on your life.'

His implied criticism made me want to snap a reply; something about how I owed my mother so much for bringing me up and keeping me safe. How it was my business if I paid her back by doing her shopping and dropping in to help her now and again. But I didn't because, and I hated to admit it, he had a point.

We got back into my car and I stared once more at the impassive front of the house. I was almost sure that I saw a flicker of movement at the top front window; maybe my mother was watching me go? My heart gave a little jump and squeeze in my chest at the thought of the lonely woman watching her daughter leave, maybe wanting to call me back but not wanting to keep me from the things I needed to do. I would come back tonight and be company for a while, I decided. Who cared if it was just watching TV and eating sandwiches, after a day confined to bed she'd be glad to have someone to chat to.

'She's tried to get a diagnosis.' I started the engine, keeping my eyes on that window, now just reflecting the light from the beck in its inscrutably dark squares. There was no more movement. Perhaps I'd imagined it. 'The doctors just keep fobbing her off.'

'Maybe if you went with her? And you could tell them how much it's impacting on her daily life, being unable to do anything for herself?'

There was a tone in Zeb's voice that I didn't understand, something sharp, almost accusatory, that made me rush to answer.

'I have offered. Granny used to offer too, she always said it was disgusting that they couldn't sort it out. But then Granny was big on the herbal medicine, and she used to give Mum draughts of various tonics and cordials that she'd made up. None of those ever did any good either. I think she lost patience after a while.'

'Perhaps it's ME or fibromyalgia – one of those illnesses that it's very hard to diagnose and the doctors can't really treat it.' Again, there was that note in Zeb's voice. Not blame, it was milder than that, but almost the tiniest bit of censure as if Mum just wasn't *trying* for a diagnosis. 'But I am curious as to how she's managing to pay the bills.'

'None of your business,' I replied, chippily. 'Or mine either. We'd better get back and oversee the band, in case they suddenly decide to start climbing trees or doing something else that might end in an actionable case of damages.'

'Plus, of course, the delicious Mika is there to be flirted with.'

'Shut up.'

But as we drove away down those lace-edged lanes, I couldn't stop wondering why Zeb was so concerned about my mother and her illness.

12

As soon as we arrived back at the gardens, Mika came over, opening the car door to help me out and putting a hand under my elbow as though I were a hundred.

'Ah, Tallie, there you are. We were beginning to worry that you'd run for the hills or something.'

I heard Zeb snort. He sounded just like Big Pig.

'No, we just had some things to do. You're fine getting on without me though, aren't you?' I couldn't help myself, I leaned in to the closeness of his shoulder so I could appreciate the dusky smell of his hair which had hints of bergamot and jasmine.

'Of course, but I missed your luscious presence.' Mika led me away from the car park. 'And Simon wants to talk to you, well, he wants a word with your PR bloke actually.' He looked over his shoulder; I looked too and saw Zeb leaning against the roof of the car, watching us go. Zeb raised an eyebrow at me and gave a smile that was a bit lopsided for my liking. I didn't know whether it was weighted with sarcasm or encouragement. 'In a minute. But I wanted to talk to you too.'

Today Mika was wearing all green. A moss green T-shirt under a washed linen jacket and over green slouchy trousers. He looked as though he had more than a little of the elf about him, particularly with his hair caught up in a beaded tie that glittered like water. I felt my palms start to sweat.

'What did you want to talk about?' My voice came out high-pitched and ragged.

'You remember you were telling me which plants you've got in the shaded garden? I wondered if you'd run through it again for me.'

Oh, he wanted to talk about gardening. That was all right then. I could cope with that. My heart steadied.

'There's lots of different types of mint, they all do well in shade.' I led the way along the narrow path that wound up to the shade garden, where the foxgloves were dipping their tall heads wisely. 'Foxgloves are good too, although they'll self-seed like mad so you need to keep an eye on them to stop them taking over.'

Mika was nodding beside me. Because of the width of the path, he was tight up against me, watching where he put his feet. He'd still got hold of my elbow. I could feel his fingers curled around the bone in a way that was slightly uncomfortable but you could not have paid me to ask him to let go. This was *Mika*! He was famous!

'Mika!' Will was down at the far side of the garden. 'We're going to shoot that final track now, are you coming?'

'Yeah, there in a minute.' Mika waved the hand not holding my arm in a dismissive way without turning around. 'Mint, foxgloves, what else have you got?'

'Chives do well. I'd normally put parsley in shade but we've got a big parsley bed further down so I don't need more.

Coriander and tansy, loveage, the bitter herbs don't need much sun.'

Mika swivelled around, pivoting around my elbow. 'That's fabulous, Tallie, thank you. I'll get my gardener guy onto those when I get back.'

Disappointment dropped through me like a pebble into the pond. I'd hoped that Mika would ask me to come to London to work on his garden, an excuse or a reason to have me close. Somewhere in the back of my tiny, unacknowledged, romantic soul I'd dreamed that we could have had some kind of future, this glamorous musician and me.

'Yes. That's fine.' I sounded flat. I *felt* flat. As though Mika's careless mention of his gardener had killed my every hope, which was just plain ridiculous.

He clearly heard and maybe understood. 'You've been great,' he whispered, pulling my elbow until I was drawn in closer, my chest touching his jacket, which rustled and draped in the way that only very expensive fabric can do. 'Really, Tallie. Letting us film here, ruining your summer season.' A finger came under my chin and tilted my face upwards. 'You're a star.'

And then Mika was kissing me. Soft lips and a drift of hair, a hand cupping my face and the scent of his skin, the taste of his mouth. I felt my brain go into suspended animation as though it wanted this moment preserved forever, whilst actively trying to suck in as much detail as possible, to keep. Mika. Kissing. Me.

I was brought back to reality by two things – Mika gradually releasing his hold on me and taking a small step back, and another snort from the main path passing the shaded garden, which told me that Zeb had gone by on his way to the cottage and was unimpressed. As my brain gradually took control of my functions again, Mika swirled away in a brush of linen and was gone, cheerily calling to Will and Tessa and I was left standing utterly befuddled.

Mika. Kissed. Me.

I found I was doing the romance-film heroine thing of touching my lips as though I half expected them to be stained or branded in some way. It wasn't my first kiss by a long way, despite my mother's seeming intention to keep me a virgin until I was fifty, but it felt as though it was.

I was prodded back to reality by the appearance of Zeb. 'Come on! Simon wants a word with me and I know you'll only go off on one if I talk to him without your permission in triplicate.'

I jolted as though he'd made me jump. 'Oh, yes, I...'

'I saw.' Zeb sounded half-amused, half-sad. 'He's doing his number on you, isn't he?'

I couldn't answer. Even though I thought his statement was wrong on every level, I still couldn't speak coherently. I just fell into step beside Zeb on the wider path that led down to my cottage, where Simon, Loke and Vinnie were discussing something with much pointing and Genevra was pulling heads off the tansy flowers.

'Just on the fence,' Simon said as we arrived. 'But get them to move the vehicles first. Ah, Tallie and Zeb. Good job.'

Simon had caught the sun during the last couple of days and his good-natured face was pink across the bridge of his nose. The strictness of the ponytail had become a bit less too, and although it was still tied back, his hair had lost some of the 'I Work In Rock Music' attitude. Maybe it was just getting to know him, but he now seemed far more of an ordinary man than he had when he'd first walked into the garden. I wondered why that hadn't come into play for Mika and the others too, whom I still found myself tongue-tied around.

'Hi, Simon.' Zeb bounced and then caught my eye. I widened mine, silently pleading with him not to mention what I'd just been doing with Mika. Simon had already warned me off once and I had had enough of lecturing from Mum on her good days. I didn't need to get it again from a man whose money I was taking.

Zeb winked. 'Right. Here we are. Let us in, Tallie, and I'll put the kettle on.'

I hadn't felt my hands shaking, but they were when I tried to put the key in the lock to open the cottage door. Mika seemed to have removed all my common sense and practicality and replaced it with dangerous levels of 'Girlie'. It was ridiculous to feel this way, I knew it, and yet here I was.

'Would you like me to do it?' Zeb sounded surprisingly kind. 'You seem to be struggling.'

Simon's attention was thankfully diverted. He was watching the band forming at the far end of the garden, each member floating in from various places to where Mika was standing. It was like watching planets form around a sun, a solar system around their star.

I handed the key to Zeb who had the door open in moments and we burst through into the kitchen which still smelled slightly of cleaning fluid although that was now overlaid by perfume, crushed leaves and curry.

'What did you need to talk to me about?' Zeb began filling the kettle. I was still struck dumb and my eyes kept swivelling to the window.

'I... err... we've just about finished filming now.' Simon stood awkwardly in the doorway. 'We need to finalise payment and agree on publicity – what we'll put up on the site for you for example.'

'I was thinking – what about buying us a new barn?' Zeb

asked quickly. 'I mean,' he added, throwing me a look, 'as a lasting legacy of your visit. We might even get a bird of prey or two, you know, goshawk or something? And then it becomes an attraction in its own right and it will help us through the winter months.' He stopped, finally running out of breath.

I stared at him. 'I thought the new barn and more animals was for the future?'

But Simon was looking out of the window too now. 'I see what you mean,' he said slowly. 'Well, as long as you don't want it to happen overnight...'

'Oh no, there will be planning permission for the barn extension and insurances to look into first,' Zeb said happily. 'But it would be something you could come and visit. The Goshawk Traders in a lovely garden with an actual goshawk, great photo opportunities.'

I stared at Simon now. *Too easy. It was too easy. This wasn't how life worked, that you wanted something and someone rich came along and made it happen. Was it?*

'Well, I would like to come back and visit occasionally.' Simon seemed to be talking to the scenery. 'I really like it here. There's something so... so *peaceful* about Drycott. And,' he added suddenly, almost as though he'd just thought of it, 'it will be nice to see what you do with the place.'

'Are you blackmailing him?' I asked, when Simon had gone back to join the band. 'Because if you are, the cottage needs a new roof and we could do with some more gravel for the car park.'

Zeb laughed. We were still sitting at the table in the long rays of afternoon sunshine, while the band packed up equipment and generally messed about like schoolchildren. I didn't want to go out. I didn't want to say goodbye.

Mika had kissed me. I didn't know what it had been, a

promise of more, a farewell or just the sort of thing he did all the time. I'd watched him swinging Tessa around and draping himself over Genevra, careless and physical and affectionate. It seemed to be how he was: touchy-feely with everyone and I was nothing special. I kept trying to tell myself that the kiss had been nothing. *To him.* To me it had been like someone half-opening a gate into Arcadia and showing me a glimpse of what could be.

'Shall I ring Ollie and tell him to come back tomorrow?' Zeb broke into my wistful dream-life.

'What? Why would you do that?'

'Because I work here. You employ me. Remember?'

I looked at Zeb now. He was draped too but not nearly as picturesquely as Mika, and over the chair rather than another person. Long limbs that seemed to have taken him by surprise by being hinged in unexpected places. Zeb always looked slightly physically awkward.

'Do you really think you want to work here? With animals? When you're a trained chef and qualified financial consultant? Isn't it a bit of a waste of education and experience? I worry that you're going to stick it for a fortnight and then realise that it's actually just shovelling shit and moving a pig and you'd rather be somewhere where you get to use your brain.'

There was a long pause. A stem of basil flopped exhaustedly in its pot and there was a short scratchy sound from behind the dresser. Otherwise everything was quiet.

'Well done,' Zeb said at last. His tone was level, not sarcastic or even particularly congratulatory, but it sounded as though he meant those two words.

I blinked. The sun had moved and was shining between us now, so I could only see him as a golden outline broken by swirling dust. 'What on earth are you talking about?'

He sighed. 'You asked me a serious question. That's the first time I've ever heard you ask something about how someone else might feel. I know you said you were trained out of asking questions but I hadn't realised it was so serious.'

I blinked again. It really was hard to focus on him with the sun glancing in at such an angle. It caught the edge of a bowl, reflected and refracted and hit me straight in the eye. 'Don't be daft.' I tried to sound authoritative and like an employer. 'I ask things like that all the time.'

'You ask superficial questions. "What's the weather like?" "How old are you?" "Would you like some milk in that?" That kind of thing. But you don't ask anything where the answer might really be important.'

I stood up. 'I have no idea what you are talking about.' I pushed away from the table and over to the sink where I began running water to wash up our recently used tea mugs. It kept my back to the glaring light which was giving me a headache, but it meant that I could see out of the window. I could see Mika too, leaning against the wall of the barn with that half-amused expression on his face, watching something I couldn't see at the far side of the garden. He was undeniably gorgeous but all of a sudden there was something calculating about him. Something about the way he stood, as though he were waiting to be admired, and his easy arrogance prickled at my skin. Behind the beauty there was something showing that looked like overconfidence. Did he really like me at all? Or had I been an entertainment to distract him in his downtime? A silly girl to dally with under the trees amid the birdsong.

You don't ask anything where the answer might really be important. Zeb's words echoed in my head, and I felt all those unasked questions from the past surging through me on a lava-raft of boiling anger. My veins solidified with it, my blood burned. I *never* felt angry, never. I might be cross, mildly annoyed, possibly suffer from that mixture of disappointment and thwarted intentions that can feel like anger, but never this fierce, driving rage that was forcing into me now.

'Stay there,' I said to Zeb.

'I'm sorry?'

'There's something I've got to do.' I pushed off from the worktop I'd been leaning against. I had to do this, and I had to do it now, while the unaccustomed fury was still in the driving seat. I marched out of the cottage and across the garden.

I'd never been *allowed* to feel anger. Any extreme emotion had been kept well tamped down, the embers smouldering and giving off the occasional whiff of infuriation like a too-damp bonfire. Granny and Mum hadn't just trained me out of questions, they'd trained me out of showing my feelings too. It would upset Mum and send her to bed for a week if I permitted myself any more than a momentary bite of annoyance. She couldn't cope with me being anything other than calm and reassuring. So, no tantrums, no teenage door slamming, no thrown accusations; I had had to stay calm and sit on my emotions.

I balled my fists as I walked, stomping the gravel underfoot as though it had personally upset me. It was all starting to make sense. I'd learned to keep it all shoved down. No anger, no fear, no curiosity. No questions. I hadn't been a daughter, I'd been one of those paper dolls that Granny had let me play with from her Sunday Box, where she kept interesting buttons and bits of shell, things to keep me out of mischief. A flat, two-dimensional creature that they'd kept in her box. It was as though Zeb's congratulating me for asking him a question had unlocked that secret compartment inside me that held back all the things I wasn't allowed to do.

All this seething emotional fallout meant that I could

confront Mika without being rendered dumb by his sheer beauty. 'Hey, hi, Tallie!' He waved an insouciant arm. 'We're nearly packed and ready to go.'

He still looked elfin, in his textured green. But now, in my state of writhing anger, his dark eyes didn't look as twinkly as they had before, and his hair just looked messy rather than attractively tousled.

'Mika.' I was slightly out of breath. 'You kissed me.'

His beautiful face creased into a frown. 'Yeah?'

'And I have to know now.' The question caught in my throat. *Asking questions means rejection. It means having to pacify and cajole and make yourself small. Not knowing is better, it means you can always pretend...* The anger rose again. 'I need to know if you meant it.'

The words came out in a single syllable, rushing into the air before I could try to stop them. Mika's frown deepened.

'Meant it, how? Like, what, wanting something more with you?' Then his face cleared and the eyes were dark and shining again. 'You might have got it wrong there, Tallie, my darling. It was just a kiss, you know? Nothing heavy.'

He stepped closer to me and the smell of him was intoxicating, as though he were trying to bewitch me. I remembered some more of Granny's hair-raising fairy stories about the Fair Folk and what they could do to people, and thought *they didn't know the half of it.*

Mika was almost laughing now. 'You're cute and I'm a terrible flirt, I'm afraid. Tessa always says it's my worst feature.' He didn't look remotely ashamed. 'Tessa and I are getting married at the end of the summer,' he said. 'That one's a secret though. We've sold the rights to some magazine or other.' Another step forward and a hand came out and touched my hair. 'So I couldn't have anything with you, even if I wanted to. She'd have my balls under cheese wire.'

The anger rolled back a little to make way for a tiny cool feeling of smugness. So he actually *had* fancied me. I hadn't imagined it all.

'I'm sorry if you took it the wrong way,' Mika went on in an apology that was no kind of apology at all, and still made it my fault. 'I shouldn't have messed with someone so naïve. I ought to know better. I'll learn, one of these days.'

There was a shout across the garden and he raised a lazy hand in acknowledgement, flicking another glance at me. 'No hard feelings, eh? You're a lovely girl and this place is amazing.' A quick step right up to me, the soft drift of hair against my cheek and the merest brush of lips. 'You work too hard,' he whispered. 'Learn to party.'

Then, like the elven being he resembled, he was gone, dancing across the herb beds towards the summons. The rest of his bandmates were waiting, carrying instrument cases and, in the case of Tessa, an enormous bunch of herbs that she'd clearly spent much of the morning picking. I briefly priced it up, and then shook my head. No point. I'd just add it on to what Simon needed to pay.

But I'd done it. The immense relief almost made me drop to the ground with the lifting of its weight. I'd confronted someone and the world hadn't ended. I may have felt mildly miffed that I'd been quite so easy to bowl over with good looks and charm and a touch of hero worship. *Naïve?* I'd give him bloody naïve, the lecherous sod. Although, I had been, hadn't I? Naïve enough to think that someone as famous and glamorous and generally a person who could have anyone in the world that they took a liking to, might want me.

Here came the burning embarrassment to fry my ears and make me feel as though I was wearing a brushed-wire suit. How could I even have thought...? Me, little Tallie Fisher, how dare I allow myself to step outside the role allotted to me by life and imagine that someone so... so... *Mika* might have been serious? I turned away and began pulling faded petals off the rose clambering its way over the wall, feeling the hot-cheeked mortification dying back to the usual background bewilderment. He *had* fancied me, he had practically admitted it. He was marrying Tessa. Nothing could have come of any attraction, because he was marrying Tessa.

Focus on that, Tallie.

Slowly, to give myself chance to adjust from fury-driven or fiery with humiliation back to base level, I walked back to the cottage. Zeb was still where I'd left him, which felt odd. Inside I felt as though I'd aged a century, as though letting out some emotion had released several pent-up decades which had settled on me like dandruff.

'All right?' he said cheerily.

'Yes,' I replied, still slow. 'I just had to have a word with Mika.'

'I saw.' Now Zeb looked down at the table, tracing a crack with his fingernail. 'I was a bit worried for a minute. You went off looking as though you wanted to rip his immaculate head off.'

'Were you?'

'Actually.' Now he looked up and met my eye. 'I was worried you were going to offer to leave with him.'

Zeb sounded serious. Although the words had been lightly spoken, almost like a joke, there was nothing amused about his expression. He really did look as though he'd been afraid that I was going to throw myself at Mika and ask to be taken away from all this.

The last of the anger drained away completely to be replaced by a different kind of warmth. The sort of warmth that feels as though it creeps out from your heart rather than being forced in from outside. A hot drink, as opposed to an acid bath.

'How could I leave all this?' I waved an arm. 'I've got seeds to bring on and a fennel bed that's still got trotter prints in it. Plus the possibility of a barn full of birds and a potential donkey.'

'Which is why' – Zeb came in now with what seemed to be a burst of cheerfulness – 'you have me as Pig Wrangler and Shit Shoveller. There's still an element of financial management creeping in to my role of course. Hence me persuading Simon to pay to build us a new barn. One with proper fastening gates that Big Pig can't open.'

There was a moment of quiet into which the future settled. No rock stars. No life on the road, being an accessory to a man who flirted like he breathed. Instead, a future here, with my herb garden and my animals.

I shook my head. 'It was too easy,' I said, clanking china as I put the used mugs away in the cupboard. 'He didn't even quibble.'

'Yes,' Zeb said slowly. 'I wondered about that.'

'I thought that maybe you'd got something nasty on him or the band.'

Zeb didn't speak for a moment and I had to look over my shoulder to check that he was still there. He was tipping his chair casually back with the sun slicing through the window frame to tattoo him with shadow. 'No,' he said slowly. '*I* haven't. But I think someone might.'

'The band?' I had a brief thought that perhaps Mika had persuaded Simon to give us whatever we wanted. Perhaps he *had* felt guilty about how he'd treated me, and this was his way of making himself feel better.

Zeb shook his head. 'Not sure.' The chair came back to earth with a clonk. 'Anyway. Do you fancy doing something tonight? I know we're about a million miles from the nearest cinema, but we could… go for a walk? Or something?'

He spoke quickly, as though he had to get the words out before common sense cut in and strangled him.

I let the china drop heavily onto the draining board. 'What?'

'You, me, somewhere that isn't here or your mother's kitchen? Might be nice.'

I turned with a slowness that seemed to be weighted with doubt. 'What?' I asked again, although the words had made perfect sense.

'Sorry, did you have something else planned?' Zeb stood up, unfolding himself from behind the table. 'What do you usually do in the evenings?'

'I pop in on my mum, I tidy up the gardens, do a bit of pruning and I… I watch TV. Mostly,' I added, honestly, because often I did none of those things; I sat at this table and stared out at the day lowering itself behind the trees and watched the dusk creeping in around the hedges. Also, I dreamed. I dreamed of what could be, what could *have* been and I looked at my loneliness with a degree of introspection which probably wasn't healthy.

Sometimes I told my hopes and dreams to Big Pig, but I wasn't going to tell Zeb that either. Tears pressed behind my eyes but I froze my face and swallowed hard. Self-pity mingled with unaccustomed confessions were making me emotional, that was all.

'Or do you already have a date for tonight?'

'Who the hell would I possibly have a date with?' A half-laugh coughed out over the tightness in my throat.

'Mika…' Zeb said slowly and carefully.

'Isn't real. Oh, he's real enough, but he doesn't want *me*. He's just playing. I knew it really, but sometimes it's just nice to dream about something that isn't this house and this garden and doing my mother's laundry because she can't get downstairs and making sure she's had something solid to eat!' The words burst out, surprising even me. 'He's got a lovely house in London and a huge garden and *somebody* must be cutting his lawns and planning his borders and I just thought, why shouldn't it be me? *Why shouldn't it be me?*'

I was crying now with the rim of the sink pressing into my back harder and harder as I leaned into it, trying to use the sensation to stop the tears. Zeb took a tiny step forward to approach me, but he stopped. 'He's a player,' I said, trying to push the tears back in with the angle of my wrist. 'Of *course* he's a player. He even told me he was, *Simon* told me he was. It's just... it feels as though this place has knocked all the dreams out of me, you know? It's "get up, weed, plant, tidy, sell, sweep gravel, feed the animals" all day, every day, like there's no other life out there. This is all I've ever known, I've been living here and doing this since I could toddle and it's like some giant Groundhog Day.'

Somewhere in the back of my head Sensible Tallie was telling me that, yes, this might be how I felt deep down, but equally deep down I knew that I was very lucky. I had a job, a roof over my head, a mother who loved me. There were people out in the world who would kill to have even one of those elements, so what right did I have to be dissatisfied?

None. I had no right. I should pull up my Big Girl Pants, realise that this was my life, and then grit my teeth and get on with things.

But Emotional Tallie, who didn't usually get much of a say,

other than crying when one of the guinea pigs died, had taken control for once and was becoming slightly hysterical.

Zeb looked somewhat taken aback, which wasn't surprising. It can't be every day that your employer breaks down in tears in front of you and admits to wanting something else.

'Er,' he said. 'Do you think another cup of tea might be a good idea?'

His diffidence made me snort a laugh. 'No. No it's fine, I'm all right really. I just sometimes get a bit… and you were there. Sorry.'

He'd rolled up his sleeves again. What *was* it about the sight of those bony forearms that made something inside me go peculiar? The way the cuffs of his shirt flapped against his skin or the vulnerability of the veins that showed on his wrists?

'I thought you loved it here.' He sounded *cheated*, as though I'd somehow swindled him out of something.

'I do. No, really, I do.' I sniffed mightily and wiped my eyes on the hem of my T-shirt. 'It's just that sometimes it all seems so… narrow, do you understand what I mean? As though if I never left this place I could just keep doing this until I die. Ticking over but never actually *living*. I love it here but sometimes I just feel as though there should be… *more*.'

Zeb came out from around the table and sat on the edge of it, nearer to me. There was an expression in his dark eyes that gave me a similar feeling to seeing his bare wrists, as though my heart were twisting sideways in my chest. 'Of course I understand,' he said softly. 'That is exactly how I feel. It's how I felt about being a chef, to be honest, and it's how I feel about the financial advice thing. Yes, it's great, it's a wonderful job and I know I'm doing a good thing, but I want there to be more. Something else. I'm not great with pressure, that's my problem, I'm a born backroom bloke, but something in me wants there to be... yes, like you said, more. Living, rather than working and sleeping. Having something, someone, a life. I've always been restless, looking for something and I didn't realise that the something I was looking for – could be this.'

We stared at one another with the dawning realisation that we had a lot more in common than we'd ever suspected.

'But what else is there for me?' I asked finally. 'I mean apart from imagining running away with a famous folk-rock band member and living a swish and fancy life in London with a gorgeous garden and a converted chapel.'

'You'd have hated London though, wouldn't you?'

'Yes, of course I would, but that's not the point.' I sighed. 'It would be something else. I'd be – I don't know, achieving something. I don't want fame and fortune, I just want...'

In my pocket my phone began to trill its message that my mother was calling again. I stood, paralysed.

'To be seen, perhaps,' Zeb said, gently. 'To make something of this place in your own right. Your mother does seem to regard you as something of an extension to herself, doesn't she?'

I pulled my phone out and looked at the screen. That old familiar guilt was tugging away at my insides, the feeling that I needed to make sure that Mother was all right. But pulling the other way was this conversation that I was having with Zeb. I hadn't realised how little opportunity I ever had to be truly honest with myself, with someone else, and he seemed to understand.

But Mum needed me.

'I should...' I held the phone up, as though Zeb might have thought I was talking about something else.

'Should you? Yes, perhaps you ought. Although...' He trailed off, staring at the phone.

'Although, what?'

The ringing stopped and the silence was as heavy as the dust-laden sunlight.

'I'm not sure. But I think there's a story here that's beginning to piece itself together. It's like a jigsaw puzzle and you are standing so close to the picture that you can only see the bits that are right in front of you.'

'Oh very enigmatic.' I was holding the phone, my mind a huge whirl of uncertainty. Should I call her back? What would happen if I didn't? 'You're like Yoda, only without the cuteness.'

'Thanks.' Zeb looked genuinely hurt.

'Sorry. You are quite cute really,' I said, then clamped my lips together.

Zeb seemed mollified. 'All right then. I'm just beginning to wonder about some things.'

'I'm wondering about *lots* of things.'

'So, shall we go out then?' Now he pushed his hands into his pockets, hunching his shoulders slightly as though he expected me to push him away. 'Or would you rather go to your mum's?'

I stared at the phone again. Why didn't she text? Why did she have to ring and then hang up, so I didn't know whether she wanted to ask me something or whether she'd fallen down the stairs and needed my help?

Zeb was looking at me and I felt my insides give that twist again. Oh God. It felt horribly as though I fancied Zeb! No. No, no, no. This just wasn't possible. I fancied Mika, I couldn't fancy Zeb as well, I just didn't have enough oestrogen in me. Besides – it was Zeb. A dead ringer for David Tennant's younger, scruffier and lankier brother with a huge side order of no career path and an extra helping of what the hell…

Mum hadn't rung back.

'I think going out would be a lovely idea,' I said, all in one breath. Mum could look after herself for a while, I'd check in on her afterwards. And Zeb really did have lovely eyes.

He brightened. 'Fabulous.'

Although. 'But...' I could feel it now, that pull of guilt and duty. Perhaps she *was* crumpled at the bottom of the stairs and that call had used the last of her energy?

'Look, how about we go for a walk, and during that walk we pass by your mother's house? You could phone her back and if she needs you then we can call in.'

I felt myself relax. I hadn't known that I was in such a state of high tension until it left me. 'I think that sounds...'

'Just bear in mind that I think your mother might possibly be playing on her illness just a touch to keep you close at hand.'

The tension coiled itself up again. 'I know. I think so too. But she's genuinely not well. I've seen her some days, she's so pale she looks as though all her blood has drained away; she can barely stand up or hold a cup and her whole body shakes. She couldn't fake that, not just to make sure I come when she calls.'

'I'm not saying she's faking.' Zeb held out a hand to me. 'Come on. You can ring her back on the way. It's a lovely evening going begging out there while we sit in here. We could be out in the fresh air comparing terrible work experiences.'

I didn't seem to be entirely myself this evening, almost as though losing my temper and confronting Mika had thrown me into another universe, one where I was much more emotional, and more open to suggestion. On any normal day, I would have answered the phone. I would have kept quiet about my feelings that I was trapped at Drycott. And I most definitely would not have taken Zeb's hand and headed off out of the cottage into the warm late afternoon.

13

We wandered lanes where the hedges were heavy with late honeysuckle, threaded with meadowsweet and splattered with beginning-to-ripen sloes, their bitter green fading to bruise-black beneath the leaves.

Zeb talked about life. About things beyond herb gardens – working in a busy kitchen where the head chef threw plates out into the yard if he didn't think the meal looked right. About the break-up of his marriage and returning to study with hours looking at business plans.

What could I offer to the conversation? I could talk about the best way to get parsley to germinate or drainage methods. I could point to things growing in hedge bottoms and tell him their uses, culinary and medicinal. I could pass occasional comment on the weather.

I felt small, boring and unworldly. Mika's telling me that I should 'learn to party' had obviously gone in deeper than I'd realised.

'You're making me feel like Mika did,' I said at last, as we strolled down towards the bridge into the village. My mother had not answered the phone when I'd returned her call and guilt and worry had steered my feet towards her door.

Zeb flickered his eyebrows. 'Flattered and swept away by passion?'

'Boring. As though I haven't really lived any life at all.' I slapped a hand on the parapet of the bridge, which made yellow and green lichen flake off under my palm into the water running swiftly and purposefully beneath. Even the river made me feel aimless.

'Living and working in the same place doesn't mean you haven't lived.' Zeb's immediate rebuttal made me feel better. At least he didn't find me boringly parochial.

'I know. I think it's because I stepped into Granny's shoes. Oh, not literally, she had tiny little feet, could never get boots to fit.' I waggled my well-shod clodhopper. 'But with the business. The only change I've made is to redo the barn so there was room for the animals. Everything else, even the cottage, is pretty much as she left it.'

'The A-ha posters being a case in point. Why not redecorate?'

I sighed. 'Time. And if I've got spare energy then I'm better off putting it into the garden – clearing new beds, weeding, sorting out the irrigation unit, that sort of thing.' It made me sound as though I were living in a loop of days, that allowed only for variations in the sandwich I ate for lunch and the occasional deviation from my usual bedtime. 'That's one of the reasons it was so nice to have the band around, throwing everything in the air a bit. It's made me see the place...' I tailed off. I *had* been going to say that it had made me see the place differently, but it hadn't really, had it?

'I want to do something that's mine.' The words came out fiercely. 'Build up something that I can point to and say "I did that", but doesn't involve toddlers patting Big Pig and an enormous muck heap.'

'We've talked about that. I'm here to take responsibility for the animals and turn them into an attraction. Perhaps donkey rides? Or if that's too hard on the insurance, we could get ducks? They eat slugs,' he added hopefully.

'You see? They're *your* ideas. Your initiative. Yes, it will all be great, an extra attraction but – it wasn't my idea.'

We coasted over the hump of the bridge and down to the stepping stones. Mother's gate hung askew, the grass of the lawn growing up and obscuring the base, and a languorous rose stem had leaped the gap, with thorns at head height.

'Do you want to pop in?' Zeb sounded as though our conversation had been the most fascinating thing he'd ever heard, and breaking it off to visit my mother might spell the end of – whatever it was that we were doing.

I looked up at the small window of Mum's bedroom and felt that tug of love and duty, irritation and pity. It all must have shown on my face because Zeb stepped through the gateway, ducking under the vicious thorny stem of the rose.

'Maybe I ought to pop in. Just for a minute,' I said, following him.

Mum was sitting in the kitchen, drinking black Earl Grey tea. This meant that she was recovering from her latest bout, but wasn't quite up to shopping or cooking yet. 'Hello,' she said, sounding put-upon. 'I tried ringing you earlier but you didn't answer.'

'Hello, Mrs Fisher,' Zeb said brightly. 'We were out for a walk and decided to call in; anything you need?'

'A word with my daughter,' Mum said, slightly frostily. I didn't know why; she'd seemed to get on perfectly well with Zeb before.

'Is that why you rang?' I asked. 'I did try to call you back – why don't you just text me, Mum? It's much easier if I'm busy.'

The tea filled the air with the cloying scent of bergamot and I wondered again how she could stomach something so strongly flavoured when she'd recently been so poorly. Surely something more neutral would be better?

'And *were* you busy?' She fixed me with a glare from above the steaming cup.

I felt my cheeks get warm. I *hadn't* been, after all. I'd been chatting to Zeb, enjoying the pretence of a social life for a few minutes. 'Well, I'm here now,' I said placatingly. 'What did you want to talk to me about?'

'Him.' My mother jerked her head in the direction of Zeb, who was blamelessly staring out of the window. 'I'm firing him.'

Zeb whipped round and, at the same time I said, 'You can't do that.'

'Of course I can. I employed him, I can fire him.' Now the steely glare moved to Zeb, wreathed in the sweet-smelling steam. 'You were taken on to increase the business takings, not to play happy families with my daughter.'

'And I've come up with a few strategies to increase the revenue,' Zeb said, sounding remarkably calm. Talking to semi-hysterical chefs when the rosti had scorched must have trained him into this level, sensible approach. 'We are talking about a new animal barn, and a proper pets' corner.'

I made shut up, shut up faces at him behind Mum's back and he finally looked up at me and stopped talking.

'Drycott is doing really well, Mum,' I said, still sounding inexplicably apologetic. 'It was kind of you to bring in a business consultant, but…'

'I think we should sell.' She put her cup down onto the table. I heard it rattle off the edge of the saucer, but she managed it second time around. 'Maximise the profits and sell as a going concern.'

'What? No!' Now the anger staged a resurgence, leaping up as though it had learned a new trick and my releasing it on Mika had given it permission to go through the routine again.

I saw Zeb's head come up and he looked at me with his eyebrows lowered, half frowning and half quizzical.

'You could go and live by the sea,' my mother said, vaguely. 'You've always liked the sea.'

'No I haven't!' I was forcing the anger back down, packing it back into that unopened trunk where it had always lived. She didn't have the power to force a sale, she could only suggest it, and even the suggestion was laughable. We'd always owned Drycott.

'Really, Natalie darling, you're becoming dreadfully forgetful.' My mother picked up her cup again. 'You always say you love the sea.'

'I love the sea, that doesn't mean I want to sell up and buy a house beside it!' I could hear my voice escalating in volume. 'I love nice cars, it doesn't mean I want to buy a house beside the A1! I love a good steak but I'm not about to move next door to an abattoir, am I?'

Now I got the pursed lips. I dreaded the pursed lips, they were my mother's ultimate weapon. She pressed her mouth closed so that her top lip concertinaed into a fan of fine lines and little tension brackets opened on each cheek. She was losing her temper but wouldn't show it. She'd just be icy towards me until I folded, and if I didn't she'd be ill and invisible for weeks. '*I think,*' she said heavily, 'that selling Drycott would be best for both of us. I'm feeling poorly again now, you know I can't cope with this sort of thing. You ought to leave now, Natalie.'

I felt Zeb touch my shoulder and turn me, moving me out of that kitchen with his body. We passed out of the front door into the overgrown little square of garden, where he stepped back to let me slow to a stop just before the gate.

'Well, that was unexpected,' he said. 'But she can't fire me, I work for you now.'

I found that I was breathing very, very deeply; my hands were curled into fists at my sides and my entire body felt as though an icicle had fallen from above, piercing me from my skull to my ankles.

'What...' My voice sounded squeaky, so I tried again. 'What the hell just happened?'

I couldn't see Zeb, he was standing behind me, but I could feel him. He was the stream of warmth in the cold that I had become. 'I think the metaphorical brown stuff just hit the air movement device,' he said slowly. 'Things are surfacing.'

Now I turned around. The intrusive rose that snagged the hedge instead of arching decoratively above the gate caught in my shirt. 'Did you know? Did she tell you that's why she hired you, why she wanted profits maximised – to sell the business as a going concern?'

My turning had clearly surprised him. 'No! No, of course I didn't know. All I was told was that she wanted to make sure that everything was running as efficiently as possible.'

The rose had torn a stammering patch across the top of my arm and I could see bright beads of blood welling through the fabric. I concentrated on those, it was easier than thinking about what my mother had said.

'But she can't sell the place. It's yours.' Zeb pushed the reluctant gate open against the pressure of the grass. The sudden release of the scent of lawn made me desperately want to be back at Drycott. It was stupid but I had the feeling that if I were there, I was safe. This place, which had been a second home to me, no longer felt as though it offered any security.

'It is mine,' I said, as we limbo'd under the flailing rose. Then again, with ferocity. 'It is *mine*.'

'Then we've no need to worry, have we?' Zeb said lightly.

I didn't even bother with the stepping stones. Instead, I splashed my way through the calf deep water of the little beck running down outside the houses to join the main river just before the bridge. The water was cold, the weed draped my jeans and there was something about the eddy and curl of its movement against my legs that made me feel better.

'No. No, we don't. She can't sell, she's only got a tiny percentage interest.' My feet sloshed as I stepped out of the water. 'Unless she can guilt me into it, and my mother is very, *very* good at guilt.'

Here came the anger again. I'd opened that secret trunk and, like Pandora's box, I'd released something that had been better contained.

There was nobody else about in the village. Away along the street I could see the corner shop, its awning still pulled across to shade the goods in the window from the relentless sun. I should pop in there and pick up some bits, Mum would have used all the milk I'd bought her yesterday. She always said it wasn't as nice as the farm shop and that they'd once sold her some out of date Battenberg so she preferred me to go elsewhere, but it was handy for last minute bits and pieces.

Then I looked at the distance. It was less than a couple of hundred metres, along a fully paved lane. There was rarely any traffic. Mum could get herself to the shop if she wanted something.

I walked on.

'Guilt I'm practically an expert in.' Zeb was just behind me.

'Having had all my imperfections and shortcomings listed for me as my marriage imploded, I've got a degree in handling guilt.'

I half smiled. We'd got that much in common, Zeb and I. His guilt over not being present enough in his marriage, and mine – actually, why *did* I feel guilty?

'So it's the money.' Zeb caught up and fell into step beside me, seemingly not disturbed by the fact that my wet shoes and jeans were spraying water with every step. 'She needs the money. I wonder why?'

I stopped on the bridge and turned to him. 'Zeb,' I said, keeping my voice as level as I could. 'I don't even know what my own father looked like. I don't know why I was brought up at Drycott instead of in the village. I have nothing to go on except little hints and Granny's mutterings. We are *not* a family that talks, as you may have gathered.'

His face twitched in something that might have been a suppressed smile. 'You're not, are you?' he said. 'It's great. You don't shout random commands at me which is very refreshing. You ask me to do something, then just let me get on and do it. You *expect* me to get on and do it, as though any kind of refusal doesn't cross your mind. It's just one of the reasons I'm enjoying working with you.'

Beneath us, deep in the river, there was the plop of a fish jumping. Zeb and I were facing one another on the summit of the bridge, surrounded by ancient stone and the smell of moving water. He reached out a hand and touched the rip in my shirt sleeve. 'You're bleeding,' he said.

I ignored that. My pulse was thrumming in my head. I must still be in shock, I reasoned to myself. *I'm not selling the gardens.*

'Oh, and if you're thinking that I'm just wanting a place to stay and all that entails, I can assure you that I came out of the divorce with some money.' Zeb's voice seemed a long way away now. All that was real was the sunlight, the water and this feeling that all my nerves were too close to the surface. 'We had a surprising amount of equity in the house. I'm not trying to get my feet under the table.'

His words weren't making sense. I was here, feeling everything so acutely: the warmth of the road coming up through my wet shoes, the sun etching the stone, the apple-pie smell of willow herb from the riverbank. The anger had gone again now, to be replaced by confusion. Why was he still talking?

'Zeb,' I said, looking up at his face. 'I really like you.'

He swallowed. 'Ah,' he said. 'Well, the feeling, as you may have gathered, is mutual.'

We stared at one another for a moment, silently acknowledging what we had said and how important it might be. 'I'm glad,' I said quietly. 'It makes all this' – I waved to indicate the house behind us – 'less embarrassing.'

'No need to be embarrassed, Tallie.' Zeb looked away and into the water below us. 'You aren't responsible for the way your mother feels.'

'Thank you. I know that, really. But I've had nearly thirty years of being made to feel that I am. Which is why my life is such a mess – I have absolutely no idea what's going on here, why my mother has suddenly decided to sell her family home and business, why she thinks I ought to go and live somewhere a long way away. It's come out of nowhere and I don't know what I should feel. I need help, I think.'

Cautiously, as though he was afraid that I might jump over the bridge to get away, Zeb took my hand. 'You're not used to asking for help, are you, Tallie?'

'Nope.'

'Then I'm flattered that you feel you can ask me.'

I glanced sideways at him. 'There isn't anyone else,' I said, and then bit my lips together. 'Sorry. Sorry. That was uncalled for. I'm just not used to this talking thing.'

Now he laughed. 'Clearly.'

But he kept holding my hand. 'I'm starting to feel things that I've been ignoring for years and I really have no idea what to do. Or why my mother has pulled selling Drycott out of a hat as an idea.'

'Perhaps you should ask her,' Zeb said gently.

I did not protest at the hand-holding. It felt nice to have someone else on my side in all this. 'I can't. In my family you don't ask questions like that. You don't ask questions at all.'

Zeb tugged my hand until I came in closer. 'That's what they taught you. But you've never wondered why? I mean, I'm pretty shocking at communication, but you and your mother, you could give lessons to an order of Trappist monks when it comes to the "not talking" thing. I never properly learned to talk to people because my parents were always so busy, we didn't do the family meals around the table talking about our day thing. Mum was out in the evenings – she was a music tutor, getting pupils through their exams – and Dad was out all day and working when he was home. I used to sit with a book in the corner wondering if they'd notice if I wasn't even there.'

'That's very...'

'And when I got married I realised that other people want me to talk about how I feel, about what's going on in my head, and I don't know how to.' He tightened his grip on my fingers until I was almost pressed against him. 'But you, Tallie, you're like a specialist at not talking about things.'

He was tall and when he moved he blocked the reflections of light on water that were spearing my vision. But most important of all, he was *here*. He was calm and he was sensible. He wasn't Mika, all over-excitement and raising my hopes of there being something between us only to dash them with his flightiness and exuberance. Mika wasn't real. What I felt for Mika was just the crush that anyone would feel for a star which had unexpectedly appeared in their bleak sky. Zeb was *real*.

I moved in closer, of my own volition now. 'Zeb,' I whispered. 'Maybe we could learn to talk to each other.'

He gave a tiny smile and the hand not holding mine came up, fingers brushing at my hair while his dark eyes smiled into mine. 'We can try,' he said. 'I guess we just go with it and see what happens.'

'You and me, is it... I mean, could we... is it a *thing?*'

'I'm not Mika,' he said solemnly. 'I've never played a washboard in my life.'

'To be honest, I'm not even sure that *Mika* is Mika.' I was enjoying this. Physical contact with no pressure, as though Zeb just wanted to be here, talking to me, and could have stayed here until dark. 'I get the feeling that he's a bit too used to being attractive and having any woman he wants. Oh, and I'm glad. About the washboard thing. I was never sure how I felt about a man who played the washboard. He's not for the likes of me.'

'Could *I* be for the likes of you? Do you think?'

I looked up at him. A hank of fringe was dangling over one eye and his head was cocked at an opposing slant. 'Can we see?' I whispered. 'Take some time and just – see? I'm not used to being allowed to feel things. I've been sitting on emotional baggage for years and I need to find out how it all works.'

Zeb smiled and gave a twitch of his head that made his hair bob about. 'Not an unequivocal "no", that's good.' He sounded diffident, but then Zeb generally sounded diffident. 'And you're not throwing things, which is even better. I think you need someone on your side in all of this.'

I bridled a bit out of habit. 'People *are* on my side,' I said, somewhat haughtily. 'My mother, Ollie, um... other people.'

'Your mother wants you to sell Drycott,' he pointed out. 'And I don't think you can really bring Ollie into this.'

I deflated. 'I suppose not. I'm not convinced that Mum is serious. She's just throwing ideas about, she does that sometimes.'

'Hm, I'm not so sure.' Zeb looked back over the river towards the house. 'She sounded pretty determined to me. Maybe she's got financial worries? I mean, how *is* she affording to keep that place?'

'Like I said, I assume Dad had insurance policies that paid out on his death.'

'Hmm,' Zeb said again. 'But that was, what, nearly thirty years ago? And she owns the house, so that will have taken a lump sum. She must have bills; where is the money for those coming from? Unless your dad was a billionaire.'

I found I was looking too now, at the mossy-roofed old house beyond the grassed-in gateway with the thorns preventing entry as though my mother was some kind of latter-day Sleeping Beauty. 'He was a guitarist in a local band,' I said. 'I don't think they are noted for being rich.'

'The Goshawk Traders aren't doing too badly,' Zeb observed, managing to sound only slightly sarcastic. 'The lovely Mika is hardly scratching round for a fiver to buy lunch.' He sighed now. 'There's just *something*. I can feel it. Too many things not said. Not *allowed* to be said.'

I thought about the band, milling around the garden. About their decision to film in the garden because Mika... hang on. Hang on a second...

'Simon said that Mika wanted to film because he liked the look of the place as they were driving past,' I said slowly.

'Yep. Bit odd, but why not, it's pretty and off the beaten—'

'But Mika said it was Simon's idea.' I still spoke carefully. All those years of being told not to ask questions, all those years of upset and silence and the unspoken censure if I dared to voice any of my concerns, hung heavy in the back of my head. It was as if the fear of repercussions made it too much trouble to even start to prod any doubts into life.

'Maybe they got muddled. Maybe it was one of those group decisions, where everyone has a say.' Zeb was looking at me with a concerned crease between his eyes.

'You said I should ask questions.' I rounded on him and he was forced to take a step back, brushing against the stone of the bridge wall and raising a little cloud of lichen and moss dust. Behind him, the sun slunk lower, dodging down between the hills as though it wanted no part of my sudden desire for knowledge. 'So don't shoot them down when I do.'

'I meant questions about things that matter. Like how come your mother, with no visible means of support, owns a fabulous semi-detached cottage with a stream at the end of the garden and yet does nothing in the way of upkeep? Why you have no pictures of your father? That sort of question. Not "who decided the band should film here?" That wasn't the sort of thing I had in mind.'

I eyed him sternly. 'Look. I have to start being assertive somewhere.' I probed around the thought of asking Mum about my father; about her decision to move home to live with her mother when Dad had clearly left her enough money to live on. Other questions loomed too in the background – what had my father been like? Kind, musical, tall was all I knew. Why would it have hurt Mum so badly to have told me more about him? I understood there'd been grief, but it all happened twenty-eight years ago, surely feelings must have been down to a quiet sadness and nostalgia by now.

But that was all too much. For now I could only deal with the small questions. How come the band decided to film with us?

'You've got a point though. We never did get a proper answer from them, did we?' Zeb had moved away from me now, as though satisfied that we'd come to a conclusion about us and were now onto other things. 'Driving past, like the area – but why *Drycott*? Why a herb garden? We need to know why they chose us so we can capitalise on that.'

'Let's go back.' I started walking, gravity accelerating my footsteps as we sloped down from the high point of the bridge. Behind us the water rushed on and a duck quacked into the otherwise silent air. 'If the band have finished filming then I need to tidy everything up and get ready to open again tomorrow.'

'Plus, I need to look into building regulations, if Simon is serious about paying for a new barn.'

Zeb strode along beside me, our lengthening shadows thrown into the hedge by the slowly setting sun, which was creeping down behind the hills as though reluctant to leave us. I flicked the occasional glance at him as we walked. He was still something of an unknown quantity, but he was *nice*. He was here and he wanted to see if we could have anything more in the way of a relationship other than grouchy boss and unwanted employee.

I didn't know yet. Maybe we could, it was too early to tell, but the sight of him sloping along, pulling stems from the verge to put between his teeth and keeping up an inconsequential chatter, made me think that we just might.

14

It took a week or two for the business to get back to normal. I struggled the A frames back out onto the roadside, turned the sign to OPEN and threw wide the gate from the car park to the garden, then waited. Ollie came back, pedalling his bike furiously through the gate and propping it carefully against the fence to return to weeding and cutting and turning the compost as though he'd never had an unexpected few days off.

The weather continued fine and bright. I put the irrigation system back through the garden and made some more herb bouquets while manning the shop. We had customers. Zeb made telephone calls, hovering at a distance as though almost afraid that our conversation of declared interest in one another had never taken place.

Questions. It all came down to questions. Why hadn't I pushed to find out more about my father? Why had Mum and Granny never talked about him? Why had they squashed the urge to ask anything out of me? It had become almost pathological now, I thought, tying up the yarrow, now beginning to break down into plate-like flowers as the season drew towards its close.

Granny would snap and avoid me if I asked too much. Mum would take to her bed, becoming immobile and unapproachable. But *why*? 'Seriously, why?' I asked a patch of dying chive flowers. 'Why couldn't they have just told me what Dad was like? Why did they have to treat it as a national secret?'

I also missed having the band around. Watching their glamorous posing around my little garden had given my life a borrowed shine, which had vanished with their departure. I didn't miss Mika at all, although I did look forward to seeing his and Tessa's wedding as a multi-page spread in whatever gossip magazine had bought the rights. I could experience a little frisson of second-hand acquaintance – 'I know these people', and enjoy her choice of designer wedding dress and their, no doubt, off the wall venue. I missed the background chat and laughter though, and the energy that had come from all the people running around and I missed the music bursting from speakers at random moments.

It had been fun. It had also taught me how much I appreciated peace and quiet.

Late one afternoon, as I was walking the OPEN signs back into the shop and watching a flock of yellowhammers forming and re-forming in the hedgerow, like small mobile flowers opening and vanishing, Simon swept into the car park in his smart convertible.

I leaned against the top of my board and watched him park carefully, flip down a mirror and check his appearance, then get out of the car.

'Hello,' I said, making him jump.

'Oh! Er, hello, Tallie. I... err... I came to... is Zeb about?'

Start asking those questions, Tallie. 'Yes, he's up in the barn with Big Pig. Simon...?'

'Mmmm?'

'You know you said that it was Mika's idea to come here to film? Well, Mika said...' Simon's expression was baffled and I found that I couldn't put the rest of the question into words. It had been a simple question so that we could understand what had attracted the band to Drycott. Not something that should have provoked the evasive look that Simon had acquired.

The fear crept over me, cold and hard as a frozen blanket. *Don't ask. Never question.* I had absolutely no reason to expect *Simon* to give me the silent treatment or to behave as though mortally offended by an innocent remark. Yet here I was, almost cowering. 'Never mind. Doesn't matter.'

I turned away and began shoving the board towards the shop doorway.

'Mika told you it was my idea,' Simon said, surprising me.

'No. Yes. Well... we only want to know because then we can advertise better,' I blurted. 'Whether you already knew about us or saw the sign or... something.' I tailed off now. That scrunched look had deepened and had become almost a cringe. 'I mean, it doesn't matter, never mind, it was just a thought. Let's go and find Zeb.'

I abandoned my A frame and began a brisk trot along the path, high stepping over the lemon balm which had flung itself full length along the gravel to form a fragrant carpet. Aversion therapy, wasn't that what they called it? Zeb was right, I had been trained not to ask questions.

My mother had trained me into obedience, in the same way as you'd train a dog – no, nobody would train a dog by withdrawing any affection or attention until it behaved, that would be cruel. She had trained me in a way that you wouldn't train a dog. The thought made that unaccustomed anger boil up again. I stopped and turned around so quickly that Simon walked into me.

'People are avoiding telling me things, I think,' I said, fast and breathless. 'I don't know why.'

Simon's face went a peculiar colour like all the blood in his skin fell back inside him, leaving him a waxy-yellow. It made me feel sick and guilty as it dawned on me that there was more to the 'Mika/Simon deciding to film here' than I could have known. 'Er,' he said, looking around as though he wanted to sprint for escape.

To my relief, Zeb appeared. He smelled of pig and had hay in his hair but his fortuitous arrival made him almost godlike in my eyes. 'Zeb! Simon's come to talk to you,' I said, very, very quickly, to prevent other questions I wasn't sure I wanted to know the answer to escaping.

'Oh. Hi, Simon.' Zeb wiped his hands down his jeans and I felt again that frisson of attraction. An attraction that gave me a buzz of warmth when I thought about it.

I left the two of them to discuss barns and money and wandered off to do some weeding. There were self-sown seedlings popping up all over the place, where the irrigation system and undergrowth made conditions suitably humid, and I needed to tidy them up before my careful planting system ran riot.

While I weeded I could think. My hands could carry out the actions without the involvement of my brain, and I went straight back to thinking about Simon's face when I'd mentioned the difference of opinion between him and Mika over who had noticed Drycott first and decided to drop in. Then that almost corpse-like expression he'd gained when I said I thought people were keeping things from me. What had brought *that* on? Simon and I had very little interaction apart from general chit-chat, so it must be something to do with Mika. But what?

Over at the pond the sun was seeding itself, tiny reflections coming to the surface and breaking into ripples as the froglets dived at my approach. It made me smile, the thought of all those baby frogs leaping like synchronised swimmers and I felt such a fierce attachment to the garden in that moment that I knew I'd never sell.

Not to make my mother happy. Not to move to somewhere 'by the sea'. The knowledge gave me peace but that was swiftly followed by the heavy dread. The weight in my stomach that pulled all my joy down with it, knowing that Mum was going to be upset with me.

'Right.' Zeb appeared as though he'd sprung through the earth and grown alongside me. 'Simon's going to come back in a while, once we've finished closing up. He wants to talk to you.'

'Oh?' I straightened up, hands full of couch grass. 'What about?'

'Plans, I think,' Zeb said, vaguely. 'We've talked money and the barn extension. I expect he wants to know what you've got in mind.'

'But he talked to you!'

Zeb gave me a very direct look. 'This is your garden, Tallie.'

'Well, yes, I just meant...'

'...so he's coming to see what sort of ideas you might have.'

I looked around. Over in the barn, Big Pig was trying out the new catch on her pen, but the string was holding and her attempts to break free weren't working, to her obvious frustration. Her thwarted snorts were audible from the other side of the garden. 'New gates, for a start.'

'Goes without saying. I've already raised the issue of proper pig containment.' Zeb had his hands in his pockets which made his arms look longer, as though he were out of proportion. 'And a really nice handwashing station for the toddlers, low level sink and everything.'

'You've thought it all through, then? The petting farm idea?'

'Yep. Let's go inside and we can talk it over.' He gave me a nudge. 'And have tea. I really need tea. Big Pig was a bit combative over the bucket just now.'

I shrugged. 'No need. You know what you're doing. I don't need chapter and verse.'

Zeb hesitated, halfway to walking down the path to the cottage. His foot stammered over the gravel. 'You're doing it again, and there's no need to do it with me.'

'What?'

'You don't want to talk. I'm not suggesting an in-depth conversation about our respective upbringings, I only want to lay out the ideas for taking the animal side of the business forward. You know, because you're employing me to do it.'

I felt stupid. Had it really come to this – that I would avoid the merest hint of talking about anything? Perhaps I'd been more shaken by my mother's expressed wish to sell the business than I thought, if I didn't even want to chat to Zeb about the future.

'No, of course, you're right. Let's go inside and discuss plans.'

'That's better.' He sounded cheerily back to being my business consultant now. 'I'll put the kettle on. I'm parched. D'you think a little café might be a good idea next to the shop? There's room, if we partition off the back end, where you store all those baskets, we could put an upper room in the new barn for storage.'

It felt odd, having someone to go over plans with. Ollie was great, he'd talk herbs all day and have wonderful ideas about new varieties and planting schemes, but he had absolutely no interest in anything else, and would wander off if I started throwing business ideas at him. Zeb was *keen*. I could see how he had made a good chef, putting new things together in combinations I would never have thought of. He was good at ideas. I found that once he began to lay out his thoughts on what we could do and his opinions on the best way to go forward, it made my creative side tingle with potential. This could work. That encouraged me to come out with some thoughts of my own and before I knew it we were drinking tea, drawing designs on the back of a tax demand envelope, and laughing. We laughed a lot, and it made me realise how little I'd had to laugh about lately. I was relaxing with Zeb, uncoiling that desperate hard spiral that kept me running, like clockwork winding down to a final tick. He was funny, that concerned Time Lord face opening up into a smile that was so genuine and engaging that it made me smile back. The tense knot between my shoulder blades softened when I reached out to hold our sketch and encountered his hand on the way.

The touch stopped me. It was as though the feel of his skin against mine brought me back to reality. 'What do I do about Mum?' I asked.

His grin died. 'What do you want to do about her? I have to warn you that I won't be party to anything illegal.' His eyes still held the echo of the smile. 'But I might offer to hold the pillow,' he muttered, and I didn't think I'd been meant to hear that.

'Why on earth does she want me to sell up? And even if I do, she's not entitled to any of the money.'

'But she could persuade you to give her some. If she needed it.' Zeb let go of the envelope and his fingers fell away from mine. 'Couldn't she?'

'No. Well, maybe.'

'So the question isn't so much why does she want you to sell, as what does she need money for.'

I thought of my mother in her frowsty room, old make-up caked onto the surface of the dressing table. Old clothes hanging in the wardrobe. The state of the garden. 'I have no idea. She doesn't seem to spend much.'

'Tallie...' My name was almost a sigh. 'No. Never mind. It's not my business. Do you ever look in her cupboards?'

It was such an odd question that it made me pull a face. 'How strange! Why would I? I check that she's got food, that the fridge isn't empty, that's all. I'm not going to start ransacking her storage, if that's what you mean.' I narrowed my eyes. 'Is there something you're not telling me, Zeb?'

'I don't think it's me you should be asking that question.' He looked almost sad now, a hint of similarity with Simon's expression earlier in the afternoon. 'But you don't ask your mother anything and it's ruining your life.'

I laughed, but it wasn't the same laughter as before. This laugh was harder and curled up at the edges. 'No it's not.'

'Simon told me you seemed upset. You think that people are keeping things from you?'

'Don't bring Simon into this, it's nothing to do with him. I only wanted to know which one of them was fibbing about deciding to come in and look around. Nothing big. He got a wee bit evasive and I decided it wasn't worth stirring things up for such a stupid reason, that's all. Maybe neither of them can remember whose idea it was. Why should they, after all? *And*, and I cannot stress this enough, it was your idea to find out. For the advertising,' I added, with a flourish that may as well have had 'ta dah!' printed on it.

'True.' Zeb nodded. 'Maybe we should both ask him in a bit, when he's over to talk to you. I could stay and referee.'

The thought struck me then that I had always intended that Zeb should be here when Simon came. But I'd just thought it, as if asking him would be too much. What had I been going to do if he'd got up to leave – fling myself across the doorway and block his exit?

I needed to learn to use my words. 'I'd like it if you stayed,' I said, cautiously. The world didn't end.

'There. That didn't hurt, did it?' Zeb said cheerfully. 'I'm not your mother, Tallie. You can ask me things, you can ask me to do things, I'm not going to treat you the way she does. If you say something to upset me, I'll just tell you and give you chance to put it right, not sulk as though it's an international sport and I'm in training for the Olympics.'

'She doesn't…'

'Yes, she does.'

'All right, maybe she does.' I looked at him and lowered my voice, until it was just audible. 'Can we really make something work with us?'

Zeb leaned in until he was only centimetres away from me. I could feel his breath against my face. 'If we want to, why not? But that's an important question, I'm glad you felt you could ask it.'

Unexpected laughter bubbled up again in my throat. 'It is, isn't it? Wow, maybe I'm improving.'

'Or maybe you're just not afraid of me.'

I looked past him, out of the window into the green twilight that was gathering at the base of the tall herbs. Scuds of cloud peppered the horizon. The weather was changing. 'I am afraid of her,' I said softly. 'I love her, I resent her and I'm afraid of her.'

Zeb's hand came up and closed over mine. 'I know.' His voice was as soft as my words had been. 'You had a hell of a childhood and you never know where you stand with her. It's enough to unsettle anyone.'

'I had a lovely childhood,' I said, still softly. 'I had Granny and Mum looking after me, and I had all this.' I was full of memories of making petal perfume by putting roses in water, until Granny taught me how to distil, of rolling in damp grass and watching the enormous stems towering overhead – I must have been very small then.

'You've been appeasing her since you were tiny.' Zeb sounded more normal now. 'I used to be a chef. Believe me when I say I know all about appeasing. When the head chef has thrown a cleaver at your head for making a lumpy sauce, you learn appeasement as fast as you learn how to get the lumps out.'

'Maybe that's it.' I stretched my hand under his. 'Maybe I've been getting the lumps out all my life.'

He jerked his head sideways. 'I'm not sure the metaphor covers everything,' he said. 'But you've been living under your mother, certainly.' A pause. 'Actually, I'm not sure *that* works either. But we both know what we mean.'

'I was afraid she wouldn't love me.' I practically whispered the words. 'I'd lost my dad and she'd go and lock herself in her room for days. If I lost her as well I'd got nothing.' Suddenly my eyes were full of tears. 'I was afraid she wouldn't love me any more if I didn't behave perfectly, and then she'd leave me too.'

'Oh, Tallie.' There was a hitch in Zeb's voice and the warmth that I felt sometimes when I looked at him flooded through me again. *Was this love?* I tried to examine how I felt. It reminded me of the feeling when I opened the curtains and looked out over the garden, or when I fed Big Pig and she was being amenable to having her ears scratched. I thought of my mother, and the warmth had hooks in it.

'I really like you, Zeb,' I said suddenly. 'I don't think I understand you, but I like you.'

'Good.' He sounded robust, as though he wanted to discourage any further tears. 'Because I'm not sure I understand myself. I've been looking for something all my life. I thought cooking was it, then I thought that maybe helping businesses might give me what I was looking for. But it turns out that what I really want in life is a bucket, a scoop of pig feed, trotters and squeaking.' He dipped his head so that he could look in my face. 'Which is weird and a little bit sad, if you think about it.'

'It's not sad.' I surprised myself with my ferocity, which made me jerk my head up so sharply that I almost bounced my forehead off Zeb's nose. 'It's really *not*.'

We were eye to eye now. My cheeks were stiffening with the drying tears, but I barely felt that because they were becoming warm under the weight of his close attention to my face. His eyes were the deep brown of very good chocolate, but somewhere inside them I could see tiny flecks of green and it was intriguing enough that I couldn't look away.

Those eyes flicked from mine, down to my mouth and back up again. 'Tallie,' he said, and my name swirled against my skin. We were both standing now, the table width between us but not separating us as we leaned in closer and closer until our mouths met. It was a brief kiss, hardly more than an affirmation of a later intent, but it made the heat rush from my cheeks to everywhere else so suddenly that my head swam.

This could be something. The thought flashed through my mind at the same speed as the hot blood flashed through my body. Then we'd moved apart and I was standing, blinking, slightly shocked. When Mika had kissed me it had felt like a demonstration. As though he'd been showing off to someone – Tessa, probably – how attractive he was, how he could kiss anyone. I'd let him and it hadn't entirely been my choice. But kissing Zeb had felt like a mutual decision.

Zeb was smiling at me, still across the table, big eyes and a bit goofy, but now his lanky uncertainty had more of an edge of assuredness to it. 'Well,' he said, and then cleared his throat. 'Well.'

'Yes.'

A silence fell. A leaf dropped from one of the basil plants over in the corner. They needed watering. I didn't move.

'We could...' I began.

'Perhaps later.'

'You don't know what I was going to say.' We were keeping our eyes on one another, both seemingly to stop the other from evaporating. I worried that if I blinked, this wonderful man would vanish and never have been. Then I realised that the death of my father and his absence from my life was making me think this way, and turned to the kettle. 'Tea?'

All that reading I'd done for research hadn't done me any favours. I still subliminally worried that anyone I had feelings for would leave me.

'Mmm.' I heard Zeb sit down again, the grind of the chair legs on the brick floor. It didn't annoy me now like it had done before. It was audible proof that he was here.

'So, what did you think I was going to suggest?'

He coughed. 'Doesn't matter. That's Simon arriving now and I don't think you'd want anything we did to be interrupted, would you?'

I glanced up. He was right. The sporty little car was parked over by the shop and Simon was checking his reflection in the wing mirror, smoothing a hand over his hair and tugging at his jacket collar. I didn't know why he was bothering, just for a meeting about financing our barn, but perhaps Simon had a 'thing' about always looking well groomed. He had to deal with the daily competition with the band members, who would look sensational wearing bedsheets and bin liners, after all.

'Bugger. I'd better get another mug out. I'll have Ollie's; he won't notice if I wash it properly.'

I started preparing the tea mugs, while Zeb went to the door to meet Simon who was retying his ponytail and looking awkward.

'Is it all right if I... oh, hello, Zeb. Didn't know you were going to be here. I thought you'd have gone home by now. Er.'

'Zeb is part of Drycott,' I said confidently, realising that I really meant it. 'So it's only right that he's here.'

Simon stepped down into the kitchen. 'Yes, I just meant... I need to talk to *you*, Tallie, and you might not want Zeb listening in.'

There was a moment of chill down my spine. *What the hell?* All I could think was that perhaps Mika had said something to Simon about me and I was about to be taken to task over my unwarranted assumptions about him?

I shook my head. Mika would have shrugged me off by now as the small distraction I had been. He'd probably even forgotten my name.

'Unless you're about to declare your undying love for me and propose that we emigrate immediately, I won't mind Zeb being here,' I said, aware that I sounded stiff and formal. 'And actually, if you *are* going to, I think I might need him.'

'Not quite, but you might want to sit down.'

'Just a second.' I poured three mugs of tea, put the milk in its bottle on the table, which my mother would have told me was the height of bad manners – didn't I have a milk jug? – and then sat down beside Zeb, letting Simon have my half of the table. 'There. All right, Simon, what have you come to talk about?'

Simon took a deep breath and adjusted his hair again. 'Tallie,' he began, and his voice sounded falsetto, so he cleared his throat and tried again. 'Oh, this is difficult. You wanted to know why we chose to film here.' He stopped again.

I looked at Zeb and Zeb looked at me. I felt as dumbfounded as he seemed. 'Sorry, Simon, you're just going to have to come out with it, I'm afraid,' I said, silently hoping that it really *wasn't* anything to do with Mika.

Another deep breath, and Simon seemed to take a run at it. He licked his lips, fixed his eyes firmly on the unremarkable surface of the kitchen table and said, 'I brought the band here. I wanted to see... I was curious about how... while we were in the area. I used to know this place very well. Tallie, I'm your dad.'

15

There was the kind of silence you could have hammered horseshoes on. The air felt suddenly thick and I seized the handle of my mug to steady myself. 'No you're not,' I said.

There was more silence, the three of us frozen into a tableau like the final scene of a play, waiting for the curtain to come down. Finally Simon moved; he inched a hand across the table and touched my wrist. 'I am,' he said. 'I'm sorry.'

I leaped to my feet, freed by his touch from the odd stasis that had held me. 'No, you're *not*!' My chair dragged and I hated the noise all over again. 'My dad died in an accident trying to get to my first birthday party! He's been dead for twenty-eight years!' I noticed the note of hysteria in my voice and stopped speaking, took a deep breath and also noticed that my eyes were burning. 'Didn't he?' This was a plea, aimed towards Zeb, who was looking from Simon to me and back again.

'Tallie.' Zeb touched my arm. 'Let's just listen to Simon, all right?' He smiled. 'If it's totally barking then I promise I'll chase him out with the broom, I've had plenty of experience at that.'

This attempt at humour burst the bubble I'd been in and I

flopped back to my seat again, shaking my head. 'This is nuts,' I said. 'You must be mistaken, Simon. There's just no way you can be my dad, he's been dead for years.'

But, whispered a tiny breeze from the window, *you've no proof of that at all, have you? Only the word of two women who never let you ask anything about it.*

Simon's face relaxed a little. 'I'm sorry, Tallie,' he repeated. 'It's true. I should never have let it come to this and I'm really, really sorry.'

The breath I took felt like my first breath ever. 'All right,' I said. 'Start talking. It's about time somebody said something about my parentage, although I warn you, if you mention anything wacky or UFO related I will invoke Zeb and the broom.'

'Er.' Simon looked from me to Zeb again. I had no idea why. Was he just giving his eyes something to do, apart from resting on me? Did he not *want* to look at me? 'UFO related?'

'The only *possible* explanation you could come up with for not being in contact for twenty-eight years would involve being beamed up and carried off into outer space,' I said. 'Twenty. Eight. Years. And I've been here, findable, at Drycott, all that time.'

Simon gave a shamefaced half-smile. 'No. No aliens. I honestly have no idea where to start. I've rehearsed this so many times, gone over and over it in my head, but in real life it's nothing like I imagined.'

'How *did* you imagine that an announcement like that would go?' I asked, acidly.

'How about starting at the beginning?' Zeb suggested. 'It might help.'

Simon sighed. He looked older now and that daft ponytail was coming untied again. I wanted to get up and give him an elastic band. I wanted to take away his tea mug and tell him to go, to never speak of this again. *I wanted none of this to be happening.* I wasn't entirely sure that I wasn't going to be sick too, there was a ferocious burning weight in my stomach as though half a pound of hot lead had replaced the tea.

'Okay. Okay.' Simon took a gulp of tea. It had clearly been too hot because his eyes watered for a moment. 'What were you told about me – about your father, Tallie?'

I wished he wouldn't keep using my name. It was beginning to sound possessive. 'Nothing,' I said, almost sulkily. 'Tall, nice, played the guitar. Oh, and I can't stress this enough, *dead*.'

I also wished my heart would stop slamming itself against my ribcage like Big Pig trying to rattle her gate open. It was distracting and made me feel even sicker.

'And that's *all*?' Simon widened his eyes. 'Wow. They weren't kidding, were they?'

'And who's *they*?' I snapped.

'Your mother and your grandmother. When they told me to keep away and that they'd bring you up without me. I didn't realise that they were going to erase me from your history quite so thoroughly.'

The last bit of sunlight squeezed itself between the flopping leaves of the indoor herbs on the sill and bathed us all in a queasy light. I didn't need its help, I already felt green. Between my heart going as though I were heading for a cardiac arrest and the tea refusing to go down my throat, I could have thrown up there and then. But I managed the words, 'I think you had better tell me,' with a degree of assuredness.

Simon swallowed another mouthful of the much-too-hot tea. His eyes skipped about again, from my face to the dresser to Zeb, and then to the window. 'This place hasn't changed at all,' he said to the wilting basil plants.

'Since it was built? It really has; we've got a flushing toilet, no pony and the garden isn't full of coal.' The anger was still coming out in my voice.

'I mean since I was here.' Simon was obviously trying to find his way into the topic; he had no more idea of how this should go than I did. 'I remember you playing on a mat there, in front of the range, you'd be about six months old I suppose. Sitting there with your chubby little arms waving about, all gummy grins and sudden shrieking,' he went on, mistily.

'If you say "no change there" I shall pour this tea over your head,' I said to Zeb. I was trying to move this along; I wanted it over, and yet – I wanted to know. Every word that Simon said sounded new, as though I'd never heard a baby described like this before. This was *me*. A me I'd never ever heard about. A me, now I thought about it, that there were no photographs of. As though I'd only started to exist once my father had... died.

'I met your mother in London,' Simon said, surprising me anew. My mother had never mentioned London before in any context. 'We were both very young, both rather inclined to be party animals.'

Again that moment of dissonance. The only kind of animal my mother could ever be compared with was something that hibernated, and the only parties she had any interest in were the rigidly anti-everything political ones.

'We came back here when you were on the way and rented a little place in the village because your mum wanted to be close to home, to her mum, which was only right. I knew then, of course...' He tailed off. Cleared his throat. Started again. 'I thought she'd change. I thought things would be different when you were born. Having a baby, having a home, I thought it would make her stop. But nothing could, Tallie. Not even you.'

That ice crystal that had sunk to the bottom of my stomach

was back. It crept up and became solid, as though a sudden frost had stiffened all the stems in the garden and fixed the blooms in a deadly immobility. He was speaking about my mother as though she were a person I'd never met. 'Stop what?'

Simon seemed to come back from whatever romantic past he had been inhabiting. His eyes snapped up to mine and there was a frowned question in them. 'They kept *that* from you too? Oh, Tallie, I am so sorry. Things should have been so very different, but I agreed, *we* agreed, it would be for the best.'

'Simon, will you stop building up your part and just tell me, outright and factually, all these things that you assume I know?' I sounded brisk now, far more like myself. 'Clearly I *don't* know, and obviously everything has been kept secret and I'm getting a little bit fed up with all the allusions and careful not-mentionings. So just tell me.'

I felt Zeb press his leg against mine under the table, just a brief touch but it was comforting.

Simon made an 'ouch' face. 'But I don't know what you don't know,' he said, reasonably. 'I have no idea how much of this is a total surprise to you and how much is me going over old ground.'

'Can we just assume that I know absolutely nothing?' I put my mug down on the table. 'Because that is about where I am coming in at. I might need the full prologue too.'

'Right. Okay. Yes, sorry.' Simon's eyes were a greenish blue, I noticed. I'd not really looked at them before, when they'd just been eyes. Now I could see that they were the same colour as mine. 'Tallie, your mother is an alcoholic. She has been since I first met her, and from what you've said about her, nothing seems to have changed in nearly thirty years.'

Of course. *Of course.* His words slammed into my brain and everything slotted into place like a toddler's jigsaw puzzle with huge chunky pieces and enormous easy-fit holes. The 'illness' nobody could get to the bottom of. Her periodic disappearances to her room, her random behaviour and never eating. My mother was so obviously an alcoholic that I couldn't understand why I hadn't seen it. Stupidity and anger were now at war in my brain for prominent emotion.

Anger won. I threw my mug across the room and it hit the stone sink, where it shattered. I was clearly getting good at this 'angry' thing. All the practice I was getting, probably.

'Just tell me the fucking story,' I hissed and I sounded as though I were about to commit a murder. Zeb's leg pressed mine again.

Simon took another deep breath. 'Right. You didn't know that either. Right. Okay. I'd better give you chapter and verse then.'

So he did.

Amanda Kiddlington and Jonathon Fisher had met on the party circuit in London. From the description, 'the party circuit' had mostly been girls who did PA jobs and young men trying to make it in the music industry. Too much alcohol, a lot of drugs, and the inevitable had happened. Amanda had got pregnant, whereupon Jonathon had done the decent thing, married her and moved with her back to her home village in North Yorkshire.

But Amanda, despite wanting to come home, hadn't wanted to quit the party. She had tried to stop drinking throughout her pregnancy but failed, she'd probably been drunk when I'd been delivered too. Her mother had tried to get her to stop, Jonathon had tried, but she was deep in addiction. The young couple had been blown apart by the arrival of a baby, my mother's drinking, *her* mother's interference, Jonathon's refusal to give up music and go to work on a local farm, and they'd split up. Jonathon had gone back to London.

'You *left* me?' I asked, aghast. 'With a drunk?'

'I honestly wanted to take you with me.' Simon sounded choked. 'I came back for you, about six months later. Not my finest hour, I have to admit. I should have gone through the courts and done it properly but I didn't think I had a leg to stand on as a single man living in squats. So...'

'It was *you*?' That smell of smoke and the scratch of a shirt against my face. 'You were the man who tried to snatch me in the supermarket?'

He dropped his head. 'Yes,' he muttered. 'I thought, once I'd got you, they'd let me keep you.'

'And what really happened?'

'We went back to court. I told them all about the... the drinking. The judge was sympathetic but it was still thought best that you stayed with your mother. They made a ruling though, that she had to have help, and your grandmother stepped in, said that Amanda could come and live with her, to be supervised.' Again his thoughts seemed to slip back a few decades. 'The court agreed. I'd just given up playing in the band, changed my name and taken over the management side, I didn't have a house, I was moving around all the time – there were several bands, all over the country. I didn't look a good bet to leave a small child with.'

'They told me you were dead.' The words sounded emotionless but only through some effort. Right now I hated everyone and everything. Even Zeb was going to get a fork in the hand if he tried to touch me.

'We thought it was best. I was travelling abroad, I couldn't keep to any contact schedule, your mother and your grandmother thought it was less confusing for you if I just stayed away. I did think I might be able to come back, to visit a few times a year, that they might allow that... But no. I was dead. And they seem to have made sure that you never asked questions. I always hoped that one day you'd find me. I wrote to you. I sent you cards and presents every birthday. When I thought you were old enough, I sent you my address, my new name so you could come and looking and you'd find me... ah, who was I kidding.'

I thought of the hours spent poring through the digitised copies of the local paper, trying to find details of the accident. Of all that research into women whose fathers had died when they were young. Trying to make sense of it all, trying to work out what had made me the way I was.

And it had all been a lie.

'Why did you change your name?' Was all I could ask.

Simon shrugged. 'Jonathon Fisher didn't sound rock and roll enough.'

'And Simon Welbury *did*?'

He shrugged again. 'I loved you,' he said, fiercely. 'I didn't know you weren't getting the letters. Your mother must have... Look.' There was a moment of earnest searching of pockets until he found his phone, contained in that 'older person' way in a case with slots for cards. In the front, where a driving licence would normally be displayed, was a photograph. Small and battered with ragged edges, as though it had been cut from a larger picture, it showed a small chubby-kneed child in a hand-knitted jacket of such chunkiness that it about doubled the child's weight. 'It's the only picture they let me have.'

'That's me?' I stared at the round face of the toddler, which stared back solemnly.

'I sent money for you,' Simon said hastily, clearly taking my momentary thoughtfulness as a feeling of rejection. 'All the time. And when the bands got successful, I was sending quite a lot of money. For you, for your education, your future. I thought – I have no idea why, because I know quite a lot of drunks – that the money was going into an account for you. One day, I hoped your mum would sit you down and explain and give you a big cheque.' He glanced around the kitchen. 'I can see I was mistaken.'

He stood up and put his still nearly full mug down on the table. 'Look, I ought to go. You've got a lot of thinking to do and this has been a bolt from the blue for you, I'm so sorry.' A hand reached out to touch me, and I recoiled. The hand withdrew. 'Yes. As I said, I'm very sorry. We were complicit in keeping you in the dark, but I didn't realise just *how much* dark was going on. I only began to realise when we chatted by the pond that day and you obviously had no idea who I was. I truly didn't know whether it was better to tell you or let you believe whatever you were told about me.'

My breathing was still snagging in my throat. I didn't think I could say anything, so I was quite glad when Zeb stood up too. 'Maybe, if you came back tomorrow, Simon? I think Tallie has quite a lot of thinking to do.'

'Yes, of course. The Goshawk Traders are off on a break now for a few weeks. I'm going to stay in York, so I can come over?' His tone was hopeful. 'I want to do what I can to make up for all the lying and years of not being there.'

'The wedding,' I said.

'Wedding?' Simon was nonplussed for a second. I could hear it in his voice. I couldn't see him because I was refusing to look up from the cracked and lined surface of my table. It still looked and felt the same as it had when he'd walked into the kitchen an hour ago, and it was the only thing that did. That permanency was comforting.

'The wedding. Mika and Tessa's wedding.'

'What about it?' he asked, cautious now, as though I were about to confess to something. Did he think I might be pregnant with Mika's child? The idea almost made me laugh.

'I want Drycott to do the flowers. Herb bouquets. Table decorations, room décor.'

Beside me I felt Zeb react, a momentary twitch of surprise.

'Oh!' Simon flickered, a moving outline. 'Well, they're getting hitched in London, some fancy venue, I think a wedding planner has—'

'We will do the bouquets and all the wedding arrangements.' I dropped the words like stones into the pond of his confusion. 'You know we can. And the magazines will feature them. I think you owe me this, Simon.'

He blinked, clearly processing and then smiled. 'Actually, I think that's an amazing idea, Tallie. It will tie the wedding into the video we've been making, link it all together.'

'But they will already have sorted flowers,' Zeb said, a tiny voice breaking our concentration on one another.

Simon waved airily, a hand that knows money is no object. 'I'm sure they can switch suppliers.' Then, with a touch more trepidation, 'Are you sure you can do it? They get married in two months, will you have enough herbs to do all the arrangements?'

'Yes,' I said, absolutely definitely. 'We bloody well will.'

'Well then.' Simon rocked on the balls of his feet. 'Well then.'

Zeb got up now and opened the back door to the rapidly gathering night. 'Give it a couple of days,' he said, as Simon moved to leave. 'I think Tallie has a lot of thinking to do and she'll have more questions for you, I have no doubt.' He threw me a look. 'She's getting much better at asking questions now, I've found.'

Simon looked relieved; the worst, for him, was over. 'Yes. I'll... I'll give you a call? If that's all right? I need to talk to Mika, obviously, and Tessa, and there will be some... some questions from them, I expect.'

'I'd think so, yes.' Zeb ushered Simon out.

'Can I tell them?' Simon asked from the doorway. 'About you and... and being my daughter?'

I had a momentary vision of Mika's face, being told that he'd been casually flirting with his manager's daughter and laughed. 'Why not?'

'I think that's a yes,' Zeb said and closed the door. We sat in silence, listening to the footsteps crunch the gravel, the gate open and shut, and then the sound of the car driving away.

I still didn't move. I stayed focused on the yellowing polished top of the table, crazed into honeycomb patterns by heat and years. It looked like the earth outside, in the summer drought.

Zeb stood at my shoulder. 'Tallie?'

My brain was full of words that wouldn't come out. *Drunk. Money. I wanted to take you. Better if I stayed away.* Then images of a magazine photo shoot, Tessa holding a bouquet of herbs. Rooms decorated with the overblown flowers of the mallow, the tight orderliness of lavender, the wide plates of yarrow.

'I am in so much trouble,' I said finally and to Zeb's obvious relief. 'I broke Ollie's tea mug.'

16

The room was warm, even though the window was open to let the moonlight in to cover the bed.

Eventually Zeb spoke. 'I feel as though I've taken advantage of your trauma.'

I rolled further into his embrace. 'You didn't. Honestly.'

'But it...'

'Was something I wanted to do. Okay, maybe it took a bit of shock to get me over the hump, so to speak, but I wanted it, Zeb. Never doubt that.'

His long arms were around me, his legs entwined with mine. We were sticky and breathless and it had been surprisingly good for an unplanned event. Zeb had turned out to be an intuitive lover with a great line in improvisation.

'But you're not in your right mind, are you? After a revelation like that?'

'If I weren't in my right mind, do you think I could have come up with the idea of doing the decorations for Mika's wedding?' I wriggled against him. Even his smell was familiar. I wondered for a moment if I were searching for something with

Zeb, a constant who didn't lie to me, but pushed the thought away. It was too soon to be examining ideas like that.

'True. True.' He stroked my hair, a gentle movement which disturbed the still air in my bedroom. 'It's a great idea and a fabulous move for Drycott. You have surprising depths, Tallie.'

'Which I feel have been well plumbed now.'

He laughed. 'Thank you for that.'

We lay and breathed for a moment. It hadn't just been my depths that he'd found surprising, my tattoo had astonished him too. His unexpected tenderness and ability in bed had made me see him in a new light. Zeb wasn't just the rather sweet, floundering in life lanky-limbed pig carer, he had a capability and a certainty that I was quite sure would come through more in real life now he'd found his 'place'.

'Did you know? About my mother?' I whispered the words drowsily.

'I had my suspicions. That's why I asked if you ever checked her cupboards. There was an empty vodka bottle under the sink, when we were round there yesterday. I'd already thought by then – an illness that she hasn't had investigated, that makes her take to her bed with such regularity, sounded like something she didn't *want* investigated.'

'And Granny knew. They both kept it from me. My mother, the drunk. Oh!' I half sat up against his shoulder. 'No wonder I went to a fee-paying school out of area. They wouldn't have wanted the chance of me hearing any rumours about her.'

'And Simon sent the money for your education. She couldn't really get away with spending that on drink. Or, maybe she could have done, but she didn't. She wanted the best for you. Tallie.'

'She kept that fact well hidden too,' I muttered. I was too

riled up to sleep. 'Everyone has been lying to me, Zeb. All my life.'

'Which is why they taught you not to ask questions.'

'It's obvious why, now isn't it. "Your father is dead," it's quite hard to think of many questions about that, other than 'how?' And "rushing to your birthday party"? It's almost as though they wanted me to feel guilty from day one.'

'I'm sure it wasn't like that.' I could feel Zeb's fringe tickling the skin along my spine.

'*How* sure?' I turned suddenly to face him.

'Okay, not that sure.'

I lay back down again, but still couldn't sleep. Beside me, Zeb's breathing slowed into a drowsy rhythm, but that relaxation eluded me. *Everyone had lied.* Mum and Granny, and I suspected that most of the village who asked after Mum's health with such solicitude, knew too. They had known Amanda Fisher all her life. But they'd known *me* all my life too! Didn't anyone owe me the truth?

Careful not to disturb Zeb, I got out of bed and went downstairs. There was only one way this ended, and that was up to me. It wouldn't be an end, of course, more like the beginning of a whole new chapter, but I had to be the one to turn the page. Otherwise we'd all just carry on in this weird, stunted life.

'Granny, you could have said something,' I muttered to the rumpled old arm chair as I pulled my gardening coat off the hook on the back door. 'You could have explained, I would have understood.'

But really, how could she? She'd had to side with her daughter; had to watch her only child drinking herself into incapability and leaving her own child to fend for herself. No wonder Granny had taken me under her wing. She'd understood that if she hadn't, I would have had nothing. After all, she'd agreed to have Mum come to live with her so she could help raise me, as an alternative to my father having custody.

My father. I tiptoed out of the front door. I had a father. Alive, well and a very successful manager to a famous band. I wondered whether he'd really changed his name because it was more rock and roll or whether it had been to prevent my family from hounding him. Then I remembered that Simon had been sending Mum money. She'd spent the money he'd been sending for me, on herself. A house. Alcohol. The money I could have used to find what I really wanted to do with my life.

I got into my car and started it up. I couldn't sleep, so I might as well hunt for my answers now. I drove the few miles to the village, this time without my usual wondering, 'Was this the place? Or this?', as I searched for the location of my father's 'death'. All those years that I'd imagined his last moments somewhere along this road. All those years that I'd studied women whose fathers had died young, searching for an identity, a commonality, and all of those years it had all been a lie.

There was a light on in the house, despite the late hour. A pink glow from the living room, which meant that the lamp was on in there. Mum might be watching television, she often couldn't sleep and sat up with dubious programmes on late night TV. I'd sat through more of them than I cared to remember, staying with her to keep her company.

Had she just been waiting for me to go, so that she could drink? Or was her bedroom rammed with empties from years of 'early nights' and 'just popping up to freshen myself up'? Why had I never noticed?

I let myself in through the kitchen. I could hear a laugh track echoing through the house, but the TV was playing its eighties comedy to an empty room. The kitchen was likewise empty, but there were no lights anywhere else. I crept up the stairs.

'Mum, are you in?' I pushed her bedroom door open, surprising her sitting on the end of the bed, in the dark.

'Natalie? Oh, you made me jump! Why are you here? It's gone midnight.'

She hadn't quite been quick enough. Not quite. The covers beside her bulged with a recognisable lump, vodka or gin by the look of it. A big bottle.

'I came to tell you that I know.' I stayed in the doorway, watching her struggle to adjust to the situation. Usually I didn't come unannounced, I came when summoned, irritably and looking for things to do, or I called out when I came into the house. Giving her time I hadn't known she needed.

'You know?' Mum was still dressed. She'd been downstairs watching TV and she'd come up here to – what? This was her house, she could have bottles in every room if she wanted, so why did she need to come into her bedroom to drink?

The answer came to me, stark as the expression on her face right now. *Because then it's all hidden away. Everything she needs is in here.*

'What is it you think you know, Natalie, darling?' I could hear the drawl now I was listening for it. Before, I would have put it down to her not being well, her inability to speak clearly down to the fatigue she felt constantly. Well, of course she did, she sat up all night drinking! The flame of anger lanced through my chest and I stepped into the room.

'My dad is alive and well. That, for starters.'

I flung open the door to her wardrobe. It was full of dresses and coats, but a momentary fumble behind the shoes piled on the floor turned up two litre bottles of vodka, one half full and the other empty.

'And this.' I flourished the bottles.

She blinked at me, astonished at my statement, at my presumption.

'You and Granny lied to me. And the money to send me to school? That I thought was just because the herbs were doing well? Turns out that Simon... that *Dad* was sending you the money for me.'

I began pulling things from the wardrobe. Two coats clonked with bottles in the pockets and there were more empties tucked inside a pair of boots.

'All the while I've thought that you had some rare illness' – I threw the coats down, pulled out a small suitcase which turned out to be rammed with bottles, mostly half full – 'you were drinking, drunk or hungover!'

She let out a little cry of alarm and tried to stop me, but she was so fragile and weak that I could push her back down onto the bed with one hand. 'Natalie, darling, you don't understand...'

'Then you have the nerve to try to persuade me to sell Drycott! What is it, are you running low on money? Is Dad refusing to send you more cash?'

Another little mew of a cry.

'So you'd happily see me out of the farm, having to find myself a job somewhere, just so you could sit and drink yourself into insensibility?'

'You're my daughter!' she managed. 'You are supposed to *help* me.'

'He's been sending you money, every month, more and more as he's got successful, thinking that you were passing it on to me. Money that could have put in a new irrigation system, or kept us ticking over during winter – you've spent it on buying yourself a house and alcohol.'

I could feel the anger draining away now, leaving me with an odd emptiness. My mother turned her worn face towards me, scrunch-eyed as though she was trying not to cry.

'You don't know, Natalie,' she said quietly. 'You have no idea.'

'No, because I was never allowed to ask. Never allowed to talk about anything that mattered. Everything was pushed down and stamped out of me so that I wouldn't dare mention anything that might upset you.' I sounded tired now. 'So the fact that I don't know why you drink isn't my fault. And, right now, I don't care. I came over to tell you that I know, that Simon has told me nearly everything. Anything else I need to know I shall ask him. So if there's anything you feel you ought to tell me, then you should do it right now, because I'm going to find out anyway.'

I got a weak headshake for that. A slow, ponderous negative that I wasn't even sure that she meant. 'I tried so hard to keep you away from musicians,' she said weakly. 'I *knew* he'd try to find you, one day.'

'And that's why you panicked when you heard there was a band filming in the gardens?'

'I *knew* he'd try,' she repeated. I saw her hand reach out and gently slide under the cover that concealed the lump that I was pretty sure was a vodka bottle. Even here, even now, she couldn't reach for me, only for another drink.

'I'm off.' I turned, leaving the detritus of my search all over the floor. 'I'm going home.'

There was a huge, empty space, unfilled by all the words we knew we should say. Eventually my mother said, in a small voice, 'Will you come over tomorrow? I might need some more milk from the shop.' Her voice was almost childlike, so whispered and broken. A child who's had a nightmare, who wants reassurance.

I sighed. 'Of course I will, Mum,' I said, and saw her relax.

'I want some bread too,' she said, her voice rising back to her normal levels. 'I fancy sandwiches for lunch. That nice bread, from the farm shop, not the packet stuff they sell in the village.'

The farm shop people were new, I thought, with the clarity of sudden realisation. They hadn't been here for generations like the family that owned the old-fashioned village grocery. She didn't want me mixing with anyone who might give her away.

'Don't push your luck.' But the normality was making me smile despite myself. I was still angry, I still felt that low burn in my stomach at the thought of the lies, and the memory of all that deflection and the stamping out of any questioning, but this damaged woman was still my mother, and she still needed me. 'No more lies. I'll help you where I can, but no more lies.'

With that, I walked out of the room, leaving the fug, the smell of alcohol and the sound of my mother crying.

17

I drove around the dark lanes for hours, thinking. When I got back to the cottage it was so late that it was almost dawn. A faint slice of lemon-coloured light lay on the far horizon behind the hills and I could see the outline of the planting scheme as I parked my car and came in through the garden. I could have parked in my usual spot and come in the way I went, but I wanted to see the herbs. I *needed* to see them, in all their rustling, dancing glory, nodding in the early breeze as though agreeing with what I'd done. They swayed, each in their appointed place, grouped like-with-like, planted for height, for use, for appeal; neat, orderly. I remembered the garden as it had been when I had taken it over. Lovely, yes, but wild. I had thought that was my mother's idea of planning, a Sleeping Beauty of a garden, letting people wander to choose their herbs by discovery among the riot of scent and flower.

Now I knew it was just that she hadn't been able to keep up a planting method. She'd let the garden go to ruin, basically, with only me keeping on top of the pruning and weeding, but pretending it was still a viable business. Buoyed up by my father's – by Simon's – financial input, she'd not needed to rely on the herb garden for income. I'd bought her out, so keen to take over and make Drycott mine that I hadn't questioned our low turnover. The bank had only loaned me the barest minimum, based on my business plan for the future, and still I hadn't questioned how she'd been keeping everything together on our woeful profits.

All because I hadn't dare ask.

I felt myself droop. Now that the adrenaline of sex with Zeb and the meeting with Simon had ebbed, I was back to being the usual Tallie. Back to worrying about causing offence, worrying about upsetting Mother. I thought of what I'd said to her and felt the horrible heat of shame creep over me. I shouldn't have rocked the boat. Let her carry on thinking that I knew nothing and let life continue as it always had, set in the aspic of lies and deceit.

Big Pig heard me arrive and snorted herself to standing. I went to lean over her gate.

'I don't know what I've done,' I said softly to her, and scratched her enormous bristly head as she snuffled around the base of her gate. The guinea pigs heard me then too, and set up a squeaky call for breakfast, so I thought I might as well get the day started and opened the feed bin.

As I tipped buckets of feed into feeders and tried to tamp down the deep cringe that had been set off by the knowledge that I had upset my mother – something I had been spending my entire life trying not to do – the thought struck me that the little hyperactive mop heads and the huge sow would have been the first to go if I'd had to sell Drycott. There would be no more mornings being greeted as though I were a captain being whistled aboard my ship. No more additions to the muck heap that teetered down by the compost bins, now all neat edges and careful structure thanks to Ollie and Zeb.

She'd wanted me to sell, to keep her in drink. I might be able to forgive the drinking – who knew what reasons she had for that, I guessed she'd convinced herself it was necessary. I might even be able to forgive the lying – no, scratch that, I'd *never* be able to forgive the lies but I could come to understand why I'd been turned into a compliant, scared, non-confrontational person, to let her life continue as it was.

But I would not forgive her wanting me to sell up. This place was in me, in my bones and my teeth and my hair, just as much as the herbal cordials Granny used to give me as a child, to help me grow 'big and strong'. Drycott was my home. I knew, suddenly and with the clarity of dawn, that it wouldn't have mattered if Mum had given me all the money that Simon had been sending. I would never have left. Other lives might have beckoned, doors might have been held open for me, but I would have stayed at my home.

Drycott and I were as entwined as the bindweed with the mallow.

In the cottage I crept up the stairs. Zeb was still asleep on his back and puffing so that his fringe rose and fell with each breath. I looked at him lying there, his feet sticking out at the bottom of the bed like a cartoon, one long arm flopped along the covers like a pale snake, and I felt a rush of affection.

Not love, not yet. But a heat that was attraction and physical compatibility, soft-edged with fondness and caring that could turn into love, if I let it. He understood me. Zeb, with his searching through life for a – well, for a life. Perhaps, just perhaps, he could find one here, with me.

I began pulling things off the walls. All those articles, all that therapy-speak that I had thought was showing me who I was, all had been irrelevant. I wasn't the daughter of a grieving widow who'd worked hard to give me the advantages she'd lacked. I was the daughter of a woman who drank so much she'd driven away a loving husband and who'd spent most of the money sent to help keep her daughter.

The noise of ripping paper, where some of the edges had been stuck to the wallpaper for ten years or more, woke Zeb. He half sat, scrubbing a hand through his hair and staring down at his bare chest.

'Oh, I must have fallen asleep again,' he said, and then, with memory obviously returning, '*Oh*.'

'These,' I said, peeling a three-page article on childhood bereavement away from the 1960s florals, 'are all *lies*, Zeb.'

'Er.' He sat further up the bed. 'Tallie, they're not. They're just not you.'

'But I thought they were!' I wailed, pulling Kate Beckinsale down to lie on top of the crumpled pile. Her face stared upwards, reminding me of my teenage self, although I hadn't been nearly so good looking or composed. Away at school, I'd searched for an identity and found that it lay here, that Drycott was who I was.

'Does it make a difference?' Zeb pushed skinny legs out from under my solar system patterned duvet. 'You're still Tallie. I'm going to put the kettle on, this is all way too deep a conversation to be having without a good sturdy cup of tea inside me. Possibly some toast, would you like some toast?'

His normality was grounding. Zeb was still the same as he'd been before all this dramatic revelation nonsense. So perhaps he was right and I was *also* still the same, even though I felt changed from the inside.

'Toast sounds nice, thank you,' I said cautiously, as though New Tallie might not yet want to eat.

'Good.' He draped himself in my dressing gown, which had been hooked on the back of the door, and, struggling arms into the fluffy sleeves, squeezed his way past me out to the staircase. 'You need some food. I might scramble some eggs – do we have any eggs? Chickens ought to be the first new addition, I think. We can pen them down by the compost to start with.'

Then he stopped on the landing and turned. 'Is it all right?' His face was clouded with anxiety now. 'If I make plans? I mean, are we still going ahead with… or are you going to sell?'

'Sell?' I was momentarily startled from my tape-unsticking.

'I thought – I don't know, maybe you'd want a new beginning? I thought you might be out roaming the acres and deciding on a different future. The pig woke me up,' he added apologetically. 'So I knew you were out there.'

'I went to see my mother.' A satisfyingly long strip of aged newsprint tore away; a story about an entrepreneur who had been orphaned tragically at the age of ten and had gone on to set up his own tech business. 'To tell her that I knew.'

'Ah.' Zeb turned back to the staircase. It creaked under his weight. 'I might need to bring out the jam then.'

'She was sitting in her bedroom, drinking. And her wardrobe was full of bottles.'

I followed Zeb out and down the staircase to the minute hallway and into the kitchen. No sun reached it yet and it smelled of long-gone dinners, dust and crushed leaves. I realised that I hadn't done anything to the cottage since I'd taken over from Mum. She, obviously, hadn't touched the place since Granny died. I was living in a house that was stuck in a time warp from the sixties, when Grandad had been alive. Nobody had decorated, nobody had painted. No wonder there were mice in the kitchen and a tatty version of Morten Harket on the landing. I'd kept this place as Mum had kept it, because I thought it was in memory of my father, when really it had just been an inability to cope, and an unwillingness to spend money on anything that wasn't drink.

Zeb moved from kettle to toaster, examining the bread carefully. 'I think we've got mice,' he said.

'Might have,' I conceded.

He spun around. 'Tallie, this place needs a good scrub, some traps down and a coat of paint, possibly in the well-known shade "fumigation".'

I sighed. 'I know. It's beginning to dawn on me what really needs doing around here. I've been so busy concentrating on keeping the gardens going that I've not really touched the house. I thought Mum was too deep in grief to touch the place, but I'm beginning to think it was laziness now.' I scraped a nail along the table, and some varnish lifted and curled under my finger. 'There's so much to do.'

Zeb pushed the bread into the toaster, flicked on the kettle and came over to stand at the window. 'Now you know,' he said. 'What's next?'

'There's so much to do,' I repeated. 'If we're providing the arrangements for Mika and Tessa's wedding…' I stared past him, out of the window, where a few sunflowers were drooping miserably, leaning against the walls. 'I have to talk to Tessa about colours. Or rather, I have to talk to whoever is arranging the whole wedding, I doubt she's been allowed to choose her own décor. I need to get out there and start picking and drying.'

Zeb caught at my hand as I waved it in a feeble gesture at the garden. 'I can help, though. I'm here, Tallie, I want to help. Not just with the animals, although I've got ideas I want you to hear, but maybe we can park that for now and crack on with preparing for the wedding?'

I looked up at him. He looked ridiculous, protruding from

my dressing gown, all angular and bony with his hair standing up in tufts and his mobile face wearing an expression of contained excitement. My heart twisted in my chest.

'We can spend the winter having a big clear out?' He went on. 'Decorate, repair, get rid of the mice.'

'There's still a fair bit to do in the gardens even in winter you know, Zeb. I don't lock the gates and put my feet up for six months.'

'Good, good. But we can get even more done if it's the two of us.' The toast popped up and the kettle steamed itself to boiling. 'Do you want it to be the two of us?'

He wasn't looking at me now.

I remembered last night. I remembered his caring, his gentleness. And, of course, there was his ability with Big Pig, if we were going to be prosaic about it. 'We can definitely try,' I said. 'But first...'

'Yes?' His head came up, as eager as Big Pig sighting the feed bucket.

'Can you tie up the dressing gown? It's a bit distracting, and Ollie will be here in a minute. You're on full view in the window and I don't want him scared off first thing in the morning.'

'Oh. Oh!' Zeb gathered the fluffy pink fabric around himself. 'That's embarrassing. Although you've seen all I have to offer already, and you haven't run screaming, so thank you for that.'

'Nothing to scream about,' I said. I moved closer, pretending to help him with the tie, but in reality stretching up to give him a kiss.

The sun, finally getting itself going, sloped a few tentative rays in through the top of the window. 'Are you really all right?' Zeb asked gently. 'That was a hell of a day yesterday.'

I thought of Simon's face, breaking the news, that scared, wary expression. He'd been afraid. Had he thought I'd throw him out and refuse to listen? And why hadn't my mother worn a similar expression when I'd walked in on her? The thought that maybe she hadn't cared about being discovered, that perhaps she was relieved that everything was out in the open, crossed my mind, to be dismissed with a inwards sarcastic laugh. She knew she'd raised me to keep the peace. She knew that I would never speak about this again. Not to *her*, anyway. I was too well-trained.

'I'm…' I hesitated. 'I've got a lot of processing to do. I've got to come to terms with the fact that everything I thought growing up was a lie. Everything I was told was a lie. Even Granny couldn't tell me the truth.'

Granny, watching her only child fall through cracks into alcoholism. Did she know why? I spared a few moments of very uncharitable thoughts about Grandad, but then dismissed them. If he'd known anything or been involved in any of this, Granny would have killed him herself with the overweight frying pan she'd wielded for most of my childhood. No. This was something only my mother could get to the bottom of. Granny had done her best to help, but hadn't known how. So she'd taken us in, kept me safe, given me a purpose. Hoping, I had to suppose, that her granddaughter wouldn't follow in her mother's footsteps. She had done what she could.

And I still had Drycott.

Which still contained herbs that needed weeding, cutting back and tying up, and a lot of hard work to prepare for a wedding.

18

The pure physical work of sorting the garden was a huge relief from dealing with the feelings and emotions which seemed to come out of nowhere to ambush me when I least expected it. I knew I was trying to distract myself by concentrating on the minutiae when I found I was changing the string I used for tying up, because my previously blameless and workaday twine was 'too hairy', and I spent half a day with the gardening supplies catalogue, trying to find some that was smoother.

My mother continued to text and ring me, needing me to help with her cleaning or shopping or just keeping her company, and I hadn't known what to do. How could I face her, how could I continue in the life we'd had before, now I knew? I'd gone over to her house the first time, aflame with what I thought was righteous anger for what she'd put me through. But, there she'd been, sitting in her kitchen with her Earl Grey tea and her make-up on, looking faded and tired and scrubbed around the edges with the scourer of life.

I'd burst through the front door, wanting to shout. But one look at her collapsed face, with her mouth pursed around the tea cup as though she were finding the taste unacceptable and would far rather have been drinking gin straight from the bottle, and all my emotions collapsed into a heap of layers. The rage fell through the middle to lie somewhere at the bottom, heating the rest like compost but not enough for a conflagration. Over the top, blanketing everything, lay pity.

I didn't know what made Amanda Fisher drink. And I suspected Mother didn't know. She'd kept me from my father, kept the money he'd sent and put it into living her own life – there was no forgiving that. But I could still feel a blunted kind of sympathy for her and the little life she'd squeezed herself into.

'It's an illness, Tallie,' Zeb told me, as we mucked out the guinea pigs together one morning. 'An addiction. She can't help it. Believe me, when you've worked with as many head chefs as I have, you learn a lot about these things.'

'But she didn't have to lie.' An enthusiastic shovelful of shavings missed the barrow. Big Pig snorted amusement. At least, I think it was amusement, but she and Zeb shared a mutual glance at my face, then they both looked away and pretended to be very interested in other things.

'I'd guess, once she started, she didn't know how to stop. After all, she got your granny to lie for her too. All that pretending that she had to keep you safe from strange men, when it was your father she was keeping you from all along. Your mum has an excuse – well, a reason. Your granny must have done it because she thought it was for the best.'

'But it *wasn't*! Ollie, can you come and take the barrow now please, it's full!'

Ollie bundled up from where he'd been sorting seed heads. 'Righty-ho!' he said and wheeled the barrow off to the compost.

Zeb and I stood and looked at one another. 'You can't know the other life,' Zeb said gently. 'Please don't be bitter, Tallie.'

'I'm not bitter. I'm processing. And you were the one who said I should start asking questions, so this is your fault.'

He gave me a grin and a small shrug, then turned back to spread a new layer of shavings. From their Simon-financed huge run on the newly empty patch of ground, the guinea pigs whistled hopefully.

'Simon has found me a family therapist you know.' I leaned on my shovel. Watching Zeb work gave me a kind of inner calmness. It was as though he'd belonged here all along and we just hadn't known it.

'Yes, he said.'

'I don't know what to say to her.'

'Just tell her the truth.' Zeb straightened up again. 'Honestly, Tallie, if there's one thing I've learned from my somewhat patchwork life, apart from what core competency is and how to prune roses – oh, and a truly excellent recipe for tagine – it's that hiding yourself away and not admitting what you really want from life doesn't work.'

'You're very wise.'

'I lost my wife because I couldn't admit that I wanted to give up being a chef. I lived through all that business admin training and learning how to read accounts, when I knew, deep down, that it wasn't what I wanted from life. I didn't know then that what I really wanted' – he leaned over, across the sweetly sawdust-scented pile and kissed me gently – 'was this.'

Big Pig snorted again and threw a snoutful of straw into the air. The little pigs squeaked and piped their annoyance at the lack of grass. Late daylight sloped into the run and, from the compost bins, we could hear Ollie singing. I looked out over the coming autumn, tinting the edges of leaves and sending flowers into seed. 'You're right,' I said softly. 'You are absolutely right.'

19

The wedding was beautiful. Well, of course it was, it had the financial power of a woman's magazine, a lot of advertising contracts and Simon behind it. Tessa wore a simple white dress and an organdie shawl, Mika was resplendent in a tweed suit with waistcoat and a bowler hat, looking every inch the washboard-and-viola-playing star. The October light was crystal clear and cool, but the sun reflected from the lake at their chosen destination with a fierce light that highlighted the gorgeousness of the guests.

These had, I suspected, been invited more to pique the interest of magazine readers than because they were close friends of the couple. It was even rumoured that Adele was there, although I didn't meet her. The 'behind the scenes' people like us were kept well away from the guests, although the rest of the band wandered through occasionally, stealing canapés and teasing the waiting staff.

Zeb and I tweaked the last table centrepiece into order for the fourth time, signalled to Simon that everything was ready, and then ran out of the marquee to hide elsewhere in the grounds of the stately home that was hosting the event.

'Do you think it went all right?' I asked Zeb for about the billionth time that day, as we watched the organised gorgeousness trooping across the lawns from being photographed, towards the reception under the watchful eye of a drone camera. 'She looks lovely, doesn't she?'

Tessa was still carrying her bouquet, handpicked by me that morning and dashed down the motorway in buckets propped upright with straw bales. The feathery greenery trailed across the bodice of her gown and made her look even more ethereal than she already did, and that was pretty bloody ethereal. She was radiant, but pale.

'She looks a bit anxious,' Zeb observed. 'But yes, Tallie, everything went beautifully.'

We peered out from behind an acer. 'I'd look anxious if I were marrying Mika,' I said. 'I wonder if it's a proper wedding or just one of those show-biz jobs and they'll be divorced in two years?'

* * *

Simon, wearing an incredibly vivid waistcoat so bright that it strobed, and with his hair up in a man-bun for which he was at least twenty years too old, walked down to the marquee with Will and Genevra.

'I hope he doesn't play the washboard at her.' I watched them be greeted by uniformed staff offering champagne flutes on a tray. 'Simon's buying a house in the village by the way, near to Mum. Did you know?'

Zeb looked at me evenly. 'He told me. Are you all right about that?'

'*I* am. I don't know how Mum is going to react, though. He did ask me if I thought it was a good idea.' I kept my eyes on the wedding party. A breeze blew across the parkland and a few hats went flying to a whoop of laughter and I caught sight of the inside of the marquee, where some of the suspended greenery was swaying. Nothing fell and I breathed again. We'd done a good job even if the local fishing tackle shops were going to shudder if we ever went near them asking for fishing line again. We'd used enough to tie up the decorations to land a fair-sized whale.

'And you said?' He was keeping his eyes on mine. There were bits of fern in his hair.

'I said it wasn't my problem. It's entirely up to them and I won't be responsible for Mum and her reaction to things again. They're adults.'

'As are we.' He hugged me then, a brief and sudden contact, surrounded by all this conspicuous wealth and class, and the smell of bruised grass. Somewhere to our left a fountain tinkled falling water and a late wren sang into the gathering dusk. 'Oh, and quite a lot of the publicity people asked for our details. I've been handing out business cards like a blackjack dealer.'

Our details. I tasted the words inside my head. I liked them. I really did.

'It was a great idea of yours to do the flowers for this wedding,' Zeb went on. 'Inspired. And it looks as though we might get some more wedding business out of it.'

'That's where the money is,' I said vaguely. Outside the marquee someone I thought *might* be Adele was deep in conversation with Simon, while Loke and Genevra were drinking champagne. Will was staring around at the grounds. He saw Zeb and me lurking and gave us a little wave. I waved back. 'Even if we did have to pull it all together at such short notice. I really should have thought it through more carefully.'

'But now we can go back and start properly planning the barn extension, and what to do with the gardens next year.' Zeb rubbed his hands together. 'I'm looking forward to it. I've got those hens arriving next week, so Ollie and I are going to build them some proper mobile housing.'

'A caravan for chickens,' I said, still watching the activity over on the lawns. I was really watching Simon, of course. My father, even if we seemed to have nothing more in common than eye colour. To his credit, he did seem to want to get to know me and my life. Plus, he was putting money into building us the new barns.

None of what had happened had been his fault, I caught myself thinking as I watched him smile and nod and adjust his hair again. None of the lies or the obfuscation or the obligation had been anything to do with him. He'd told me how he'd wanted to meet me over the years, had even driven past Drycott a few times, but had always chickened out. He'd been too afraid of the repercussions with Mum and, reading between the lines, I thought he'd really been waiting for her to die before he came out of the woodwork. Funny how a parent you'd never known could be more sympathetic than the one you'd grown up with.

More laughter. The clink of champagne flutes, and then everyone was heading into the marquee for the four-course dinner, dancing, and more photographs. The Goshawk Traders were, apparently, going to play a set and I hoped Tessa would get to change out of her wedding dress before then. Our dried and fresh herb arrangements were going to look stupendous in the pictures.

'We should go home,' I said. 'There's nothing more we can do now.'

Zeb nodded. 'It's been a long day. Ollie's looking after Big Pig tonight, so we can go back and fall into bed. Unless your mum needs you to pop round?'

His tone was so carefully neutral, whilst containing so many questions that the sentence almost bulged. I shook my head.

'I've pulled back a lot on helping her, you may have noticed.'

'I have. And you're obviously struggling with that, so I thought I'd ask.'

There was a small silence, broken only by the persistent wren.

'I *want* to help her,' I said, slowly. 'But it's hard to get over what she's done.'

'It's an illness,' Zeb reminded me again, carefully.

'I know. But I don't have to like it. And I don't have to tiptoe around her any more in case she "gets ill". She already is ill, but if she won't help herself then it's not my problem. I won't let her starve and I won't let her house fall into disrepair, but I'm not popping round every time she summons me. She can go to the shop for herself.'

He nodded. 'Okay. That sounds healthy.'

Now it was my turn for the small smile and the sideways shrug. 'My therapist advised it. A watching brief, I think they call it. Now, are we going to head back or shall we wait to see if we can scrounge any more of those hors d'oeuvres? I liked that mushroom one.'

'Too much cream,' said the ex-chef. 'But yes. Let's go home.'

We left the wedding party without a backward glance.

EPILOGUE
TWO YEARS LATER

The wedding was beautiful.

The church was decorated with all the herbs of high summer and smelled of a really good kitchen, slightly overlaid with the scent of pig. Big Pig had, against my better judgement, been our ring bearer. While seeing her little trotters, polished and scrubbed, mincing down the aisle to Zeb, with the ring cushion balanced on her head like a duchess teaching deportment, had been cute, it had also been fraught with danger. However, she'd behaved impeccably, Ollie had sufficiently managed his fear of strangers to escort her into and out of the church, and she'd featured in so many photographs that she was going to get ideas above her station if we weren't careful. I felt, in my gorgeously embroidered gown, that I had slightly been upstaged by half a tonne of Tamworth sow.

Now we stood as dusk gathered, in the middle of our gardens. I was still wearing my dress – green and stitched with tiny ferns all across the bodice – as we waited, hand in hand, for the sun to set.

'What a lovely day,' Zeb said finally. 'Nice of Mika and Tessa to come, what with the baby being so tiny and everything.'

'Bit of a surprise Will and Loke being together though. I really thought Will was going to marry Genevra.' I watched the last swifts tearing across the sky, trying to beat the sun. 'Simon never really talks about the band when he's here, does he?'

'He's got a lot of parenting catching up to do.' Zeb was staring at the sky too. His excellent grey suit was peppered with petals from the lavender at our feet. 'He's probably going to start telling you you have to be home by nine and not to talk to strange men.'

'Bit late for that.' I nudged him and he laughed. Hand in hand we wandered up to the new barn, where the goats and hens had been closed in for the night. The building smelled of new wood and animals and resounded to sleepy clucks and rustling straw.

'Your mum stayed sober.' Zeb handed some hay to Winnie, goat-in-chief. He'd had to be persuaded about the goats, but now he loved them. 'She did well.'

'According to Simon, she's getting help.' Careless of my dress, I sat on the top of the gate. 'I don't know if it's going to work, but she's showing willing at least. I think she wanted to look good in that dress she was wearing. She and Simon have been having some long talks lately, now she's got over wanting to kill him.'

'More wedding bells?' Zeb scratched Winnie on the neck.

I shrugged. 'Let's finish enjoying ours first. And get over the four we have to do the flowers for next week.'

'Yep. Better get an early night then.' The sun dropped its last rays behind the scoop of hill and the birds finally fell silent. 'Let's go and celebrate.'

So we did.

* * *

MORE FROM JANE LOVERING

Another book from Jane Lovering, *Happily Ever After*, is available to order now here:
https://mybook.to/HappilyEverAfterBackAd

ALSO BY JANE LOVERING

The Country Escape

Home on a Yorkshire Farm

A Midwinter Match

A Cottage Full of Secrets

The Forgotten House on the Moor

There's No Place Like Home

The Recipe for Happiness

The Island Cottage

One of a Kind

The Start of the Story

Happily Ever After

Once Upon a Thyme

ABOUT THE AUTHOR

Jane Lovering is the bestselling and award-winning romantic comedy writer who won the RNA Contemporary Romantic Novel Award in 2023 with *A Cottage Full of Secrets*. She lives in Yorkshire and has a cat and a bonkers terrier, as well as five children who have now left home.

Sign up to Jane Lovering's mailing list here for news, competitions and updates on future books.

Visit Jane's website: www.janelovering.co.uk

Follow Jane on social media:

- facebook.com/Jane-Lovering-Author-106404969412833
- x.com/janelovering
- bookbub.com/authors/jane-lovering

BECOME A MEMBER OF

THE SHELF CARE CLUB

The home of Boldwood's book club reads.

Find uplifting reads, sunny escapes, cosy romances, family dramas and more!

Sign up to the newsletter
https://bit.ly/theshelfcareclub

Boldwood

Boldwood Books is an award-winning fiction publishing company seeking out the best stories from around the world.

Find out more at www.boldwoodbooks.com

Join our reader community for brilliant books, competitions and offers!

Follow us
@BoldwoodBooks
@TheBoldBookClub

Sign up to our weekly deals newsletter

https://bit.ly/BoldwoodBNewsletter

Printed in Dunstable, United Kingdom